"If you are a fan of secrets, intrigue, and strong female characters bent on revenge, then this series is definitely for you." —*The Not-So-Literary Heiresses*

"Addicting! . . . Kyra Davis writes a fast-paced, mysterious, and very sexy story." —*The Blushing Reader*

"Kyra's ability to toy with her readers and her characters' psyches is an unusual talent, I think. I also really love her love/sex scenes. . . . [They have] a voyeuristic feel." —*Bookish Temptations*

"Had me on the edge of my seat from start to finish." —*Love to Read for Fun*

"If you like a killer suspense romance story, this book is for you." —*It's Andrea's Book Blog*

"There are awesome sparks that ignite the sheets . . . Hot! It was the heavy atmosphere, the secrets and mysteries that made me turn the pages." —*New Books on My Shelves*

"Fast-paced and interesting. . . . Kudos to the author for showing her talent to write a vastly different genre than her usual mystery." —*Literary Marie's Precision Reviews*

JUST ONE NIGHT

The runaway international bestseller!

"Gives *Fifty Shades of Grey* a run for its money. . . . But this novel gives some depth, respect, and sexual tension to the genre." —*New York Journal of Books*

Books by Kyra Davis

Just One Night

The Pure Sin Series

Deceptive Innocence
Dangerous Alliance

Dangerous Alliance

KYRA DAVIS

POCKET BOOKS

New York   London   Toronto   Sydney   New Delhi

Pocket Books
A Division of Simon & Schuster, Inc.
1230 Avenue of the Americas
New York, NY 10020

This book is a work of fiction. Any references to historical events, real people, or real places are used fictitiously. Other names, characters, places, and events are products of the author's imagination, and any resemblance to actual events or places or persons, living or dead, is entirely coincidental.

Copyright © 2014 by Kyra Davis

All rights reserved, including the right to reproduce this book or portions thereof in any form whatsoever. For information, address Gallery Books Subsidiary Rights Department, 1230 Avenue of the Americas, New York, NY 10020.

First Pocket Books paperback edition January 2015

POCKET and colophon are registered trademarks of Simon & Schuster, Inc.

For information about special discounts for bulk purchases, please contact Simon & Schuster Special Sales at 1-866-506-1949 or business@simonandschuster.com.

The Simon & Schuster Speakers Bureau can bring authors to your live event. For more information or to book an event, contact the Simon & Schuster Speakers Bureau at 1-866-248-3049 or visit our website at www.simonspeakers.com.

Cover design by Anna Dorfman
Cover photograph © Serge/Getty Images

Manufactured in the United States of America

10 9 8 7 6 5 4 3 2 1

ISBN 978-1-4767-7426-8
ISBN 978-1-4767-5687-5 (ebook)

To my husband

prologue

You don't know me.

Did you think that you did? Maybe you looked at my long black hair and lightly tanned skin and mistook me for the pretty Latina caricatures you see in sitcoms or prime-time dramedys. It's possible that I tricked you into believing that you understood my ambitions and motivations.

You may even think you know my name.

But you're wrong.

Travis Gable thinks he knows me. Travis with his smooth smile and chilly blue eyes. He's a creature carved out of greed and malice. And like any real demon, he's very smart and very observant. And yet he doesn't *see* me, not really. Even though he hired me to be the personal assistant to him and his wife. I've been in his home, his office, his limo; he's let me see parts of his world that he likes to keep hidden in the shadows. That was his mistake.

Travis's wife, Jessica Gable, thinks she knows me too. I like to think of her as a professional socialite. A woman of fashion and breeding. She gets her clothes from Bergdorf's, her facials from the spa at the Mandarin, and her temperament from the pharmacy. She self-medicates in the hope that it will help her tolerate her husband. It also helps her tolerate herself. Just as Travis is comforted by the belief that he can manipulate me, Jessica is empowered by the idea that she can torment me without my ever fighting back.

Travis and Jessica call me Bell, which is short for Bellona.

But Bellona isn't my name. It's more of an idea. I chose that name for myself because I like its origins:

Bellona, the Roman goddess of war.

Travis and Jessica don't know me at all.

And of course Micah Romenov thinks he knows me very well. His niece shared a prison cell with my mother, and like his niece, Micah is a criminal. Russian mafia to be precise. My mother, Julieta Jiménez, helped get his niece on a better path, and Micah has helped support me ever since. He thinks that I'm a little lost and that I can be controlled through threats and bribes. He calls me Sweet.

But I've never been lost. I know exactly where I am and where I'm going. As for the threats and the bribes? He might as well be threatening and bribing a storm. Like any hurricane, I'm simply going to do what I want. You might be able to prepare for me, but no one is going to stop me.

Oh, and in case you haven't figured it out yet, I'm definitely not sweet.

So please, allow me to introduce myself. My name, my *real* name, is Adoncia. Doncia for short. I was only ten when my mother was arrested for murdering Nick Foley. My mother had been Nick's maid. She had also been his lover . . . at least until Mrs. Foley found out, and my mother was both fired and dumped. So she had an obvious motive.

I didn't know she was innocent.

But this is what I know now:

Fact: Nick was a VP at HGVB Bank. The G stands for Gable. Travis's father, Edmund Gable, is the CEO and Travis is a managing partner. And the Gables have shadowy connections and business associations that the world doesn't know about. Micah is a good example of that. My mother thought Micah was on my side, but the truth is, he's always been aligned with my enemies.

Fact: Nick had a secret. It had something to do with HGVB, and while I don't know exactly what it was, Travis and Edmund most definitely did. They saw Nick as a potential whistle-blower.

Fact: When I was ten, my mother found Nick's body. That was planned. They wanted her on her knees, crying over her married lover's body with blood on her hands. Jessica was in the neighborhood when it happened, staying at her parents' house while they were vacationing in Belize. Jessica testified in court. She said she heard a gunshot shortly after the time my mother arrived at Nick Foley's house.

Fact: Jessica lied. Less than a year after the trial was over, she was married to Travis. That was her reward, the Gable last name.

Even at ten, I should have been smart enough not to believe it when the police, the state, and the jury concluded that the woman who was the center of my world was actually evil. But pain and fear had dulled my intellect. I learned to hate the woman who had once read me all my favorite fairy tales. I learned to hate everything she loved.

And the thing she loved most was me.

So after ten years of being a good girl, I changed. Just like that. I charted a path of self-destruction. No one could handle me. I was moved from foster home to foster home until I eventually found myself in a facility for homeless teens.

It wasn't until I was almost seventeen that I began to suspect that my mother was innocent. I tried to prove it. I tried to get the police to reopen the case. I tried to get the public defender to return my calls. But of course I wasn't able to do any of that. No one wants to talk to a discipline case.

In retrospect, I should have driven to see my mother before I launched a campaign to reopen her case. I should have told her that I knew she was innocent. That's what I should have done *first*.

Maybe if I had she wouldn't have made that noose.

You see, Micah, Jessica, Travis, and his father,

Edmund—they don't know me at all, and yet in a weird way, they created me. They turned me into a weapon.

Do you think you know me now? Now, after I've confessed to all my rage and spewed my venom?

You do? That's almost funny.

Because there's much more to me than anger. I know, I know, I'm surprised by that too. I thought I was made of ice. But that must not be true, because recently someone has reached inside me and unleashed something . . . lighter. This person can actually make me laugh and want to dance. He makes me blush and tremble and lose control. This man, he . . . he *warms* me, and when he does I don't melt. I become stronger.

In the end, there's only one person who truly knows me, the most unlikely person in the world,

Lander Gable.

Edmund's youngest son and Travis's half brother. Lander, a man who I thought was my enemy all because of his last name.

But really, a rose by any other name.

Lander's mother passed away not long after mine did. Like me, he blames Travis and Edmund. Like me, he wants revenge.

And *with* me, he's gonna get it.

chapter one

When I step inside the restaurant, the first thing I notice is how warm it is, in both temperature and ambience. I pause a moment just inside the doors to take in the notes of gold and the arched ceilings. Everything in this place speaks of elegance and well-mannered sophistication. I wasn't born for this, but then, neither was the man I'm meeting. That's okay, though. We both know how to fake it.

"Hi," I say as I approach the hostess. "I'm meeting someone, perhaps you could tell me if he's already here? The reservation is under—"

I stop short as someone takes my arm from behind and addresses me in a perfectly distinctive Russian British accent: "Sweet, thank you so much for inviting me to dinner."

I turn and smile into Micah's dancing eyes. His bald head reflects the lights above him in an almost comical way. "Of course, Micah." I glance back at the hostess before lowering my voice a bit. "I was just . . . I needed to talk to you."

"Oh? What about?"

An elderly couple enters and glances nervously at Micah, noting the tattoos that are peeking out from beneath the collar of his perfectly pressed thousand-dollar dress shirt.

Biting my lip, I lower my gaze to the ground. "I just . . ." I hedge, before blurting out, "I have something to confess."

"Ah." He drapes his arm over my shoulders amiably as he turns his attention to the hostess. "Terri, take us to my table and tell the bartender to send over two double martinis immediately. He knows how I like them." He turns back to me and says in a stage whisper, "Confessions should always be paired with Stoli."

I laugh as I know I'm supposed to. Micah never takes himself too seriously, not even when he is condemning men to death.

When we reach "his" table, he usurps the hostess by insisting that he pull the chair out for me himself. "This place is exquisite, isn't it?" he asks as he takes his seat. "Did you see the way the white floral arrangement picked up the gold lighting? Such attention to detail! The place is fit for a motherfucking czar."

A pretty waitress with bright red hair and a nervous smile comes with two martinis. She hands Micah his first and waits for him to taste it. I suspect that she's a fairly new hire, but someone has trained her on how Micah likes to be served. He sips it delicately as if he's tasting champagne, and then flashes our server a satisfied grin. "My compliments to the bartender."

The waitress's shoulders visibly relax as she hands me my drink and mumbles a promise to be back soon before beating a fast retreat.

"So!" Micah raises his glass. "To confessions!"

I laugh nervously and clink his glass before bringing mine to my lips.

"So, whatcha do?" he asks as he scans the menu. "Tell Uncle Micah all about it."

"You know what I did," I say quietly.

"Do I?"

"Yes." I take another gulp of my drink. "I've done everything you thought I was doing. I got the job with Travis because I wanted to destroy him."

Micah's eyes leap up from the menu, his face growing serious for the first time. "I hope you heeded my warning, Sweet," he says in a tone that is as sinister as it is calm. "If you did anything to interfere with Travis's ability to perform his professional duties at HGVB, you would also be interfering with *my* business. I don't take kindly to people who fuck with my business."

"I didn't," I say quickly before lowering my eyes to the table. "But I wanted to. I wanted to make him hurt."

"And why's that?"

I hold my tongue. He knows the answer.

"So." He speaks slowly. "You're admitting to everything now, are you? You're telling me you think Travis is behind setting your mum up for offing her lover?"

"I did think that, yes."

"You *did*? Past tense?"

"Yes, past tense," I say, finally meeting his gaze. "I know the truth now. I know the whole story."

Micah presses his lips together, his eyes never leaving mine. Around us I catch snippets of laughter and the clinking of forks against china. The whole room seems to be buzzing except for our table, where everything is disturbingly still.

"What," he finally says, "do you think you know?"

"I know who the murderer is, Micah."

"Do you now?" He reaches for his martini. "And who would that be?"

"Don't make me say it."

"Forgive me," he says, breaking to take another long sip of his drink, "but I must insist that you do."

Again I bite down on my lip as I crumple the cloth napkin in my hand. "The murderer," I choke out, "was Julieta Jiménez."

Micah's quick inhaled breath serves as an exclamation mark. It's the reaction I wanted. "I finally get it," I say, with a little more certainty. "My mother was the one who killed Nick Foley."

Micah doesn't say a word. He barely moves. The waitress comes back to the table for our order, but it only takes one glare from Micah to get her to stammer an apology for the interruption and scamper off.

"Last we met," Micah says, "you told me that your mother was innocent. You insisted on it."

"I did. I was wrong."

He raises his eyebrows questioningly. "What's changed?"

I shift uneasily in my seat. "When my mother was arrested . . . well, she didn't have much. Almost everything was sold or given to Goodwill, but of course I got to keep a few trinkets. A necklace with a little crystal heart pendant, a pair of leather gloves that were given to her by an employer, and . . . and she had a diary."

"She did? I would have thought that would have been confiscated by the police for evidence."

I shrug. "I think they missed it. It didn't actually look like a diary, more like a notebook. It could have easily been something I was using for school. I did start to read it, but . . . well, I was ten and I was so angry at her. I put it aside before I got more than five pages in. And then later it was just . . . it was just too painful."

"But you've read it now," Micah says evenly.

"Cover to cover."

I give Micah a moment to process this. "Are you trying to tell me that your mum confessed to murder in her diary?"

"No, that wouldn't have been possible. She didn't have the opportunity to write in it after the arrest, and she was arrested at the scene of the crime."

"That's true." I can hear the confusion in his voice. I've never seen Micah show any uncertainty before, but it's clear that I've thrown him for a loop. "If she didn't confess to the murder, what makes you think—"

"She confessed to *wanting* to do it. It's right there in the diary, Micah. She was so hurt, so . . . so angry. She imagined killing him. She actually says she wants to shoot him, that she wants his blood on her hands for breaking her heart. She *wrote* that, Micah!" I summon up tears that blur my vision and my hands tremble slightly as I lift my martini, making the vodka slosh over the edge of my glass.

I'm a very good actress.

"I didn't think she was capable of this, but . . . but, Micah, not only was she capable, she followed through with it! She imagined it and then she *did* it! This doesn't just mean she's guilty, it means it was premeditated! She thought this out!" I put my glass down and cover my face with my hands.

After a moment, Micah reaches across the table and pets my hair. "Don't shed tears over this, Sweet. Nick Foley deserved to die for what he did to her. Somebody disrespects you? You hurt them. Your mum did the right thing."

I pull back from his touch and wipe impatiently at my tears. "Even if that's true, did she have to be so stupid about it? She *wrote down* the fantasy before she lived it! What if someone else had found that diary? She wouldn't have gotten thirty years, she would have gotten life! Although given that she ended up committing suicide, maybe she didn't care about that. And that means . . . that means she didn't care about being with *me*. She didn't just kill Nick, she abandoned *me*."

"She wasn't a professional criminal," Micah reasoned. "She was a wronged woman with a debt to settle. She made some mistakes, maybe she was a little careless in her actions, but in the end, her heart was in the right place."

"She was a murderer."

"Murderer, vengeful angel . . ." Micah waves his hand in the air dismissively. "I'll leave the semantics up to the poets and lawyers. All I know is she was your mum and you shouldn't hold this against her."

"Micah, that's insane."

"Is it?" he asks as he gestures to our waitress that it's safe to approach. "Is being angry at her going to get you anywhere?" The waitress comes back with her pen poised, ready to take our order. "You gotta try the salmon," he advises me. "Tender, seasoned to perfection, and good for the heart. You must always take care of your heart."

"The salmon, please," I say weakly as I hand off my menu.

"Make that two," Micah says jovially. "And get the lady another martini. She's having a rough time of it today."

I nod in agreement as our order is taken off to the kitchen.

"Your mum was a good woman in a bad situation," Micah reasons, returning to the subject at hand. "Don't you ever forget that."

I respond with a halfhearted shrug.

"She *was*," Micah insists. "I bet there was lots of lovely things in that diary. I bet she talked about how much she loved you, didn't she?"

"She did," I say grudgingly.

"And I bet she talked about Nick. I bet she was quite eloquent in her expression of her love for that fucker."

"She did love him," I whisper.

"Of course she did! That's why she was so upset! Tell me, what else did she say about him? Did she talk about how he wooed her? How he made her feel special and trusted? Did she write of the secrets he confided to her?"

I'm very careful not to show my pleasure at his last question. "She wrote a little about how romantic he was. But . . . the secrets he was confiding to her?" I ask. Outside I can hear the muted wail of a siren as it fights its way through New York's traffic. "Why would Nick tell secrets to some maid he was just sleeping with?"

"To gain her trust of course!" He pauses as my second martini is placed in front of me along with a bread basket for the table. "Some men are clever like that," he says once we're alone again. "Tell a woman one secret and she'll think she's special. Works every time. It could be about anything. Maybe something about his past, his family, his work . . . anything at all, really. But then, *you* read the diary," he says with a laugh that is just a tad bit forced. "You tell me!"

"If he told her any secrets, I didn't recognize them."

I select a roll, tearing into it slowly. "Anyway, I burned the diary."

Micah blanches and then leans forward, his forearms on the table. "You burned it? It was one of the only things you had left of your mother."

"I have a necklace and I have her gloves." I finish the last vestiges of my first drink and immediately reach for my second. "I'm trying hard to just remember her for who I thought she was when I was little. I don't want to keep a book around that undermines that."

"Ah."

Looking at Micah, I can't tell if he's relieved or disappointed. "I'm sorry I didn't initially believe you about Travis and his father," I add. "I should have known you would never steer me wrong. It's just . . . he seemed like someone who was capable of doing something like that. But then obviously I'm not quite the judge of character I thought I was."

"Now, now, it's understandable. We all get a bit unreasonable when emotions are involved."

"I suppose. But I swear, Micah . . . the way he treats his wife . . ."

"Domestic relationships are complicated things." He selects a roll and drops it onto his plate. "People fall in and out of love, blame each other for their own shortcomings. It's a fucking tangled web we weave," he says as he reaches for the butter.

"I guess. But . . . I don't know, Travis takes things pretty far. The other day he was right in her face, screaming at her. He threatened her life, Micah . . .

and yes," I say, quickly pushing on as Micah tries to interject, "I know people say things they don't mean all the time, but the way he was with her . . . I thought he was actually going to hit her—and he might have if Javier and Edmund hadn't shown up when they did."

For a very brief moment, Micah freezes, a piece of bread halfway to his mouth. It's only for a moment, but I catch it.

"Javier and Edmund? My Javier? The guy who was in the limo with us who offered to pay for a little time with you?"

I feign embarrassment but continue. "Yes, of course. I'm telling you, Micah, if you had heard the things Travis said to Jessica—"

"Why were Javier and Edmund there? How do those two even know each other?"

I shake my head as if bewildered. "I don't know. They clearly had made plans, because when they showed up, Travis apologized for not being ready for their dinner. I don't know where they all went . . ."

Micah stares at me for a beat, I see a quick flash of anger cross his features, and then, just as quickly, he regroups, casually tearing off another piece of bread. "Hell, I don't need to keep up with Javier's social calendar."

"So, he doesn't work for you?"

"*For* me? No. With me occasionally. I'm the one who introduced him to Travis, and you know what? It's great if Travis has now introduced him to his dear ol' dad." Again he digs into the butter, putting so much of it on his bread that you can barely tell that he's eating anything *but* butter. It's not how Micah normally eats.

I sense stress eating. *Good.*

"I think I'll have another martini too," he continues. "It's that kind of a night, don't you think?"

I smile sweetly, nod, and excuse myself to use the ladies' room. Once I get there I take out my phone and see the text from Lander:

All good?

I respond with one word:

Perfect

And it's true, our plan is starting off absolutely perfectly.

chapter two

The dinner goes long, and when Micah offers to have his limo drive me home I accept, although I have plans to stay at Lander's. Micah knows I'm seeing him, but I don't see any reason to advertise how close we've become. Besides, the plans Lander and I have made for our evening aren't entirely romantic. Earlier in the day Lander began to show me the evidence he's been gathering against his family. He insists that he doesn't have enough to seal their fate . . . yet. But still, he's collecting clues, arrows that will point us where we need to go and signs that will help us plot our journey.

But Micah can't suspect any of that. So I ride through the East Harlem streets in a limo and camp out in my small studio apartment for almost two hours before taking a cab back to see my partner in crime.

When I arrive at Lander's it's almost midnight. He opens the door wearing light cotton pants and an open robe, both the color of dark steel. His bare chest is a compelling advertisement for his strength and physical discipline. But his mussed light brown hair and sleepy hazel eyes are almost childlike . . . sweet. Not for the first time I'm struck by how odd it is that one man can at times be so very gentle and then suddenly become so very dangerous.

"Perfect?" he asks as he takes my coat, brushing his fingers against my neck as he does.

"He bought every word."

"Did he give anything away about who this Javier is, or who he works for?"

"He told me that Javier works *with* him, not for him. That's all I got tonight, but I'll get more." I turn and lean my weight against the door. "I was good, Lander."

He laughs despite himself, his eyes moving slowly over my form. "We're going to make this work for us, Doncia. And I've gotten more information from one of my men," he says, referring to the many private detectives he has in his employ. "We're getting closer." He reaches forward and slides one finger into the waistband of my skirt, using it as a kind of hook to pull me forward, taking me off-balance. "Go, make yourself comfortable and meet me in the dining room. We'll pick up where we left off this morning."

Thinking about this morning brings a smile to my lips. It hadn't all been business.

It only takes me a moment to go to his room and

slip out of my shoes, and then, after only a moment's thought, my clothes, choosing one of Lander's Kiton shirts that he's carelessly draped over a chair as a nightgown, rolling the French cuffs up to my elbows. When I meet him in the dining room he smiles appreciatively as I take in the scene.

The dark oak table is covered in papers, timelines detailing the activities of brutal men and surveillance notes passed along by the private detectives who took to the shadows to stalk our prey. There are photos of criminals—some with menacing tattoos, others in suits with brilliantly white smiles—and reports detailing the violence and corruption both groups are spreading over the world.

And in the middle of all this evidence of evil are two crystal champagne flutes, filled to the brim and rising from the chaos like roses bursting from a field of weeds.

But of course, that makes sense. This is what working with Lander is like. We're down in the mud, using our bare hands to dig up the ugliest secrets we can find . . . and yet even as the filth cakes under our fingernails, Lander finds a way to bring a little elegance to our pursuit.

Aware of his gaze, I move to the table and take my seat beside him. "Shall we begin again?"

His smile. It's the smile of a righteous outlaw. He reaches forward and taps a photo on the table while lifting his glass to his lips. "Have you ever seen these men?"

I lean forward, impatiently pushing my hair out

of my face when it threatens to block my view. "They look familiar but I'm not sure why . . . maybe from television? Are they reality stars or something?"

"In a way. Do you remember when the FBI busted that huge gun trafficking operation in Texas? They were smuggling guns into Mexico for a cartel. In fact, the smugglers were thought to be an extension of the cartel itself."

I look at the men again. "They're not Mexican," I say definitively. The men are fair, but that's not why I know they don't share my mother's nationality. It's an American myth that all Latinos have dark hair and tanned skin. But these men seem to uphold stereotypes that belong exclusively to a rather specific American demographic. One is wearing a UFC T-shirt; the other is wearing a baseball cap with an eagle on it. Their skin is pasty, which makes the UFC fan's Iron Maiden tattoo stand out all the more.

"They're white supremacists," Lander explains. "In some ways it was rather clever of them. No one expects the Klan types to team up with Mexican drug dealers. But in the prisons it's not at all uncommon for the two groups to join forces against the black inmates, so apparently they decided to just extend the alliance into the outside world and make a little money off it."

"What does any of this have to do with Travis? Is he a white supremacist now?"

"Travis doesn't care about a man's skin color as long as the color of what's in his pocket is green." Again Lander taps the picture, this time moving his index finger over the man wearing the baseball cap. Unlike his companion, he looks fairly clean cut. He's wearing a nice pair of khakis paired with a black polo shirt. Only the eagle on his hat indicates any kind of connection to the working-class culture. "I happen to know that my brother had lunch with this guy less than a week before his arrest. Less than forty-eight hours after meeting Travis, Kliff opened two accounts at HGVB: one for his legitimate but only marginally profitable gun stores, and one personal account. Kliff deposited over a hundred thousand dollars in each account. And any transaction over ten thousand dollars—"

"—has to be reported to the Feds for tax purposes as required by the federal Bank Secrecy Act, aka the anti-money-laundering law," I finish for him.

Lander arches an eyebrow, appreciation flashing in his eyes.

"You think I would snake my way into your life without studying the rules of your world?" I ask, incredulous.

He pauses for a moment before reaching forward and touching my face, letting his fingers slide along my cheekbone to the contours of my ear. "Adoncia Bellona," he says, pronouncing both my real name and my alias with an equal measure of affection. "Sweet warrior." He laughs softly and shakes his head as his fingers dance down the line of my jaw. "If you wanted to destroy me you took the wrong path."

"Did I?" I stand up and slowly straddle his lap, now weaving my fingers through his hair. "Have you ever had another enemy get this close to you? Has an opponent ever before had the opportunity to strip you of all your defenses and make you cry out their name?" I'm pushing his robe off his shoulders, watching a new and mischievous glint light up his eyes.

"And yet," he says, his hand now pressed against the small of my back, pulling me toward him. "Here I am, not destroyed."

"Mmm." I reach behind me, picking up the photo of the two men, and then hold it up in the small space between us. "Tell me," I say, running my finger over the form of the man with the eagle hat, "what happened to dear Mr. Kliff's accounts? Were his transactions reported?"

"They were."

I lean back so I can look into his eyes. I hadn't expected that answer.

"It was documented less than an hour after Kliff's arrest and only two hours before the arrest was shared with the media," he clarifies. "So the reporting was delayed, but, yes, it did happen."

"Someone tipped Travis off," I say thoughtfully.

Lander nods. "He was a little careless about it. Not significantly careless, but it was enough to help me understand what I needed to look for."

"Money laundering." I say the words slowly, taking some pleasure in their acidity. "But this morning you showed me evidence of three other HGVB accounts that are clearly held by fronts."

"I did."

I shake my head and drop the picture back onto the

table. "Three huge accounts! I mean, you have a *fruit company*," I say, putting imaginary quotes around the words, "that opened up an account in an HGVB Cayman Islands subsidiary and wired over a million dollars to the Cypress account of a known Russian gangster. Over a million dollars, Lander! That's got to be enough to lock these people up!"

"It might be," Lander admits, "if the people you're talking about are the individuals running that particular subsidiary. HGVB is a multinational behemoth. There are a lot of things that can happen that won't ever come to Travis's or my father's attention. Or at least, they could argue that in court. You see, I don't need three illegal accounts. I need one illegal account that has their fingerprints on it. Otherwise they'll just throw the government a low-level scapegoat and keep on doing what they're doing."

A shudder runs up my spine even as I try not to allow my face to show how that remark affected me. I'm well aware of the Gables' ability to deflect attention with scapegoats. "What about the Iranian thing?" I ask hopefully. "You said you thought they were doing business with them, didn't you? That they were violating US sanctions. Can we tie them to that?"

"Yes, I thought I glimpsed something on my father's computer when I was visiting him. But when I went back to check . . ." He shakes his head. "I'll find what I need to make that one stick. It's just going to take time."

"Hmm." I look up at the ceiling as I conjure up a morbid fantasy. "I'd really like to send Travis to an

Iranian prison . . . or maybe Saudi Arabia or some POW place in the Middle East. Can you see Travis sleeping on a concrete floor, subsisting on moldy bread and the rare glass of water? I wonder if he could keep his famously imperturbable composure under those circumstances."

"I understand they're gouging out the eyes of their prisoners in some of those places," Lander muses. "It might be a bit much."

"You're right," I agree, twisting slightly away from him as I pick up my champagne flute. "I like Travis's eyes. They're such a pale blue; it's that blue you get early in the morning right after sunrise."

"How romantic," Lander says coolly.

"I guess, although I don't really mean it in a romantic context." I tip the glass against my lips before bringing it to his, watching carefully as he drinks. "I just like his eyes, that's all. And it's important that he keeps them. Otherwise, how will I ever see him cry?"

Lander cocks his head as I take the glass away. "You are a dark angel, aren't you?"

"No, I'm just me. Your sweet warrior. And you?" I run my fingers down his chest, his muscles making little hills and valleys for me to trace. "You're just my lover, my only ally, the gunpowder to my cannon." I lean in, nibble on his ear. "Tell me, how do we light the fuse? What do you need to prove what you know about Travis's and Edmund's dealings with Iran?"

"Just a match made of all the usual materials," he says. I can feel the slight pressure of his palms against my thighs, moving up and down, warming me to new possibilities. "A few incriminating emails or memos would be good." His hands move up to my hips, pushing the shirt I'm wearing higher so now it gathers at my waist along the sides and falls in soft folds between my legs, concealing myself from him . . . but only barely. "And of course I'll need files, accounts, digital records; all the things that they're hiding."

"I'll find them." The promise comes to my lips easily with an assurance that I know I haven't earned.

Lander pauses a beat and then reaches up to push back a lock of my hair. "It's been four days since we took Jessica to the hospital," he says quietly. "Travis called to tell you he'd let you know when he would need you to come back to work and he hasn't called again since then—despite the fact that Jessica was out of the hospital in less than twenty-four hours. I assume she still needs an assistant, and yet she's not calling either, and considering the dynamics of that relationship, we have to assume that if she's not calling it's because Travis told her not to. I think we have to entertain the possibility that he's lost trust in you."

For a moment I don't speak. I allow my eyes to move up, to the wall behind him, seeing memories rather than what's actually there. "I'll get his trust back," I whisper. "I know how."

He nods. I can tell he doesn't fully believe me, but he doesn't challenge me either. "Yesterday when you showed me Jessica's schedule I noticed that she has an appointment tomorrow at three thirty."

"Her appointment with Dr. Wolper—only one of

the many doctors who give her prescriptions for her favorite drugs. She won't miss that. Why?"

"Travis will be in meetings all day tomorrow. I want you to go to see Jessica earlier in the afternoon. I want you to convince her to let you in, lead her to believe that Travis has given you the go-ahead to resume your duties for her if it helps. But get in there and find a way to stay after she leaves for Dr. Wolper's."

"Why? What do you want me to do?"

"It's what I want *us* to find. Travis bought a personal safe a while back. I have no idea where it is, and from what I can tell Jessica doesn't even know it exists. But I do think it's in the penthouse somewhere, just waiting for the right person to discover it and unlock its secrets."

"Ah," I say, my smile returning. "You mean the wrong person. A person who's wrong in all the right ways."

"Like you."

"Like me," I agree, smiling mischievously. "And I know how to break into a safe."

"Do you really?" Lander asks, clearly impressed.

"If it's a combination safe, yes. I did pick up a few tricks during my juvenile delinquent days. It takes a while but I can do it."

Lander shakes his head. "I probably shouldn't, but I find that incredibly sexy."

"Why, thank you!" But then my smile dies on my lips as the challenges of the task ahead begin to weigh on me. I gently place my forehead against his, weave my fingers into his hair. "Promise me. Promise me we'll get them."

"I promise you, Doncia," he says, caressing my nickname with a gravelly whisper. "Travis, my father, and all their cohorts." He takes the now-empty flute out of my hand and casually throws it toward the fireplace, punctuating the moment with the sound of breaking glass. "We'll get them all." He places his hands on my thighs again, this time grasping them firmly as he tilts forward and lifts me up and onto the table as he stands before me, my legs spread open, my weight leaning backward as I support myself with my hands. "Together, you and me."

I love the sound of that. With Lander what was a dark task of revenge now feels like an adventure. Like he's Zorro and I'm his lover, Señorita Lolita Pulido. Or he's Robin Hood and I'm a feisty Maid Marian. It's a dark fairy tale, the kind I used to gobble up as a kid.

It's exhilarating.

With one hand Lander unbuttons the Kiton shirt I wear and pushes the fabric aside so that I'm completely exposed to him. His eyes move over me slowly, touching me like a feather that both tickles and arouses. I wait for him to touch me for real. But he simply leans forward to take the other champagne flute. "If I had my way you would never be dressed," he says softly. "Hiding you in clothes, it's like draping a masterpiece with a veil. And you know," he adds, putting his fingers under my chin, tilting my head even farther back so I can only look into his eyes, "I do like to show you off. Just like in a gallery, I want them to see, but not touch. No one but me." His fingers slide down the center of my neck. "Isn't that right, Adoncia."

"Yes," I whisper.

"Then say it."

"No one touches me but you."

Lander nods and takes another sip of his drink as I stay there, posed for him, wanting to touch him but sensing that it is not my turn to be the aggressor. There's something commanding in his stance. He's holding me in place with a look, making me wait as I battle with my own impatience and anticipation. With one hand he traces a line from the inside of my knee, up my leg, to that hollow spot beneath the muscle of my thigh, right where the skin sinks toward my sex.

"You thought you were going to destroy me," he says thoughtfully.

"Yes," I whisper.

His eyes move back to mine and there's fierceness there, perhaps even a savagery. His fingers move to my clit, circling it slowly, toying with me as I tremble. "You were wrong."

His fingers slip inside me and my eyes fall closed. I press my hips against him as I hear the sound of another glass breaking against the fireplace. There are pictures on this table; articles and reports, sins that crinkle beneath my palms as I rock against the polished wood surface. His fingers continue to work me as I bite down on my lip, only to then cry out as I feel the wetness of his tongue. My eyes fly open and there he is, tasting me as his fingers continue to move. The unexpected pleasure rips through me and a deep, guttural moan slips from my lips. My arms are trembling so much they can barely support me. It's almost too much. But I don't move; I keep my position as he does with me as he likes, bringing me to a place of ecstasy, making me weak as he strengthens my desire.

When he finally pulls away, standing again between my open legs, I can barely speak. I curl my toes around the fabric of his pants and look up into his eyes, silently pleading for his permission to remove them.

He only has to give me the slightest nod and I pull down on the steely gray cotton, easing the pants down his legs.

And when I see him now, like this, I too am reminded of a masterpiece.

"Only me," he says again. "I am the only one who will be with you like this. I'm the only man who will even use your real name. Adoncia, it's mine to say, and this"—his fingers caress my hardened nipples as I shudder again—"this is mine to touch."

I'm aching for him, my need is broadcast in the shallowness of my breath as I once again whisper, "Yes."

And with that he grabs my hips as I link my legs around his thighs, dragging me forward as he presses inside of me, filling me, going so deep that the sensation is almost all I can process. And yet the crinkling of the papers reminds me that we are making love on a bed made of sin.

I lower myself down until my back is against the table too, moving my arms to my sides as I lift my legs so that they rest on his shoulders. He lifts my hips up, supporting me as much of my lower back rises off the table. It's a fluttery friction as he rotates his hips against me, touching every nerve ending, making me cry out his name.

I can hear the subtle, staticky sound of papers tearing on the table as I thrash against them. The men beneath me are evil and perverse, lusting after nothing more than power and money.

But the man above me is Lander.

He presses in harder, farther, and this time it takes me over the edge. The orgasm is overwhelming and again his name touches my lips as I feel him coming inside of me, feel him throbbing as I pulse against him, taking him in. His essence, his scent, everything.

He's the only man who will touch me like this. The only man who has the right to use my name.

And the men beneath me?

We'll rip them to shreds.

chapter three

The next day I take the bus across the park to Travis and Jessica's penthouse. I could have taken a cab; Lander left me the money for it before he took off for work. But although there's a luxury to taking cabs and limos, the bus offers me the familiarity that I'm currently craving. Pretending to be one thing for Micah, one thing for Travis, another for Jessica . . . There are so many roles to play. But here, right now, I'm just Adoncia from East Harlem, taking the bus to the West Side. Even the grime on the bus windows puts me at ease.

I reposition my oversized purse on my lap; its heavy weight helps center me as I prepare to put part two of the game plan into motion. In front of me a teenager with dyed black hair whispers in the ear of a girl with lip piercings and heavy black eyeliner. There's something almost sweet about their rebellion.

It's as if they're still innocent enough to think that a few piercings and hair dye will make the world see them as dangerous. They haven't figured out that the really dangerous ones never use fashion to advertise the threat they pose. They don't have to.

My eyes travel back to the window as I consider my situation. Lander was right. Travis has lost trust in me. Worse, he correctly suspects that my loyalties are with his brother. How did he piece it together? Have I done something to tip him off? No, more likely he just saw something in me. Maybe my eyes dance a little more now, whereas before they only stared. Maybe my smile seems more genuine; maybe he sees the changes in me that you would expect to see in a woman who is falling in love.

Falling in love.

I've never said the words aloud. Never even hinted at them. I'm not even sure I know what they mean. All I know is that when I'm with Lander, even when I *think* of him, something inside me shifts.

I wonder if there are feelings that he has for me that he hasn't vocalized. I wonder if he feels what I feel.

It's been so long since someone loved me.

I chuckle to myself, rejecting a path that could easily lead to self-pity. I've earned every wound I've suffered. I accept that. It's my mother who deserved better. Once I have my vengeance, I'll dedicate it to her.

Which brings me back to Travis. I meant what I said to Lander: I *know* how to regain Travis's trust. It would be simple, really. All I would have to do is decimate everything that makes what I have with Lander *real*.

That's what would happen if I gave in to Travis's request, since what he really wants is for me to sleep with him. He would also accept my sleeping with someone else—he's stated as much. It's not that Travis desires me, or if he does, it's beside the point. He just wants me to prove in no uncertain terms that I'm not loyal to Lander. He wants me to behave in a way that would hurt his brother should Travis choose to expose my sins to him. Perhaps more importantly, Travis wants to be sure that he can turn Lander against me if it ever serves his purposes.

And of course part of it is about power and control. Travis wants to control everyone in his life. My submission would be his victory.

Unless of course my loyalties are not with Travis *or* Lander. If I'm only loyal to the memories of my mother, shouldn't I do whatever I need to do in order to avenge her? Gaining Travis's trust has always been a means to an end, and it is true that I was willing to sleep with Lander when I thought *he* was my enemy . . .

. . . but no, not Travis. I just can't. Furthermore, it's not necessary. The trick is to make him think I'm willing to submit, find a way to hold him off. He just needs to believe that he's *going* to have me . . . at least until I've woven my noose and placed it around his neck.

I sigh and stare out the window. The leaves on the trees along the street are ridiculously green, screaming rather than stating their vitality. When I'm with Lander, when he's inside of me, I have a taste of that. It's funny that after years of pursuing men who made me feel numb, I now find myself brought to life by the touch of a man I once thought I hated. Even when he challenges me there's a certain pleasure in it.

And yet I haven't told Lander anything at all about Travis's proposal. Not a word. It's not that I don't trust Lander, I just can't predict him. I don't know how he would react. Is it the kind of information that would spur him to confront his brother and thereby screw up *everything*?

And secrets aren't the same as lies, are they?

The bus pulls to a stop two blocks from Travis and Jessica's place and I file out along with a few brow-beaten businessmen and upbeat interns.

My purse bangs against my side with each step I take down the sidewalk. I steady it with my hand and mentally run through the things I'll say to Jessica when I see her.

The doorman and security of Travis and Jessica's building greet me warmly. They all know me by now. Still, security calls up to Jessica before letting me go up to see her. For a tense moment I think she'll refuse me admittance, but shortly those fears are put to rest and in no time I'm riding up in the elevator.

When I get to the top floor, Jessica's waiting in the doorway. She's dressed in a peach shift that hangs stiffly around her slender form. Her hair is bundled up at the base of her neck and a perfect string of large pearls is around her neck. She looks like she could have been ripped from the pages of *Town & Country* magazine . . . except she looks a little fragile today. And there's a slump to her shoulders that indicates exhaustion or defeat, maybe both.

"Travis didn't tell me you would be coming today," she says, her voice assuming almost a mechanical quality.

I smile and shrug. "Perhaps I should have called first. I know Mr. Gable doesn't always remember to share my schedule with you."

"Oh, he doesn't forget. He just doesn't see the necessity of it." She turns at that and walks inside. Quietly I follow her, closing the door behind me.

Last time I saw Jessica she was drunk, sloppy, and mean. But right now, as she leads me into her office, she just seems sort of . . . blank.

Almost everything in Jessica's office, from the furniture to the art, is either a stark white or an onyx black. It's all very postmodern, which is more Travis's style than Jessica's, but then her preferences are never allowed to take precedence over her husband's.

She gestures toward the desk, and without a word I go to my usual spot behind the computer. She remains standing and moves to the window, looking out at the city.

"I suppose we should talk about . . . what happened," she says softly.

I raise my eyebrows in surprise. Jessica had been such a mess last time I was here it's hard to believe she even remembers anything of that day's events. But if she does, what part does she want to talk about?

Does she want to apologize for doing her level best to demean and insult me? Does she remember throwing out vaguely classist and racist statements? Or maybe she wants to talk about how she told everyone who would listen that I was a whore? There are so many ways we can go here.

"I know I was . . . a bit unpleasant that day."

I don't answer. That feels like a bit of an understatement.

"I suppose I should apologize." She turns to me, apparently expecting a response. "I don't believe I'm a good person," she says after I fail to answer her. "Now that I think about it, I'm not sure that anyone in my life ever even suggested that being good was important."

I consider not answering again but find myself asking the obvious question despite myself. "Do you want to be a good person?"

"Hmm," she says, considering. "I'm really not sure. I mean, in the end, where would it really get me?"

I can't help but laugh at that and she answers me with a quiet smile of her own.

"Do you think you're a good person, Bell?"

"Once upon a time, maybe, when I was truly young."

Now it's Jessica's turn to laugh, although even her giggles have a sort of hollow quality that is more disturbing than joyful. "Yes, well, it's easy to be good at five, although I'm sure there are more than a few kindergarten teachers who would argue the point," she quips. But then her smile melts to nothing. She turns away from me and back toward the glass. "What do you think it takes to be truly good?" she asks. "What tools must you have access to in order to achieve that?"

"I think," I say slowly, "maybe . . . maybe love. I think that being a good person requires some kind of experience with love."

"What kind of experience?" The sun is bright today, providing a glaring backdrop to Jessica's delicate silhouette.

"Oh, I'm not sure it matters," I muse. "The love of a parent, a sibling, or a teacher . . . maybe a lover."

"Travis knows what love is," she says.

"I highly doubt that," I say, the words flying from my mouth before I can stop them. I look nervously at Jessica, but she doesn't seem offended.

"No, no, he does," Jessica assures me. "He was in love before. And from what I understand she even loved him back."

A flash of memory, Lander saying something about a woman Travis once cared for but it didn't work out . . . he didn't know why . . . or something like that. "Do you know who she was?" I ask.

"Hmm?" Jessica had spaced for a moment, or maybe she was thinking about things outside of this room.

"The woman who Travis loved," I press. "Do you know her name?"

"Oh yes, it's Cathy." She pivots on her heel and crosses to the love seat. "Cathy Earnest. Common, don't you think?" She lowers herself onto the white leather cushions, her gaze still on the window. "It has no grace or prestige to it. If she went by Catherine at least she'd sound important."

"And why did Travis and Cathy break up?"

Jessica's eyes dart back to me but then she looks away just as quickly. "She's married now," she says, ignoring my question. "To Eli Lind, another awful name. But he's rich enough . . . not Gable rich, but still, perhaps she's happy."

"She could be," I agree. "But there are a lot of unhappy women married to wealthy men."

Jessica looks down at her hand and studies her wedding ring. It's a standard-issue solitaire on top of a plain white-gold band. It's pretty and expensive, but it has little individuality.

"Do you think Travis is over it?" I ask.

Jessica blanches, her eyes still glued to her ring. I realize immediately that she thinks I'm asking her if Travis is over his marriage to *her*.

"I mean," I say quickly, trying to clarify myself without letting on that I know she's misunderstood, "you two have been married for just under ten years. That's enough time to get over an old flame, isn't it?"

"You'd think so, wouldn't you," Jessica says dryly. "If you ask Travis, he was over her before we even started dating. He told me that their relationship was just a fling and that she was nothing to him. But then, as I'm sure you've come to realize by now, Travis is a liar."

I lean back in my chair, making it creak. "I only

know of one honest man and they crucified him over two thousand years ago. Men might have taken the wrong lesson from that because they've been lying ever since."

Again Jessica giggles and this time her laugh sounds almost genuine, almost. But the sound dies quickly as she presses her point. "The truth is," she says quietly, "Travis will never be over Cathy. Not really. And he will always hate every woman who has the audacity not to be her. You see," she says, her eyes moving back to me, "Travis knows love. I believe he may even know how to be kind, which makes his decision to embrace hate and cruelty that much more devastating."

For a moment neither of us say anything as her point sinks in. Then she breaks out in a hysterical little laugh. "Come to think of it," she says, "Travis and I might be a good match after all."

You're a perfect match. You're the kind of woman who would bear false witness against an innocent mother in exchange for marrying into the "right" family, and he's the kind of man who would ask you to do it.

"By the way, I'm better now," Jessica says, pulling me out of my thoughts. I shake my head, not understanding.

"I've thrown out the Vicodin and the codeine; they're all gone. As are the vodka and the bourbon. You won't find a single liquor bottle in the house. Since that night you took me to the hospital, the only thing

I've taken is Xanax during the day and a Valium or two at night to help me sleep, and I don't drink anything stronger than wine, and I've even cut back on that. I've turned a corner, as they say."

For a second I think she's joking, but her expression says otherwise. Only wine, Xanax, and Valium . . . in the last four days.

"When you didn't show up for a few days I was afraid Travis had fired you. He wouldn't tell me. He's barely talking to me."

"He hasn't fired me," I say truthfully.

She nods thoughtfully. "Last time I saw you I accused you of trying to sleep with him."

"Mrs. Gable, I swear I have no interest in sleeping with your husband."

"Yes, I know that now. I shouldn't have said it . . . or at least I should have said it differently." She takes a deep breath before continuing. "I should have said you're *going* to sleep with my husband."

"I really want you to try to hear me when I tell you, I'm absolutely not—"

Jessica holds up her hand to stop me. "You say that because you think your disinterest will be determinative," she says with a sigh. "But Travis always gets what he wants. *Always*. And if he wants you?" She shrugs, suggesting my fate is both inevitable and inconsequential.

"Mrs. Gable, that isn't going to happen."

Jessica rolls her eyes as if she finds my protests more exasperating than meaningful. "Listen, I'm just trying to tell you that *when* you sleep with him, I won't hold it against you. I'm . . . I'm letting go. This is my personal growth."

"Your personal growth," I repeat.

"Yes. I've been a bit tightly wound. That's why I was drinking too much. I was wasting my energy worrying about things I have no control over." She pauses a moment and looks me over, taking in my shoes and the cinched-waist blazer and camisole, all bought at my favorite consignment store. "Where are you from?" she asks. "Brooklyn? Florida? Or are you an illegal?"

Are you an illegal?

Those had been the words the police detective, Sean White, had asked my mother before he arrested her.

Are you an illegal?

My mother on her knees, sobbing, sick, covered in the blood of the man she had pinned all her hopes on.

Are you an illegal?

She hadn't even been a person to Detective White. Just a thing to use. She was used to bring a case to a close, used to help the Gables get away with murder, used to get Sean White a cushy, high-paying job at HGVB Bank.

Are you an illegal?

My nails dig into my palm as my hand clenches into a fist that I have concealed under the desk. "I was born here," I say, working hard to keep my voice level, calm, pacifying. "I'm an American."

"Ah, but not exactly from an important family,

right?" Jessica sighs and stretches out her legs. "My point is that it's highly unlikely that you'll marry well and you're certainly not going to be a captain of industry. At best you're going to be, well, a decently paid servant like you are now. So really, what does it matter if you have sex with my husband? If you can't marry rich you might as well have sex with the rich, maybe get a Fendi bag out of it . . . perhaps even a generous Christmas bonus. And besides, he's not a bad lover. He's very . . . technical. He knows how to touch a woman; he might even be able to make you like it." She closes her eyes and inhales deeply, only to let the breath leak out through clenched teeth so that it comes out as a hiss. "That's the ultimate humiliation, you know," she whispers. "Enjoying the touch of a man who doesn't care about you; a man who will never see you as anything more than a whore. But"—and with this her eyes pop back open and her smile returns—"in your case that's basically what you'll be, so, really, you'll have nothing to lose."

She watches me and waits for me to respond, but I don't say a word. I'm afraid that if I so much as breathe I'll lose the sliver of control that I'm holding on to and I'll strangle this bitch.

But Jessica takes my silence as acquiescence. She relaxes back into the cushions and stares up at the ceiling. "You see? We've both grown. We've both learned to accept the inevitable and embrace the silver lining rather than get lost in the storm clouds. It's good, don't you think? Now," she says, not waiting for me to answer as she gracefully crosses one leg over the other, "shall we get to work?"

For the next few hours we go over the Evites she's been sent and the donation requests from various charities she has supported that would like her support again (yes to the symphony, no to the veterans, and so on).

But mostly we work on the fund-raising dinner for senatorial hopeful Sam Highkin that's to take place on Tuesday, only four days away now. We need to put together a final head count, make sure the seating charts are perfect, touch base with the quartet she hired for the event as well as the florist. I'm to go down to the venue tomorrow to make sure they know exactly what to do and have everything they need. It's clear by the bored tone in Jessica's voice that she's done all this a million times before. She obviously has no passion for it, although to be fair, Jessica is rarely animated when she's not dangerously drunk.

At two thirty Jessica checks her watch. "I actually need to get going soon. I could ask you to stay and work, but . . . maybe we should just make it a short day," she suggests.

Jessica has left me in the penthouse alone many times before. The fact that she seems reticent to do so now means that she's picked up on something. Maybe from me, more likely from Travis. But no matter, I'm prepared for this.

"Sure," I say with a chipper smile. I stand up from the computer and slip my purse over my shoulder. "If it's all right, I'll just use the restroom and then be on my way. Maybe we can then just quickly go over the things you need me to work on before you leave?"

Again Jessica checks her watch. "I have to be in the limo in about ten minutes."

"Plenty of time," I assure her and leave the room to go to the bathroom down the hall. As soon as I close the door behind me I pull out the wrench from my purse. "Time to get to work," I whisper to myself.

❧

Minutes later I walk out into the hall and rush into the office. "There's some kind of leak under the bathroom sink," I tell her urgently. "I just turned it on and it went kind of crazy."

"What?" Jessica quickly follows me into the bathroom. I turn on the faucet and immediately water gushes from the pipes under the sink.

"But I don't have time for this! I have to make this appointment! It's . . . it's . . ."

I place a calming hand on her shoulder. "I'll call down to maintenance and make sure it's taken care of. You go, do what you need to do."

She looks at me and then down at the water. "Travis should be home a little after five. It has to be completely fixed by then. If he finds out I left without making sure this was handled . . ."

"Mrs. Gable," I say, keeping my voice at its most reassuring tone, "Mr. Gable will never even know there was a problem."

Frustrated, Jessica looks at her watch again. "Fine.

The number for maintenance is in my office in the top drawer of the desk. If they *can't* fix it quickly, call me."

"Of course, Mrs. Gable."

She nods and turns to leave, but then hesitates and turns back. "Will you still be attending the Highkin dinner with Lander?"

"I believe so, yes. Assuming he still wants to take me."

"Yes, I'm sure he does," Jessica says, somewhat ruefully. She pauses a moment to study me before adding, almost casually, "When you two took me to the hospital I was in a bad way. The doctor says that if I had indulged in another drink I might have slipped into some kind of alcoholic coma, maybe even died."

"Oh." I lean on the bathroom counter as I consider the implications of that.

"You may have saved my life," she adds quietly as her gaze drops to the water pooled on the bathroom floor. "Perhaps one day I'll be able to forgive you for it."

I remain silent as she turns and walks down the hall. As I hear the front door open and close I turn and look into the mirror. Anger and pain have defined over half of my life. I had thought that had made me hard, efficient, ruthless when need be, the perfect instrument for revenge. I had originally planned to let Jessica die and then make it look as if Travis had killed her. But when the moment of truth came, I couldn't do it.

The woman in the mirror looks confused, frustrated, maybe even a little bit scared. She's not as callous as I thought she was, as I *need* her to be. This woman in the mirror saved Jessica's life. I stare hard into my own eyes. "I think," I say aloud, "I'll have to find a way to forgive myself for that one as well."

I inhale a cleansing breath and then bend down to fix the sink before pulling out my cell and making a quick call. "I need a plumber," I say. "Can you be here in about fifteen minutes? Yes? Great."

I hang up and use a white monogrammed towel to soak up the mess.

chapter four

As I wait, I search Jessica's office for the safe. It seems doubtful to me that it would be in Jessica's office but one never knows. I look behind the wall art, I get on my knees and look under the furniture just in case it's a floor safe, but nothing. I get up and brush myself off and am about to try another room when I notice Jessica's iPad on the chaise longue. Carefully I pick it up and type in the four-digit password that I figured out weeks ago. I check her history, but to my relief there's no evidence that she's found the new email account I set up for her, or the message board that I have been posting on using that email as her identity.

The message board is for abused women. I wanted the police to be able to find a digital trail that made Travis look extra guilty once Jessica's body was found.

I always used Jessica's computer and I was careful to use it while she was napping so none of the posts happened at times when witnesses could testify that she was away from the IP address the posts came from. Every detail of my plan had been thought-out.

Lander still doesn't know that I ever even *wanted* her dead. Maybe he wouldn't care . . . or maybe he would. Maybe if I told him about my original plans he would look at me differently.

I'd rather lie to him forever than let that happen.

There's a knock at the door and I quickly go to answer it.

And there stands my man, in a baseball cap that hides his face from the overhead cameras, and a nylon navy windbreaker.

"Thank God," I say with a smile. "The plumber is here."

He quickly walks in and I close the door.

"How'd you get past security?" I asked.

"I got in through the service entrance."

"And no one stopped you?"

"No, they stopped me, a few even recognized me, and then I made up a story and paid them enough to pretend to believe me."

"Well," I say, eyeing the cheap windbreaker. "You're certainly not dressed to be noticed."

Lander takes off his jacket and drapes it over my shoulders. "It looks better on you."

"You're too sweet."

"Mmm. Have you started looking for the safe?"

"It's not in Jessica's office."

"Well, that's a shocker," Lander says dryly. "I don't

think he'd keep it in his room either. I'm going to start in the guest room, you go search the maid's room."

"Ooh, you're so sexy when you're handing out orders."

Lander laughs, and using the collar of the jacket pulls me forward. "You'd better be careful," he says, his voice a low, teasing growl, "or the next order might be a bit more salacious in nature."

"Promises, promises." I lean forward and kiss him slowly, biting his bottom lip gently before pulling away. "Aaand, I'm off," I say, suddenly pushing him away playfully and hurrying off to my destination. Jessica and Travis don't have a live-in maid. Neither one of them wants a stranger living with them. Jessica sometimes refers to the maid's room as Travis's library, or when she's feeling sarcastic, Travis's meditation room. It's small and the only furniture is a desk with no drawers, a chair, and two large bookcases, big enough to almost completely cover two walls. From the first, I pull out hardcovers and paperbacks three at a time before replacing them, looking for a hidden safe. Books about presidents, wars, dictators, economics, religion, history . . . being a serious book addict myself I'm actually a little impressed.

But I'm not finding a safe. So I start pulling books from the second bookcase. Here there are a few true crime books, a few thrillers . . . George Orwell is here, as is Aldous Huxley. I find *Fight Club* and *The Silence of the Lambs*. The only thing all these books have in common, aside from their dark outlook on human nature, is that they're all written by men. Except . . .

I pause as I pull out a book by Alison Weir, *The Lady in the Tower: The Fall of Anne Boleyn*. That surprises me. Obviously Boleyn's story is dark and it centers around the themes Travis seems to love—power, money, ruin—but Weir has a distinctly feminine sensibility that seems in contrast to the other books on these shelves. I start to open the book and two photos fall out, along with a folded-up piece of stationery.

I bend down and examine this unexpected treasure. The first photo is of a woman. Her thick brown hair is cut into a short, flapperlike bob. She's slender but curvy, with what I would consider an athletic hourglass figure. It looks like the picture was taken on a boat and she's holding on to a rail, the blue of the ocean behind her. Her smile looks almost devilish.

The next photo is of Travis and this woman together. I can't tell where they are . . . inside somewhere, perhaps at a convention center or a hotel. Behind them there are people mulling about, but Travis and this woman clearly aren't concerned with them. She is completely focused on the camera, her head tilted coquettishly to the side and her smile small and seductive. Travis, on the other hand, doesn't even seem to be aware of the camera. He's just completely absorbed with her. And the smile on his face . . . It's so odd. I've never seen Travis smile like that. It's . . . *genuine*. In this picture Travis actually looks happy. Maybe even . . . joyous? Is that possible? Could Travis be joyous?

I tuck the pictures back into the book and unfold the stationery. It's a letter:

Dear Travis,

    I can't wait to meet your father. I just know he's going to love me (doesn't everyone?). Seriously though, I'll be on my best behavior. And I love the necklace you gave me! I can't stop looking at it! Julie says it makes my eyes sparkle. But if your eyes can't sparkle when you're wearing hundreds of thousands of dollars in diamonds then you might as well just give up, right?

    But even without the diamonds our last weekend together would have been perfect. You're the first man who has ever really understood me. And believe me when I tell you, I understand you.

    I know how you feel about sentimentality . . . the same way I do. So I'll skip the really gooey stuff and just say this: You're going to be bigger than your father. You're going to take on the world and I'm going to be right by your side taking it on with you. We'll have the best of everything, but most importantly, we'll never be alone. You'll always have a partner in me and I swear on my life, on my father's <u>grave</u>, I will never hurt you.

    I will never leave you.

I love you,
Cathy

I check to see if the letter's dated. It is . . . it was written about twelve years ago.

He's kept it all these years.

Carefully I put the letter back and then pull out my phone and Google Cathy Earnest Lind. There are about three hundred thousand results on Google, and just over seventy-eight hundred when I plug in *Cathy Lind* and put quotation marks around the name.

I go to Google Images and scroll through her pictures. She's still pretty . . . maybe even beautiful. There are pictures of her on the red carpet for various functions, one of her standing by her husband's side while he shares a laugh with New York's mayor. She doesn't have a Wikipedia page or anything like that, and if she works I don't see any evidence of it here. But her husband, Eli, is a renowned oncologist at the Memorial Sloan Kettering Cancer Center and his father is a named partner in one of New York's more respected law firms lauded for its willingness to do certain cases pro bono if it truly believes in the cause. Eli is known as a generous philanthropist and appears to be a genuinely good guy. The weird thing is, she doesn't seem like a genuinely good girl. I obviously could be wrong about that, but there's just something about that letter she sent to Travis. If nothing else, her letter made it clear how important money and power were to her, and while everything she said was affectionate, none of it was exactly, well, nice.

Still, to keep it all these *years*. As the letter noted, Travis is not a sentimental guy. But he is meticulous, so the possibility that he might have just forgotten about these pictures and this book seems unlikely.

And that means that Jessica may have been right, Travis might still be hung up on this woman. Maybe he's even obsessed with her. It's certainly easier to believe that than that he might actually be capable of love.

Using my phone and my credit card I'm able to run a quick online background check on Cathy and get instant results. Now I have her birthdate. I also know that she has no children and no siblings and that both her parents are now gone. I have her address, the date of her wedding, and it seems that she does a lot to support local and state politicians, donating both time and money.

She likes to support politicians . . .

Oh, this is too good.

A new strategy starts to map itself out in my head. It's a little risky, but if it works, I'll be back in Travis's good graces and he'll never even come close to sleeping with me, not merely because I'll refuse, but because he won't want to. And if things really work the way I hope they will, Travis will become distracted, maybe even distracted enough to make a mistake.

It's a scheme that is ripped right out of the fairy tales and myths that I used to read so often: the strong man brought down by his infatuation with a woman he cannot have. Love. It.

I'm almost giddy as I rush back to Jessica's office and find a spare invitation to the fund-raising dinner. Using Jessica's fountain pen, I carefully write out Catherine's address on the envelope. And then I turn the invitation over and write a personal note in the kind of penmanship one might expect from a man:

Dear Mrs. Lind,
I've been impressed by your work in the
political field over the last several years and believe

*we share many of the same values and goals. I
hope you will come to my dinner where I will
detail my vision for both the state and the city of
New York. The dinner fee will of course be waived
for you.*

Thank you for your time,
Sam Highkin

I smile as I wave the invitation in the air for a moment, letting the ink dry before sealing the envelope.

"Doncia, did you search the maid's room?"

I look up to see Lander standing in the doorway giving me a peculiar look.

"Almost done in there. I, um, got distracted."

"You got distracted," Lander says flatly.

"Look." I rush over to him, holding the sealed invitation, "I found something—"

"Will it help us put Travis in prison?"

"Well, not directly, no."

"I can't be here for very long, we have to stay focused."

I bristle slightly at his tone. "No one is more focused than I am," I say as I carefully put the invitation into my purse, which I place on the chaise longue. "I'll finish the maid's room, and you should check his kids' rooms. Then I'll meet you back in the master bedroom. Does that work for you?" I ask, almost sarcastically.

He smiles slightly, as if amused by my irritation. "I doubt it's in the children's rooms, but I'll check."

"Good." I push past him back to the maid's room

and resume my search, which turns up nothing, of course. And even if we do find a safe, who's to say that there will be anything interesting in it? As far as we know, Travis is using the safe to store his Rolexes.

I stand in the middle of the room, double-checking to make sure that there isn't something I missed. I haven't actually been working for Travis and Jessica for that long. The fact that I've gotten them to trust me as much as they do is an accomplishment I'm actually quite proud of. But Lander, he *is* a Gable. He's a VP at HGVB and he's been trying to dig up dirt on his family for almost as long as I have. So why hasn't he turned up a smoking gun yet? Because he's looking for the wrong things, *that's* why.

Frustrated, I leave the maid's room and go back to the master bedroom. Minutes later, Lander meets me in there. "I've checked the kitchen and dining room too," he says. "Nothing."

"Maybe he doesn't have a safe anymore." I look behind the dresser and then the bed.

"He has it. I talked to the people at the store who sold it to him. He paid for home installation—it wasn't a temporary item. So . . ." He gestures with his hand as if to say that it has to be here somewhere.

I give him a look. I'm still not sure I'm buying this. But instead of protesting I go into Travis's closet. It's huge. All the clothes here are expensive and there is enough space on the bar to prevent anything from getting wrinkled. There are built-in drawers and shelves that stack almost to the ceiling . . . in fact . . .

"Lander?" I call.

"Yes." I turn to see him leaning against the doorframe.

"Do you see something odd about these shelves?"

He cranes his neck up to examine them. "They're not very practical," he notes. "They're so high you can't get to them without a stepladder."

"Yeah," I agree, turning my gaze back to the shelves again. "I can't even really see if there's anything on the top one."

I feel him move behind me, his breath now in my hair. "You can't see portions of the wall behind some of those shelves either."

"There's a ladder in the laundry room," I say quietly.

"I'll be right back."

In less than a minute Lander is back by my side, stepladder in hand. I take it from him eagerly and climb to the top as he holds it steady.

"Well?" he asks hopefully.

I place my hands on the edge of one of the shelves as I scan its surface and see . . . nothing. Nothing but dust bunnies and a dead spider. All of the shelves are empty. "No dice."

"Damn it," Lander grumbles as I begin to step down. But then something catches my eye.

"Doncia, are you all right?"

"There's something in the door."

"What do you mean there's something *in* the door?"

"The top edge of the door. There's a round metal thing in it; I mean it's *in* it. It looks like someone drilled a hole and put it in there."

"What kind of thing?" Lander asks.

"Maybe it's a washer? But then why . . ." I climb down and move the stepladder to the door before climbing right back up again. "It definitely looks like a washer . . . and . . . yeah, someone made a hole in the door specifically to fit this thing in. You can tell." I try to get my fingernail into the very small space between the washer and the wood to pull it out but it's not working. Still, just doing that gives me a better sense of what I'm dealing with. "Lander," I breathe, "it's not really just a washer. That's just a makeshift lid to something."

"Get down," Lander orders. I do so quickly and he takes my place on the stepladder. "Do you have a nail file?"

I don't, but it doesn't take me long to find one in Jessica's bathroom. When I bring it to Lander he digs into the hole, but he still can't get the cylinder out.

"It's a genius hiding place," he mutters. "But how the hell does he get it out of . . . Doncia, go to the kitchen and see if you can find a magnet."

"They have a stainless steel refrigerator, why would they have a magnet?"

"Just go."

I rush to the kitchen and start a serious search. It takes me about five minutes to find a magnet wedged way in the back of a junk drawer. It's a small, old-fashioned horseshoe magnet at that. Now why would they have this? I bring it to Lander, who takes it and places it above the washer . . . and the washer connects with it immediately. Slowly he pulls out a metal cigar tube. "Well," he says slowly, "isn't this interesting."

"What's in it?" I ask.

He climbs down and opens the tube. I hold my hands out like a child waiting for candy. And like a benevolent adult he pours the treats right into my palm. Two keys, taped together so they almost look like one, and a USB stick.

Almost reverently Lander takes the USB stick from my hand, holding it up to the light as if he's examining a fine jewel. "If this is what I think it is, we may have them," he whispers.

We both fall silent as we examine the delicate little device in his hand. It was meticulously hidden, the way truly damning sins should be. Between his thumb and forefinger Lander holds something that is capable of holding an ocean of information . . . and if it does, it could be powerful enough to open the floodgates of hell.

Lander turns to me, his eyes dancing with the light of possibilities, his smile broad and unaffected as he slips the flash drive into his shirt pocket. "We may actually have them."

I giggle and throw my arms around his neck, clutching the keys in my hand as his lips press against mine. When we finally break away I squeal, "We might have them!"

Lander laughs and picks me up as I wrap my legs around his waist. I feel like there should be music, confetti, fireworks, everything! This could be the defining moment of my adult life!

And I'm sharing it with Lander.

I bend my neck and find his lips again and this time the kiss is even more passionate. My free hand moves into his hair as he pushes me up against the hard wood of the open door. His kiss, his strength, the heat of his body . . . it all feels like delicious victory.

"I want you," I whisper as his lips find my throat. "Right here."

I feel his smile against my skin as my nipples harden, scratching against the lacy fabric of my bra, pressing against him, broadcasting my desire. And all the while the words *we have them, we have them, we have them* are echoing through my mind.

While I cling to him, his hand moves to my panties, which are already wet for him. He pulls them aside and I groan as his fingers find my clit, his heat mingling with mine.

My entire body shudders against him and I bite down on his shoulder, practically ripping the fabric of his shirt with my teeth as he continues to play with me. His erection is now against the most sensitive skin of my inner thigh, the rough fabric of his trousers a frustrating reminder of all that separates us.

"Enter me," I whisper. "Here, in this room."

"In the home of our enemies," Lander replies as he uses his free hand to unfasten his belt. This is everything I've wanted, everything I've worked for . . . and so much more.

"Adoncia," he whispers.

I open my mouth to say his name in response but the word that comes out is "Triumph."

I taste the salty skin of his neck as the fabric of his pants falls lower. Now I can really feel him. He removes his hand from between my legs and uses his cock to massage me, teasing me, bringing me to the brink of a new, luscious insanity.

Because that's what this is. This risk we are taking is insanity. Our victory dance could be our undoing.

And yet I know it won't be. Because I'm Adoncia, his sweet warrior.

And he's *Lander*.

When he thrusts inside me he fills me with his power even as I embrace him with mine. I feel the flash drive pressed against me, wedged right there between our two hearts. Such a mechanical piece of evidence serving as such a sweet aphrodisiac as his mouth finds mine. I cross my ankles as my legs circle his hips, my sex tightening around him as he continues to grind against me, hitting every nerve ending as my back presses against the open door whose secrets have been exposed.

The orgasm rocks through me and this time I do say his name, calling it out as if it's my battle cry as he comes inside of me, pulsating with conquest and passion.

For a moment neither of us move, forehead to forehead, eyes closed, our breaths mingling in chorus, the mysterious keys still clutched in my palm. It's a perfect moment.

There's a sound . . . like the jiggling of a doorknob as someone prepares to enter the penthouse.

My eyes open wide in panic, but gently, Lander puts his hand to my mouth.

We hear the door open and then Travis's voice.

"I don't know what you're talking about, I never meet clients in my home," I hear Travis say. I wait to see if there's going to be another voice but there's just silence and then Travis speaks again. "You know when I've met Javier. You helped me set those meetings up. My father never involves himself with this side of the business. Yes, Micah, yes, I know." Travis's voice gets louder then softer as he walks down the hall, first toward us, then farther away.

Slowly Lander lowers me to the floor and readjusts his clothes as I pull down my skirt. Glancing at Lander's watch I confirm what is now an irrelevant fact . . . Travis wasn't supposed to be here for another hour at least.

Regardless, he's here now. Still struggling to catch my breath, I creep toward the door. Behind me, Lander carefully climbs up the stepladder and replaces the now-empty cigar tube.

Quietly, *oh so* quietly, I place my ear to the bedroom door.

"I'm not lying to you," I hear Travis say. "I have no need to. Even if Javier was here, it shouldn't matter."

I turn to look at Lander, who is staring pointedly at the stepladder. I don't need him to speak to know what he's thinking: even if we're able to sneak out of here, we can't put it back.

With the silence and stealth of a stalking tiger, he folds it up and then lays it on the ground before pushing it under the bed. He gets it so that it's lying under the center of the mattress. Someone would have to get down on their knees to find it there. Of course if they find it missing from the laundry room . . .

I squeeze my eyes closed. I can't let my mind go there yet. I have to deal with what's happening right *now.* I put the keys in my pocket and press my ear to the door again. I can still hear Travis talking on the phone; now it sounds like he's moved into another room, but I can't quite tell what room that is, and I can't tell if he's in a position where he'll be able to see the hall that leads to the front door.

Lander comes up behind me and gently moves me aside. He listens for a moment and then opens the door a crack. I can hear Travis a little better now. If I had to guess I'd say he was in the living room. Lander puts his finger to his lips, takes my hand, and leads me out of the room.

"I see." I hear Travis's voice floating down the hall, but when I look over my shoulder he's still out of sight.

He's in another room, talking on his phone, I assure myself. *Just get to the door and get the hell out of here.*

"I'm surprised," I hear Travis say as we get closer and closer to freedom. "Isn't this a little beneath your pay grade, Micah?"

If I wasn't so freaked out right now I'd love to eavesdrop on this conversation. But then I hear more footsteps. Travis is in the living room . . . and it sounds like he might be moving toward the hall.

Lander speeds up his pace, pulling me along, and then quickly, silently, he opens the front door and we slip out. I close the door behind us with barely a click.

Immediately my legs start trembling with relief and the aftershocks of repressed panic. I bend over, resting my hands on my knees as I inhale deep, shaky breaths.

"Doncia, we have to go."

"Yes, I . . ." But my voice trails off as I'm struck with a new, sickening realization.

I've left my purse in Jessica's office. Worse still, that invitation is in my purse.

"Adoncia, now!"

I don't respond and instead count slowly to ten and then, backward from ten to one.

"Doncia—"

I pull myself up, smooth out my skirt, my hair, run my fingers around my lips to ensure there's no smeared lipstick. And then, after exhaling one more time, I place a hand on each of Lander's cheeks. "I have to go back in."

"Why the hell would you do that?" He's still whispering but I can hear the edge in his voice.

I consider telling him about the purse but something stops me. I don't want him to think I feel pressured to walk back into the lion's den. I don't want him to think he has reason to rescue me. I want this to look like a choice. And if I can convince him of that then maybe I can convince myself too.

"It's time," I say slowly, "for me to gain back Travis's trust."

"*Now?*" Lander asks. "You don't even know if that's possible! You—"

"If Jessica comes home and tells him I've been here before I get to try my hand at this then it *won't* be possible. And we don't have time to discuss this. You should go."

"Wait—"

I turn around and ring the bell, giving Lander no choice but to quickly retreat. I watch as he strides around the corner toward the elevator, but I'm under no illusion that he's going far.

Still, now that he's out of sight some of the fear creeps back in. What if Travis has already found my purse? What about the stepladder? How often does he check his little hiding spot to pull out that USB stick? What if—

The door swings open and Travis stands before me, looking as cool and menacing as he's ever been in his life.

"Hello, Mr. Gable!" I say, flashing him my sweetest, most guileless smile. "Is this a bad time?"

chapter five

Minutes later we're both in the living room. The cognac Travis had apparently made himself while I was sneaking out is now sitting on the coffee table, neglected. Travis is sitting on the black leather sofa, staring at me without even a hint of warmth.

"Bell Dantès." Travis says the name like he's referring to a particularly dangerous and contagious virus. "I believe I told you I didn't need you to come in today."

"I . . . I know," I say, my hands clasped in front of me like a little girl ready to confess her misdeeds to a teacher. "I was actually here earlier. I did a little work for Jessica. I'm afraid I left something in her office."

"My wife called you in?" He reaches for his drink, takes a leisurely sip. I think of Lander with his champagne flute filled with Cristal. There is something very sexy about the way Lander drinks. But the way Travis cradles his glass, it's just . . . intimidating.

"She didn't call," I admit. "I came of my own volition."

Travis doesn't say anything for a moment and then takes his glass to his lips one more time before asking, "Are you here to confess?"

My pulse goes into overdrive but I work to keep my face impassive. "Confess what, Mr. Gable?"

"That you're the one who called Lander and asked him to come and help Jessica when you thought she might overdose, even though I told you to leave her be."

"No! Of course not! Mrs. Gable called him. They both said as much when Lander showed up."

"Lander's a con man," Travis says dispassionately. "And Jessica was simply parroting him. She was so out of it she would have said anything. But the truth is that my brother has never been on my wife's drunk dial list."

"It wasn't me, Mr. Gable."

"I don't need you, Bell. You can continue to fuck my brother if you please him but I have no use for you."

"Mr. Gable, the only reason I'm still seeing Lander is because you *asked* me to!"

"You've fallen for him."

"No!" I shake my head vigorously. Outside the windows the sky has turned an icy blue that almost matches Travis's eyes; it's as if his menace has spread all over the city.

"Your protestations are sweet, but meaningless. Go. Be Lander's girlfriend du jour, ask him to pay you for services rendered because you won't be getting another paycheck from me."

"You said you were going to give me a chance to prove my loyalty."

"When the hell did I say . . ." And then his voice fades off. I don't know that I've ever seen Travis look surprised before, but as he begins to grasp what I'm referring to, his eyes widen slightly, his head tilts almost imperceptibly to the side. "What exactly are you suggesting, Bell?"

"You know," I say quietly, holding his gaze.

"Yes, I think I do. Still, I'd like to be sure we're on the same page."

I think about my purse in the office, I think about the envelope inside. "You asked me to sleep with you. You said that if I did it would prove that I wasn't loyal to Lander."

"I said you needed to sleep with *someone*," Travis corrects. "I certainly don't want to be accused of pressuring you to sleep with a man or woman who doesn't appeal to you. As long as it's not Lander the choice is yours."

I step forward, stand before him as he looks up at me. I actually like standing over Travis like this; it makes me feel powerful. Of course I'd like him lower still, on his knees, uselessly begging for a reprieve from the punishment I hope to heap upon him.

Or I could simply have his head on the chopping block while I wield the sword in my hand.

I think of that sword as I reach down and stroke his cheek, feeling the prickly hairs that have just begun to fight their way back after the morning's shave.

"I've made my choice," I say quietly. "I choose you."

He grabs my hand and pulls it away from him. "Don't be too tender. This won't be a labor of love, you'll simply be making a point."

"It's more than a point," I counter. "I'll be proving myself to you. I want to work for you, Mr. Gable. Lander thinks he's fooling me. He's trying to act like I mean something to him, but I know he also plans to toss me aside soon enough. That's what men like him do. But you? You've always been very straight about what you want and what you don't."

"Of course. I don't care enough about you to lie," Travis says dismissively. And yet I notice that he still hasn't let go of my hand.

"But you care about what I can do for you," I reply. "You know that I'm smart and resourceful. You know that if there is one person who can find out Lander's secrets, it's me. You know I can help you with the business you like to do in the shadows of HGVB, away from the prying eyes of regulators and inspectors. I don't know exactly what kind of business that is," I add when I see Travis's eyes darken, "but you like that too. You like that I don't ask too many questions. You," I say, slowly lowering myself onto his lap, "like my moral ambivalence."

He allows me to pull away my hand so I can slide my arms around his neck as I continue to stare into his eyes. "I can do so much for you," I say again. "Professionally . . . and in other ways too. You won't love me, you don't even have to like me. But trust me, Mr. Gable, you want me on your side."

The smile forms slowly, stretching across his face at a sinister pace.

Travis never looks more evil than when he smiles. "On your knees, Bell."

A cold chill runs through me and yet I return his grin. "Your wife will be home soon."

"No matter. She can watch if she likes. Or she can just wait until we're done. She doesn't get a say in my activities." Before I can react he slides his hand between my legs and finds my panties. I jump, still sensitive from my recent lovemaking. "My, my, you must be sincere because you're already wet. It would seem now is the perfect time for us to consummate our business deal."

"But if Jessica tells Lander I slept with you," I say, gently but firmly pulling his hand away, "I won't be able to get information out of him. I'll be of little use to you then. For this to work, we have to keep this a secret."

He pauses, but only for a moment. "Jessica is very good at keeping secrets. It's one of her few talents."

"Your children will be home soon too."

Travis doesn't respond to this. His eyes move away from me as he considers the situation.

"In four days Lander will be taking me to the fund-raising dinner for Sam Highkin. I'll sit with him, let him whisper compliments in my ear, but when it's all over I'll claim that there's some work I need to do in order to wrap up the event. It'll be my duty as a personal assistant."

"And how will you perform your duty?"

I raise my eyebrows. "I'll follow your instructions. The dinner is just a stone's throw away from both The Peninsula and The St. Regis. They're both lovely hotels."

"So they are." He runs his hand up and down my leg. I work hard not to flinch. "And then after I'm done with you, I'll send you off to Lander," he says with a laugh. "So you can service him for me. Let him think he's the only one. Just keep lowering his guard."

"Whatever you like, Mr. Gable," I say. I keep thinking about the sword, I think about my objective, I think about anything and everything other than his hands. "I work for *you*," I whisper.

As the words leave my lips I hear a key in the door.

I bring my lips to his ear. "Soon," I whisper, and scrape my teeth against his lobe before sliding off his lap. I move quickly to a spot by the window, doing everything I can to look innocent as Jessica walks in.

"Oh, Travis . . . I thought you would be home later." She looks from me to him, and despite her words earlier she flushes with humiliation as she asks, "Am I interrupting something?"

Travis raises his eyebrows but I quickly shake my head. "No, no, I was just leaving. I left something in your office and I'll be on my way."

I rush out before anyone can stop me, feeling more grateful to Jessica than I ever thought possible. Of course, even as I grab my handbag from the office I realize that there's still the problem of the stepladder under the bed. But there's simply no way of moving it now.

I go to the door and throw it open to find the nanny, Kamila, reaching for the door as two children stand by her side.

Travis and Jessica's three-year-old daughter, Mercedes, peers up into my face. "I know you!" she says brightly before skipping past me, followed by her much more sullen seven-year-old brother, Braden.

"How are you, Bell?" Kamila asks with a friendly smile.

"Okay," I say, and then thinking about the series of close calls I've just had I say it with more emphasis. "I'm *okay*."

Kamila laughs, undoubtedly thinking I'm simply happy to have survived another day working for the Gables.

"See you later, Kamila," I say as I swiftly move around her, striding toward the elevator and pressing the button over and over again until it opens.

When I get to the ground floor I shoot out of the building as if it's on fire. *Walk, don't run, to the emergency exit—but do walk fast.* I try to steady my breathing as I move down the street, but as I turn the corner a hand reaches out and grabs me.

Of course it's Lander, glaring down at me. "We're a team," he says, his voice cool and calm, a perfect contradiction to the frustration and anger that is reflected in his eyes. "You don't get to make decisions about putting yourself at risk without my input."

"Oh I beg to differ," I say, yanking my arm away. "I'll work with you to bring down the bastards in your family, but you don't get to tell me what risks I can or cannot take."

"You say that as if your safety isn't my business," Lander counters. "It is."

"Really? And why is that?" I want the words to come out as a challenge, but even to my ears they sound weak, like a plea.

Because I know exactly what I want him to say. I want him to say, *It's my business because I love you*.

I want him to say those words. I want him to cleanse me with them, washing away the memory of Travis's touch. And maybe if he can say it, I can say it too. *I love you*. God, I haven't heard those words since my mother died . . . before then, really. In the last few years that I visited her she had stopped being so expressive of her feelings. I had thought she was guilty, and although she wanted to be understanding I know a part of her hated me for that.

I made the one person in my life who loved me, hate me.

So please, Lander, tell me you love me. Tell me I'm worthy of that. Tell me there's more to my life than revenge.

Lander looks down at me, the anger and frustration subsiding and being replaced by something else, something I can't quite identify. "Because we're a *team*, Adoncia," he says. "Team members look out for each other. They take responsibility for each other. It's the only way to win."

I squeeze my eyes closed. Travis and Jessica have been bombarding me with insults and indignities for a good portion of the day, but nothing they've said or done has hurt as much as what my lover has just said to me now.

When my eyes open again I stare out at the taxis that are weaving through traffic. At the pretzel stand across the street, at anything and everything except Lander.

"We'll win," I say quietly. "As far as we know victory might literally be in your pocket." I reach forward and pat the pocket containing the flash drive. "But we're going to have to play the game until we seal the deal. And to that end I'm going to need some information. Tell me everything you can about Cathy Earnest Lind."

chapter six

Twenty minutes later I'm taking a cab to Cathy Lind's home in Park Slope, a highly gentrified neighborhood in Brooklyn. Lander is going back to his place to sort through whatever information is on the USB drive. He didn't have that much of interest to tell me about Cathy. Lander was away at college for most of the time Travis was with her. But he does remember meeting her a couple of times and apparently Travis was very different when he was with her. Maybe not *better* exactly. It was more that he was too focused on Cathy to bother tormenting the other people around him. Anything that can distract Travis from tormenting is worthy of attention.

Of course all of this might be moot if whatever is on the drive is particularly incriminating. That's what I'm hoping for, *praying* for. And considering how well Travis hid that thing it's certainly possible. It's a minor miracle that I spotted it at all. I probably wouldn't have if everything else in that penthouse hadn't been so immaculate and perfectly crafted. A washer in a door just didn't make sense in that environment. Still, I have to hand it to Travis for creativity.

As for the safe, well, we didn't find it, but I'm still not convinced it was all that important to begin with.

And then there are these keys. I pull them out and hold them up to the diminishing light. Lander and I haven't even really talked about these. Maybe whatever's on the USB stick will tell us what secrets they can open.

I find a safe spot in my purse for the keys and tuck them away before fixing my eyes on the traffic-filled street that stretches before me. In many respects, it feels like things are starting to go our way.

Which makes me worry about that stalking predator named Disappointment. That beast has gotten its claws into my heart one too many times and I've yet to build up an immunity to the pain.

&

By the time I get to Park Slope the horizon is streaked with shades of orange and purple and the icy blue sky has turned into a dusky gray. If I'm lucky Cathy's husband won't be home yet. But if he is, I'll deal with it.

It's not hard to find Cathy's place. Her block is lined with brownstones that mask their steep real estate listing prices with a distinct middle-class sensibility. The cars parked here are mostly shiny new hatchbacks and the clean sidewalks provide safe passage for the women pushing their seven-hundred-dollar strollers toward home. But the women are moms, not nannies. The people who live in Park Slope don't consider themselves to be elitists. They raise their own children and cook their own wild-caught salmon and quinoa.

It's hard to imagine Travis being obsessed with a woman who lives here.

Of course, Cathy doesn't live in one of the town houses. She lives on the top floor of the historic building on the corner. Constructed of brownstone and brick with copper and terra-cotta flourishes, it's both elegant and approachable. I climb the steps and walk into the building's first floor, or what the locals would call "the parlor floor," and find a desk staffed with employees who can help me.

"Bellona Dantès?" the woman at the desk asks, repeating the name I've given her before calling up to Mrs. Lind. "Am I pronouncing that right?"

"Perfectly," I say, all sugar and spice. "But I'm just the acting courier. I'm here to deliver an invitation to a dinner at which senatorial hopeful Sam Highkin will be speaking and laying out his plans and aspirations for New York."

The woman nods and makes the call. "Mrs. Lind? Yes, I have a woman here who would like to hand deliver an invitation for a dinner featuring . . ." She pauses and looks down at her notes. "Featuring Sam Highkin . . . He's running for the Senate? Right. Then shall I have her leave the invitation with me?"

"Tell her the dinner is being hosted by Mr. Travis Gable," I say in a stage whisper.

"Wait," the woman says into the phone, "the courier also wants me to inform you that the dinner will be hosted by Travis Gable. I'll have the invitation here at the desk until . . . What? Oh, very well. Yes, right away."

The woman at the desk hangs up the phone, looking puzzled. "She asked that you be sent right up."

She leads me to the elevator and uses her key that allows the elevator to go to the residential floors before leaving me to my task.

My heart's beating a little too fast as the elevator lifts me to the fourth floor. I don't fully know what to expect. I don't know how I'll be received. All I know is that I have to convince her to come to that dinner.

When the doors open I'm faced with a woman wearing a sleeveless, hooded top with a large white rose appliqué on the front paired with a short, white A-line skirt. It's a hip, casual outfit that probably cost her upward of fifteen hundred dollars. Her dark hair, now much longer than the bob she had worn during her younger years, is loosely pulled back into an upward twist, giving her a windswept look that is both sexy and sweet.

But her still posture speaks of nothing but trepidation. Her eyes are a little too wide and she's not smiling. "Travis sent you?" she says in what is little above a whisper.

"Mr. Gable would like you to attend," I say as I

hand her the invitation. When she doesn't move I say, in a softer tone, "He'd like to see you."

Her lower lip begins to tremble. Catching herself, she looks away, putting her hand to her cheek. "Please," she says, "come in."

She leads me through what is truly a magnificent flat. It's a ballroom converted into a forty-two-hundred-square-foot, five-bedroom apartment. The windows are trimmed with stained glass through which the encroaching night slips in and gives everything a smoky glow. It's bigger than Travis's place, but is still probably about an eighth of the price. Regardless of how much they gentrify Brooklyn, the prices and the prestige will never reach the heights of Manhattan real estate.

She leads me into a ridiculously spacious kitchen with mahogany cabinetry and gestures toward a bar chair by the island as she opens the freezer and takes out a bottle of Grey Goose.

"He really wants to see me?" she asks as I pull myself into the chair.

"Yes, very much so."

Cathy takes a swig from the bottle. Then, realizing the faux pas, turns to me and asks, "I'm sorry, would you like some?"

"No, thanks."

"Really, I insist," she says. "Come make it as you like it. There's tonic water in the refrigerator."

Reluctantly I get up, retrieve the tonic water, and pour myself a weak drink.

"I'll have the same," Cathy says.

I look up at her, a little startled by her presumption that I'm serving both of us, but don't argue as I pour and hand her the drink. She's a little awkward and clumsy in the way she takes it from me. It makes me wonder how much she had before I got here.

"Thank you," she says as she lifts her glass to me before taking a sip. "I haven't spoken to Travis in years," she says. "Shall we sit?"

This time we both sit at the island, across from each other. For at least a full minute neither of us says anything as Cathy sips her drink and stares out into space.

When she speaks again I can hear the raw emotion in her voice. "So . . . he's leaving her?"

The question takes me aback. "I . . . He didn't say. Look, I'm sort of breaking the rules here. I'm really Travis's personal assistant. I've also just started dating his brother so Travis and I have developed a familial relationship."

Cathy breaks out in a laugh. "A familial relationship?" she repeats. "With Travis? What kind of family are we talking about here? You mean a familial relationship like it existed within the Tudor family? Complete with civil wars and decapitations? That kind of family?"

I sit back in my stool. "Oh," I say, trying to keep my tone as casual as possible. "Are you a Tudor aficionado?"

"A bit, certainly enough to see the resemblance between them and the Gables," she says wryly, then adds with a self-effacing smile, "I actually am into the Tudors. I've always been a bit obsessed with Anne Boleyn."

"*The Lady in the Tower*," I note.

"Yes! Oh, I got that book for Travis when I was trying to explain my fascination! He didn't get it at first but . . ." She lets her voice trail off. "I'm sorry, I'm . . . I'm talking about things that don't matter. None of that matters at all anymore."

"I think it matters," I say gently. "You know, Travis didn't want me to tell you that the invitation is really coming from him." I push the invitation over to her. She fingers it but doesn't open the envelope. "He had Sam Highkin, that's the candidate the dinner's being thrown for, he had him write a personal note to you . . . or maybe he had someone else write it. I don't know. He just . . . he wants to see you, but he's proud, Mrs. Lind. He doesn't want to admit how much he's missed you."

She lets out another little derisive laugh. "It's been over a decade." Then her face grows solemn, almost angry. "Over ten years. That's how long this charade has lasted. And why? Because he's weak, that's why. Only a weak man sticks with a marriage of convenience for ten goddamned years. And he had *kids* with her! That must have made daddy-Edmund happy."

I run my hand across the counter. She's hinting at something big here and I'm dying to find out what it is. But I have to handle this perfectly. I can't push too hard; she might clam up. And I can't do anything that will keep her from coming to the dinner on Tuesday.

"Do you think Mr. Edmund Gable would be upset if his son split with his wife?"

"Well, Edmund's the one who insisted Travis marry her, so I would think so," she says irritably. "I'm better suited for Travis, you know. And I'd be a much better standard-bearer of the Gable name. You hear stories about Jessica all over town! By now she could probably drink Charlie Sheen under the table. No one takes her seriously; they take the Gable *name* seriously, but not her."

"Why would Edmund Gable want his son to marry Jessica?" I ask, keeping my voice soft, not pushy, and certainly not as eager as I'm feeling.

Cathy toys with the envelope, tapping one edge on the counter, then the other. "What was your name again? Bellona?"

"People call me Bell."

"Well, Bell, if you come up with an answer to that question I'll give you ten thousand dollars. Hell," she says, taking another sip, "make it twenty. Twenty thousand dollars for the reason why that woman is so damned important to the Gables' family fortune. Twenty thousand dollars if you can tell me why Travis gave up *me*, a woman he loves, a woman who has more class in her little finger than that junkie he's married to has in her whole body, why he gave up *me*, for that pill-popping basket case."

There are a few clues in Cathy's little tirade aside from the suggestion of a slightly inflated, albeit bruised, ego. One of them is her use of the present tense. She didn't say Travis *loved* her, but that he loves her. Perhaps that's her ego speaking. Or maybe it's something else.

"Do you miss him?" I ask quietly.

She straightens her posture and sucks in a slow, steadying breath. "Don't be ridiculous, I'm a happily married woman," she says primly. "Eli has given me everything Travis wouldn't. Look." She waves her hand around, gesturing to the room as a whole. "Look at this place! And you know, Travis isn't the only one who dabbles in New York politics. I've helped many a man, and woman, get elected. People respect the Lind name too, you know. My husband may not have Travis's money, but people *like* Eli. And you know what? If Travis had married me people would have liked him too. That's what a good wife can do for you. That's what *I* could have done for him. We complemented each other. We compensated for each other's weaknesses and we enhanced each other's strengths. But Jessica?" She shrugs. "As far as I can tell, she's nothing but dead weight." She brings her thumbnail to her mouth and nibbles on it lightly. "He really wants to see me?" she asks again in an almost girlish whisper.

"Yes, he does, Mrs. Lind. But . . . he really can't know I told you that. I just . . . I thought you should know. Still, if we could pretend that you just received that in the mail?"

She looks at me for the first time since I walked in the door. She narrows her eyes as she examines me, as if she's trying to bring me into focus or something. "You're quite pretty, aren't you?"

It's an odd question and I'm not sure how to respond. "Thank you?"

"Are you his mistress?"

"No," I say, by now almost bored with the question.

She looks away, takes another sip of her drink. "I was offered that position. I could have been his kept woman. *That* was going to be my consolation prize. It's the same offer Henry the Eighth initially gave Anne Boleyn. She refused it, as did I. But her refusal got her a king, while I got Eli." Her hand caresses the invitation. "I *chose* Eli," she says, squeezing the disappointment out of the words.

For a minute or so we just sit there. I can almost see her walking back in time, to a moment when she was on the cusp of having it all. I try to imagine it, try to envision Travis loving someone and being loved back. But I can't quite do it. It's easier for me to believe in unicorns than it is for me to believe that Travis was ever the kind of man who would hold a woman's hand.

Cathy continues to toy with the invitation, her hands moving over it a little more roughly now, as if she's using it as a rope to pull her back into the present. After another minute or two she takes a deep breath and asks, "Where is this dinner?"

"The address is on the invitation."

"What, you can't tell me?" she snaps. "Would that ruin the story you've concocted about me getting this in the mail?"

"No, no," I say, rattling off the name of the place and the address.

"Really?" She scrunches up her nose in distaste. "Did Jessica pick that venue?"

"Actually, I think it was Mr. Gable's choice. It's a rather impressive place, historic even. And since it's on a Tuesday night I don't know if they'll have other events going on. We may have the whole building to ourselves."

"Oh." She hesitates before adding, "Well, I hear it's much improved since the remodel. I assume I will not be asked to pay into this man's campaign. I know who he is and he goes against everything my husband supports." She squints down at the envelope before adding, "Travis can't expect my loyalties to turn on a dime just because he's finally reaching out to me, not after all this time."

"You won't be asked to pay a cent," I promise with a smile. "You'll practically be the guest of honor."

chapter seven

As soon as I leave Cathy's I call Lander.

"Well?" I ask eagerly. "What's on the USB?"

"It's encrypted. I'm working on it."

I pause a moment, standing on the corner of the street, the sky above me now as dark as a city sky can get. "Encrypted."

"This is good, Adoncia," he assures me. "It means that what's here is important."

"But what if you can't crack the encryption?"

"Then I'll hire someone who can."

I nod and inhale the cooling breeze. I've heard so many tales of hackers doing the impossible. The advancements in hiding information will always be five steps behind the advancements in uncovering it.

But still, I'm not fond of this turn. Tonight, tomorrow, Sunday . . . At some point Travis is going to find that stepladder. And then there's the dinner on

Tuesday. I have Cathy as a kind of weak insurance policy. If she comes I might have an easy out from my promise to Travis, but what if she *doesn't* come? What if I've miscalculated and seeing her has no effect on Travis at all? Or worse yet, maybe he'll be all the more eager to be with me, using me as a release for his rage and unspent passion. I've suffered too much pain not to know that the worst is always possible. And if *this* worst-case scenario plays out I will have to make a choice: revenge or Lander.

Perhaps that's not a choice at all. Despite everything he makes me feel, Lander is a man. A man who has never said he loves me. A man with his own agenda, his own priorities. A man who shares the same genetic code as all the other men who have disappointed me, from my father on up.

"Where are you?" Lander asks. "I'll send the limo."

"I'm going to sleep at home tonight."

There's a brief silence on the other end of the line. "Doncia, I'm going to figure out this encryption. There's nothing to be upset about here."

"I know," I lie. Because I don't *know* anything except that certainty is for suckers. "I haven't been home in days. I can't keep wearing the same two outfits. Besides, Micah might be watching my place. I'm not sure if it's good for us if he thinks I'm spending every night with you. It might get back to Travis."

"Then I'll spend the night at your place."

"No!" The word shoots out of my mouth so fast that I even startle myself.

"If you like, I'll be discreet. If Micah's men are

watching they won't recognize me," Lander says. "Although since he knows we're dating I don't see the problem. But when you consider how dangerous Micah is, and Travis for that matter, I would feel more comfortable if we stay close for a while."

For a while. Not forever.

"We should stick close," I repeat after a moment's hesitation, "because team members look out for each other?"

"Of course." And then in a voice slightly softer, "I *will* look out for you, Adoncia."

"I can look out for myself," I say, a little too sharply. "Work on the encryption, that's your job and only responsibility for the night. Leave the rest to me . . . including my protection detail."

I hang up the phone before he can respond.

I don't know why I'm being like this. I'm acting like a girl in the most stereotypical way. I hate that.

I have no reason to be irritated with Lander, I think as I find the stairs that lead down to the subway. *He hasn't done anything wrong. The problem, as usual, is with me.*

Standing beneath the ground, waiting for a train, I can't help but dwell on that. *I'm* the fucking problem.

That's what my second foster family called me. A *problem child*. They didn't say it to my face, not at first. But I heard the whispers. I listened to the murmurings after I was supposed to be in bed.

❧

"She's damaged, a problem child," the mother would say.

"Let's just cut to the chase," laughed the father, "she's fucked-up. There's no helping this one. We got ourselves a dud."

It had been odd . . . going from a child who was loved to being a child who was nothing more than a burden. I had helped form that narrative; there was no doubt about that. But still . . .

"There's no helping this one. We got ourselves a dud."

I was eleven. And now I knew it was too late for me. There was no point in trying to be anything more than a problem. I was raised and loved by a murderer. I was contaminated; like a fruit tree in a field exposed to radiation, everything I produced would be poison.

So the choice was not: Shall I be healthy or sick? It was: Shall I be sickening?

Or shall I be lethal?

In the end, I chose the latter.

❧

When the train pulls up I'm almost in a meditative state, thinking about how I came to be the way I am. Was it really all circumstance? Or was I predisposed to be . . . well, a problem?

I sit across from a woman with a round face and a shoulder-length bob, probably in her late forties or early fifties. She clutches her purse protectively, keeping her eyes to herself. Wary, guarded. On her finger is a tan line where a ring used to be.

Here is a woman who is just now learning to live with the failure of love and the loss of a future she once took for granted. That's something I know how to do. I almost wish I could trade places with her, not because I want to give up Lander but because my relationship with pain is so intimate, by now it almost serves as a security blanket.

It's odd; I've been pushing people away for so long I don't know how to pull someone to me. I don't know how to ease into happiness, so instead I'm floundering in it, like an unskilled swimmer who just fell into the deep end.

As the train jolts back into motion my gaze moves to the other passengers. It's a fairly integrated crowd. People of all different races and religions, male and female, some clearly gay, some straight. There's no way to pinpoint who here is a problem just by looking at them. You can't tell by what they're wearing. The guy dressed like a thug might be a virginal lightweight, hoping that his clothes will scare people into thinking otherwise. The guy in the suit might be a serial killer.

People looking at me, dressed in my feminine, secondhand business attire might think that I'm a nice girl.

And who did I think Lander was when I saw him? A spoiled rich kid, a man who expected everything to be handed to him and would hurt whoever he needed to hurt in order to protect his family's name and status.

I was wrong.

And when people see Travis, when they just see him without knowing his name, without hearing his voice, what do they think? Do they think he's respectable? An upstanding example of the 1 percent? A gentleman?

Lander says that Travis's mother abandoned him when his father offered her the money to do so. And I don't think Edmund was exactly a loving parent either. Mostly Edmund paid Travis's mother to leave so he could marry someone else without having to worry about messy things like shared custody or paying out child support. And this new wife would soon give Edmund another son: Lander.

Lander loved his mother and she loved him. That was never in question. Due to his father and brother's interference he wasn't able to be by his mother's side during her last months of life. He didn't even know she was dying. It was a horrible way to lose someone. I get it. Lander was created by loss.

Travis was created by rejection. At a young age he was forced to face the fact that his parents weren't good people. And at some point Travis must have realized that he too was toxic. And instead of fighting the inevitable, he's spent his life finding ways to increase and perfect his toxicity.

I have more in common with Travis.

That's good. My mother once told me that when you choose a partner you should find someone to balance you. Someone who is strong where you are weak, weak where you are strong.

But when it comes to enemies? Commonality can be an asset. I am not weak where Travis is strong or vice versa. It's an even playing field . . . or at least it was. Being with Lander, allowing him to make me feel something other than rage . . . it's so confusing, even dizzying at times. I need to even the playing field again, and that's what Cathy's for.

It takes one train transfer and about an hour to get me to my stop in Harlem. And when the doors open I get out quickly, walking through the well-lit station, up the stairs and into the darkness.

chapter eight

As I walk home from the subway station I find that I feel more delicate than I normally do. The gray-black sky and littered streets have a surreal quality. Things are changing, although I can't quite put my finger on what those changes are. I pass Mary, a homeless woman I often talk to. She puts her finger against her lips and holds up an open coloring book. It's a picture of a child, deep in sleep. Mary has colored part of the nightgown that covers the girl's chest red, and that red seems to spill onto the blankets and then to the floor. Her heart is bleeding.

I take a Clif Bar out of my purse and place it on the ground in front of her. She closes her hand around it, offering me a wide, yellow-toothed grin. "You're a good girl. I bet your mama's proud of you."

"She used to be," I say quietly. "A long time ago."

"I like talking to you," Mary says as she drops the

Clif Bar into her lap, "when it's not so close to bed-time."

Before I can respond her eyes turn back to the picture. She begins to rock back and forth slowly, her voice rising in song. "*Hush little baby, don't say a word, Mama's gonna buy you a mockingbird.*"

It's not like Mary to brush me off, but as I said, tonight everything feels a little strange . . . a little off. I back away, unnerved by the song and the bleeding-heart girl.

And I don't see *him* until I'm almost at my building. He's standing by the stairs, on the street, one hand in his pocket, posture relaxed. The dim street-lights pick out the natural highlights of gold that ebb and flow through his straight brown hair.

His eyes are already set on me; he must have been watching me approach for some time. There's no escaping him.

"You don't belong here," I say when I'm within hearing distance.

"I don't really belong anywhere," Lander says mildly, "and I told you, I'm going to look out for you. It wasn't an offer or a suggestion."

I shake my head, look around the street nervously. I've never invited Lander here. I've never even told him where I live.

"As you can see," I say tersely, "I'm fine."

"Only if you have a loose definition of the word."

"What the hell is that supposed to mean?"

He steps forward, into my space, unnerving me the way he always does. "What's wrong, Adoncia?"

he whispers. He raises his hand, traces the curvature of my ear with his finger. Before Lander I didn't know how sensitive I was there, how just a touch can make my heart speed up a bit, just enough to warm me.

"Talk to me," he says.

But I don't know what to say. I wasn't prepared to see him here tonight . . . I wasn't prepared to *ever* see him here. I infiltrated his world with manipulations and seductions, but I never imagined he might infiltrate mine.

Once again I scan our surroundings, which are as dangerous as they are familiar. There, under the nearest streetlight, is a broken bottle; there, next door, a gang insignia is spray-painted on the wall; there, in the far corner, a drug deal is going down, next to bags of garbage. East Harlem hasn't really kept up with the gentrification of the rest of New York, although there are rumors that it's coming. After all, we're right next to one of the richest areas of Manhattan, Lander's neighborhood. Books and movies have glamorized and exalted the virtues of the sliver of the Upper East Side that Lander inhabits. *New York* magazine claimed it's where "the New Yorkers who run the world live."

New Yorkers who run the world all living just a few train stops away from East Harlem. It makes sense I suppose. Royalty likes to live near their serfs.

"Adoncia," he says, pulling me out of my thoughts.

Reluctantly I move my eyes back to him. "I don't bring people here."

"Are you ashamed?"

"No!" I snap, jerking away from him.

"Then is this the part of your story you don't want me to see?"

Stubbornly, I look back to the street. "It's not safe to just hang around out here. Not at night."

"Then invite me in."

I laugh. It's an odd seduction, but then, when have we ever been normal?

"I'll go back with you," I say, finally acquiescing to his earlier request. "I'll stay at your place tonight if it's that important to you."

"No, take me into yours."

The smile dies on my lips and I protectively cross my arms. "It's a studio. It's too small for company."

"We'll manage."

"I only have a twin bed."

"Then we'll have to stay close. You'll make my shoulder your pillow."

In the distance I can hear the laughter and howling of a group of guys as they prowl down the streets toward where we are. Lander calmly holds out his hand.

"The keys," he says simply.

The first time Lander took me to his home he told me to undress for him. He stood back and admired me, insisting that I watch him as he watched me. It had been difficult to resist covering myself. It had been difficult to expose myself so completely to a man . . . no, not just a man, to a *Gable*. But even then I didn't feel as vulnerable as I do now, laying my keys in his hand.

"Good," he whispers.

The whisper is too gentle for this place, too tender considering the strength of his demand. What compels me to obey? Why am I allowing this?

These are the questions that run through my head as he opens the door to my building. Now, standing by Lander's side, I see for the first time what's *not* here in the small foyer of my building. There's no security desk, no sitting area, no luxury. Tiny metal mailboxes line the wall, the paint is chipped, the floor beneath our feet is scratched and sullied. And yet I find myself feeling protective of this grittiness and lack of pretense. This is where I'm from.

But when I turn to him, ready to defend this place, I stop. There's no judgment in his eyes, just interest. He's simply observing. He smiles ever so slightly as he looks down at me. "Take me to your apartment."

It's such a simple, reasonable, and terrifying request. With measured steps I climb the stairs, with Lander right behind me. I don't know if he's looking at me, or the dingy walls, or the worn carpet that silences our footsteps. But then again, maybe it's *all* me, from my Kenneth Cole heels to the water-stained ceiling. It's the me I show the world and the me that I don't.

The hallway leading to my apartment has never seemed so long before, and yet I suddenly wish it was longer. Standing in front of my door I try again to come up with a way to dissuade him from entering, but of course that's impossible. Lander has made a decision. There will be no dissuasion.

"I've never let a man in here." My voice is so low

even I'm not sure if I'm talking to him or to myself. "It's always only been me."

"And tonight," he says, evenly, "it's us."

I stand to the side as I watch this man put my key in my door. I watch his wrist twist slightly with the knob, watch as he opens it and steps inside . . . me.

Just like his dining room table, my desk is covered with papers, all of them dealing with the Gables. The difference is that while Lander's papers are reports from detectives he's paid, mine are newspaper clippings and notes that I've made from articles I've found online or in the library. Under the window is a briefcase filled with money given to me by Micah, as untouched as it is unwanted. Under the desk and in the corners of the room are stacks of books, lovingly categorized by genre and author. But there's no bookcase, no shelf to elevate them above the linoleum floor. Clothes cover my bed and hang from a clothing rack I bought off a vendor to help compensate for my lack of closet space. On the counter located in the part of the room that is my kitchen sit two boxes of Clif Bars and an unopened bottle of merlot. And next to the merlot is a book about how to talk about wine. I decide quickly that this book is the worst part of the room. My naked attempt to fit into Lander's world lying there for him to see. The books placed under the desk are discreet but not much better. Books on history, art, tennis, chess, and finance . . . all subjects I versed myself in to make myself into a woman Lander would want. It makes me squirm. I'm folding into myself. But Lander doesn't seem interested in any of that.

Instead he looks at the books in the corners. Books that I love, from *The Princess Bride* to Mary Shelley's *Frankenstein*. He crouches down, runs his fingers over the bindings as if the titles themselves were made of braille rather than a simple font. F. Scott Fitzgerald, Maya Angelou, Anne Rice—they're all there to greet him. When he stands and walks to the desk, his eyes settle on the only personal photo there—a photo of me and my mother. I'm the one wearing the pretty pink princess dress, with a rhinestone tiara in my hair. My mother is curtsying to me and I'm giggling madly, happy in my little Disney fairy tale.

"She looks different," Lander notes.

It hits me that he's comparing my mother in this picture to how she looked when he saw her. The first time he met Julieta Jiménez was when she was screaming at the woman whose husband she was sleeping with. The next time would be on the witness stand as she pleaded her innocence to an unsympathetic jury.

In a flash I'm by his side, snatching the photo from his grasp. "She *was* different," I say. "She was happy."

"Was she happy often?" he asks. "Before Nick Foley's death?"

I open my mouth to insist that she was, but instead of words, memories come. Memories of my mother crying late at night, after she thought I was asleep. Memories of her looking wistfully at cabs as we waited for the bus in the rain. Memories of her mumbled apologies when a woman whose house we were cleaning angrily accused her of using the wrong polish on the silver. "There were times," I say once I've found my voice. "There were times when she was happy. She was happy when she was telling me fairy tales. And it made her happy when she talked of her dreams for the future, a few dreams for her, lots for me."

He nods as if to say he understands, but I wonder if he really does. I wonder if he knows what it's like to rely on dreams for happiness. I put the photo face-down as he walks around the small space, looking up at the empty walls and the flickering light fixture. "You can't afford better than this?"

It occurs to me to take offense but I find that I can't. "Maybe I could," I admit. "But New York is an expensive city."

"But you *could*," he presses. "You could have found things to put on your walls too. You could have found the money for a bookcase. I know Travis pays his assistants extremely well. And even if you weren't working for him, you could have pursued other careers that would have afforded you more than this."

"That's not where my focus has been," I say bluntly.

"No, it hasn't been," Lander acknowledges. "It's been on punishing others." He stops and turns to me, radiating a new kind of energy. "You've also focused on punishing yourself."

I stare at the wall behind him, unwilling to explore his line of thought.

He moves close to me, putting his hand around my waist, his lips by my ear. "Life is not meant to be a punishment."

"Meant to be?" I repeat with a quiet laugh. "All

those children starving around the world, is that meant to be? The people who are killed in genocides, the women who lose their kids to violence, the kids who grow up to *be* violent despite having loving parents—is any of that *meant to be?*" I step back, pulling away from him. "Haven't you figured it out by now?" I ask. "There is no *meant to be*. There's only what *is*."

"Maybe," Lander says, his eyes never leaving mine. "But more often than not, what *is* is what we make of it."

I laugh again, this time more lightly. It's a pleasure engaging in a battle of wits with a man like Lander.

Again he studies the room, absorbing its shabby details. "There's something I'd like to see."

"What's that? A poster perhaps? A piece of decent furniture?"

"You." He turns back to me, his eyes alight with a new idea, or perhaps a new vision. "I want to see you wearing nothing, stretched out on this bed, on top of these piles of clothes that make up your costumes."

I cock my head to the side. "This is my home and *you* are an uninvited guest," I say, a little teasing, a little provocative. "What makes you think you can ask that of me here?"

"Because it isn't your home," he says, his voice both gentle and steady. "Not as it stands now. It's just a place where you sleep and where you plan. And now I'm the one holding the keys."

I hesitate for a moment. It's just a game after all. There's no reason not to play along. But as I slowly take off my jacket, my shoes, my shirt, I find myself trembling slightly as he watches. I'm unsure of myself, unsure of this moment as my skirt falls to my ankles, my bra falls to the floor. I wait for him to touch me, but he only watches and waits, his eyes drinking me in as I finally bend down to remove my thong.

When I stand again, I'm conscious of the flickering light, of how it reflects on my body, on my flaws.

But the way Lander is looking at me, you'd think he was looking at something perfect.

Slowly I walk to the bed, then lower myself, stretching out on the mattress full of clothes, feeling silk, cotton, and leather against my skin.

He steps closer, but he doesn't reach for me. The only thing that touches me are his eyes, which are drinking me in, memorizing my details.

"When was the last time you touched yourself, Adoncia?"

My mouth drops open, and for a moment I feel innocent, like a virgin. "It's not . . . That's not something I really do."

"No?" He leans down, lets his fingers run gently up my leg, making me inhale sharply at the pleasure of it. But when I try to touch him he steps away.

"I want you to touch yourself now, slip your fingers between your legs. I want you to make yourself wet for me."

I bite down on my lip. I'm trembling again and the truth is, I'm already wet. But still, I follow his instructions, slowly, hesitantly moving my hand between my legs, touching myself here, on this bed, under my roof, caressing my clit, toying with it, embracing the hedonism of it as my body begins to move against the clothes beneath me, my eyelids half-closed.

Lander reaches forward, takes my free hand, and places it on my breast. "Go ahead," he urges, his voice soft but insistent. And almost of their own volition my fingers pinch my hardened nipples as my other hand continues to bring me closer and closer to a climax. I am literally writhing before him as he watches me.

"Yes, Adoncia." I hear his voice as it weaves into the pattern of my moans. "Give yourself this pleasure. You won't deprive yourself, not while you're with me."

"Lander," I gasp, but he puts a finger against my lips.

"Shh." He leans forward, whispers in my ear. "I want to see you come."

I thrash my head from side to side; I can feel how close I am. I have never once been able to bring myself to orgasm with my fingers. But here, under Lander's gaze, I can feel the explosion coming. Feel it building inside of me. My own titillation and unbridled desire take control as my fingers move faster, as I become wetter and my body aches and tingles.

"Slip your finger inside yourself," Lander whispers. "You know what to do."

And I do, touching myself in so many ways. And that's when it comes, the wave of rapture crashing through me, making my back arch and my last semblance of control dissipate. And it is in that moment that I feel Lander gently pulling my hands away, feel his body on top of mine, his arms wrap around me as he rides with me into another wave. I feel his lips against my neck, feel his tongue as he tastes my skin, hear him as he whispers, "You are more than a vessel for rage."

I try to absorb the words but I can barely think right now as I cling to him, as he presses inside me deeper and deeper. He pulls away from my grasp, using his arms to lift himself, staring down at me as he continues to rock against me. I meet his rhythm, thrusting my pelvis against him so now my clit is rubbing against the very base of his cock. "Lander," I whisper again, and this time he doesn't silence me. His breathing is staggered with mine as my bed creaks. For so many years this room has been sterile and austere, a place where satisfaction meant revenge, where passion came from hate.

But now we're baptizing this room with different emotions, different desires, different energy. And he's right. Now, in this moment, I am not a vessel for rage. As Lander presses into me again and again I am simply a woman who revels in being alive.

When the climax comes again, he comes with me, calling out my name as I cry out to God. For a split second I have a vision of a supernova lighting up a starless sky, pushing the boundaries of what is . . .

. . . and what can be.

chapter nine

The next morning I wake up with the sun. Unlike Lander, I don't have blackout drapes. Still, usually I can sleep through the sunrise.

But now I find myself pressed into the side of my lover, like I'm Eve just taken from his rib. And as I blink my eyes and adjust to the morning light I realize . . .

. . . this room looks a hell of a lot worse in the daytime.

How is it I never realized that before? How could I have missed how depressing this place is?

Because it wasn't my focus.

As quietly as possible I get up and try to figure out a way to make the room look marginally presentable before Lander wakes. But of course there isn't really anything I can do. I have no storage space, and even if

I did my problem isn't just that what I have is sort of all over the place. My problem is what I *don't* have: pictures on the wall, decent furniture, anything that is even remotely ornamental or a single wall that isn't suffering from chipped paint or water marks.

But as Lander pointed out, this isn't my home. Not really.

I study Lander as he sleeps peacefully in my bed. How many beds have I been in over my life? Every foster family, every children's services facility, every shelter, every lover, they've all had beds. Until now the only bed that hasn't served a purely utilitarian purpose was Lander's. Even the beds of my past lovers were nothing more than places where I could find much-needed distractions.

Well, no, that's not quite right. In a way those beds were places for me to further destroy myself. Places where I learned to be deadly.

And then, of course, there was the bed I was in when I was a little kid. That was my safe place. So much for that.

I turn to the window and focus on the fading shades of pink streaked across the sky. Everything's changing . . . and I don't know what that means.

"Adoncia."

Just the sound of his voice does something to me. But I don't turn around. I don't really want to see his expression as he takes in my apartment in this light for the first time.

"Time to get up," I say in as cheery a voice as possible. "We have work to do."

❦

While Lander showers I throw on some jeans and a T-shirt so I can go down to get the mail that I neglected the night before. Jessica has a list of chores for me to do: check in with the venue for the dinner, with the florist, with the staff of the candidate. But mostly I have to figure out how the fuck I'm going to get that stepladder out from under her bed and back into the storage closet.

As I trot down the stairs with the mailbox key in my hand I run through my options. There must be a time when Travis, Jessica, the weekend nanny, and the Gable children will all be out at the same time . . . right? But how do I get in while they're out? I know Jessica will leave me in the penthouse alone if she thinks I need to be there, particularly now that Travis is acknowledging me as a welcome presence. But it's a weekend. Travis doesn't need to be at the office. The kids don't need to be at school. This is going to be hard. Maybe if I play lookout Lander could . . .

My thoughts freeze in place and then evaporate as I'm faced with a new challenge to process. Outside my building, double-parked right in front of the entrance, is Micah's limo.

Slowly I pivot, staring up at the stairs. I could get Lander . . . and then what? The last thing I need is for him to try to protect me from Micah. I don't *need* protection from Micah . . . probably. And even if I did, there *is* no protection from Micah. Not even Lander could help me with that.

There's a knock at the door. Reluctantly I turn to see Micah, standing on the other side of the glass, smiling like the Cheshire cat.

Smiling back takes all the effort in the world. I crack open the door. "Micah," I say as calmly as possible. "It's Saturday, don't you know you're supposed to be sleeping in?"

"Don't *you* know that I almost never do what I'm supposed to?" Micah chuckles. "What's with the wary tenant shtick? You can't open the door all the way for an old friend?"

"Of course." I force a laugh and open the door a little wider. "I suppose I'm just a little surprised, is all. I'm not used to company this early."

"Good, good." Micah pushes the door open a little more. "You know, being friends with me is good for you. It's healthy. Not being friends with me?" He shrugs. "Not so healthy. And our friendship is good for me too!" he adds. "I need a friend like you right now."

"Come on," I say, somewhat taken aback. "You never *need* anybody for anything."

"No, that's not true. No man is an island and all that shit."

"Right," I say, thinking again about Lander in the shower upstairs . . . or is he out? How long before he starts to wonder where I am? How long do I have before he comes striding down the stairs?

"Would you like to take a morning ride?"

"Um, sure . . ." I say, glancing behind me. "Let me just run upstairs and get my coat."

"No need, there's a heater in the limo. It even has heated leather seats to keep your ass warm. That's when you know you've made it. When you're poor you're subject to the whims of the weather. So when you can have a warm ass on a cold day you know you're in business."

Another forced laugh from me. My cell is in the apartment. I can't even text him.

"Just around the block," Micah says reassuringly. "I only want a few minutes of your time."

I think I hear a door opening and closing upstairs. Maybe not; that could have been something dropping on the floor, it could have been the door of another apartment . . . or it could have been Lander.

If he does come down here, what will he be walking into? Is Micah threatening me? Is "just around the block" a euphemism for "I'm going to blow your brains out"?

If that's the case and Lander comes down, he'll be in danger too.

"Yeah," I say, with a decisive nod. "I can go for a drive. Shall we go now?"

Micah offers me his arm and I quickly link mine through his and allow him to lead me out. He's walking at a decent pace but I subtly push him to move a little faster. "It's chilly," I explain when Micah gives me a funny look. He laughs and ushers me into the limo, and in an instant we're off . . . off to God knows where.

"So," he says after a few seconds of silence, "how's your houseguest? Is Mr. Lander Gable going to be worried about you?"

I feel my cheeks color as I determinedly stare out the window.

Micah laughs. "It's all right, Sweet. There's lots of ways to heat up a room when the temperature dips. I'm sure Lander's better than any space heater. Still, you should be careful."

"Why's that?"

"The Gables . . . they're a complicated lot, and as you know, they're not known for treating their women well."

"You're talking about Travis," I point out, and then after a moment's thought add, "and their father, Edmund."

"Right, so what makes you think Lander is so different from the man who raised him? Or the man who has run beside him all this time? Is he some kind of fucking anomaly?"

"He could be."

"Yeah, he could be. Statistically speaking, what do you think the odds are?"

"I thought you said I could trust the Gables." It's hard to keep the sarcasm out of my voice.

"No, what I said is that they didn't shoot Nick Foley. There are a lot of untrustworthy people in the world who aren't murderers. I've been doing business with the Gables for years now. Years! I know damn well they aren't capable of bloodshed. Both my instincts and my information are too solid in this area for me to have misjudged them in that regard. But do I still trust them as businessmen? That I'm not so sure about. Like I said, they're a complicated lot."

"So, when you say you've been doing business with them," I say, trying to sound casual, "do you mean that you've been banking with HGVB?"

"For my legitimate business assets, that's all. But still, these men are my bankers, they handle my money and a lot of my investments. I've referred friends to them."

"You mean like Javier." Outside I spot Mary digging through the garbage in hopes of finding something she can use.

"I spoke to Javier and Travis," Micah replies. "Neither one of them will admit to meeting at Travis's place with Edmund. That's not good, Sweet."

That's enough to bring my eyes to Micah. "Why would they deny it?" I ask as innocently as possible. "I mean, I saw them there and it didn't seem like a big deal so . . . Wait . . . did you tell Travis you spoke with me? Micah, if I had known that was supposed to be a secret I wouldn't have even brought it up! It was really just a side note, what I was *trying* to tell you about was how Travis treats Jessica. But if this meeting *was* a secret for whatever reason, and Travis thinks I let the cat out of the bag . . . Micah, he'll fire me in a heartbeat! He'll probably have me blackballed! I—"

Micah silences me with a pat on the knee. "I didn't tell anyone I spoke to you about this."

"Oh, thank God," I say, breathing a real sigh of relief.

"If I told him that, I'd have to tell them *how* I know you," Micah continues. "And once Travis knows that you've lied to him about your name, your work experience, your whole history, well, that *would* be a problem. And if he found out who your mother was . . ." Micah finishes his sentence with a low whistle.

I shift uncomfortably in my seat, suddenly aware of how the air in the limo feels thin, as if I'd need to breathe deeper and faster just to fill my lungs. "I don't understand," I whisper. "Did I do something wrong?"

"No, no, not at all!" Micah says, as if shocked by the suggestion. "You know you were wrong about the Gables. You've changed your ways, that counts for a lot."

"What else do I need to do?"

"First of all, you don't *need* to do anything. We always have choices. There are smart choices and there are stupid choices, but they're still choices. For instance, I'm going to need some information about your employer and your six-foot bed heater. You could help me with that by keeping your eyes open, keeping track of their appointments and meetings and letting me know ASAP if you ever see Javier in their presence again. That would be the smart choice."

"And the stupid choice would be to refuse," I say, finishing the thought for him.

"See? You figured it out right away. You're a smart-choice kinda girl, aren't you, Sweet?"

I turn back to the streets of Harlem. We seem to be driving around aimlessly. Travis has asked me to spy on Lander, which I'm pretending to do. I *am* spying on Travis and sharing what I learn with Lander. Now Micah wants me to spy on all the Gable men for him. This will make me more than a double agent.

What this will make me is crazy. Literally insane. I'm going to have to have more personalities than Sybil to pull this off.

And yet to refuse . . .

I take a deep breath and then blow it out through pursed lips before turning back to my companion. "I don't know what I'm looking for," I point out. "What do you think Javier and Travis are up to?"

"Javier is . . . He's interested in pursuing a career as a pharmacist."

I can't help but smile. Micah is just too much.

"I've always taken an interest in the pharmaceutical industry," Micah continues. "I've made investments in it and I've even considered opening up a pharmacy of my own. So with that in mind, I've told Javier that I will support his . . . his education and invest in his pharmaceutical training if he agrees to eventually help me toward my own goals."

"Your goals of opening a pharmacy," I say, for clarification.

"Exactly!"

I shake my head, still confused. "And you now think he's trying to . . . open a pharmacy with the Gables?"

"Hardly." Micah laughs and takes two bottles of water out of the minifridge, tossing one to me. "The Gables are bankers. Nothing more, nothing less. But if Javier is doing business with them that he doesn't want me to know about, that means he has funds that he doesn't want me to know about too. And *that* makes me wonder if Javier is being financed by someone else who is also interested in opening a pharmacy, right in the neighborhood where I like to conduct my business. You see my dilemma, don't you?"

"I see it," I say. "You're Duane Reade and you don't want CVS taking over your market share," I say, warming to the metaphor. "Does Travis know Javier's an aspiring *pharmacist*?" I put a special emphasis on the last word.

"Travis," Micah says between sips of Evian, "knows everything."

This is turning into a productive morning after all.

chapter ten

When the limo finally turns back onto my street, Lander is already out front of the building. Even from two city blocks away I can see the anger radiating from him. His posture and his walk remind me of a street fighter, not a corporate executive.

"You want me to talk to him?" Micah asks as we approach.

"No, no," I say quickly. "I got this."

"Don't forget who this man is." Micah taps his finger against his chin as if trying to dislodge words from his jaw. "He's a Gable. Perhaps more importantly, he's a fucking investment banker. These guys play with money that no one ever sees. They make investments on islands that no one ever goes to. Theirs is a world where nothing is as it seems."

"So? I would think that would work well for you."

"Oh, it does. But people who are trained to hide

and disguise investments usually apply the same principles to themselves. I don't care how romantic the guy is, he's not looking for a wife, Sweet. He's looking for a good time . . . and he may be looking for something else. Something less obvious."

"Like?"

Micah shrugs. "There are many ways to use a woman," he says as the limo slows to a stop in front of my building. "Your mother certainly found out a thing or two about that."

The comment stings and I have to bite back a retort. Fortunately I'm now home, so I won't have to sit here and continue to listen to Micah use my mother as a cautionary tale.

"I'll keep that in mind," I say as casually as possible, and get out before he can add more.

The limo rolls away quickly as Lander strides toward me. "What the fuck were you thinking?" he explodes, grabbing me by both arms.

"It was only Micah."

"*Only* Micah," he repeats. I don't know if I've ever seen him this angry. "*Only* the Russian mafia."

"We knew he might be watching me. We knew that your coming here was a risk," I snap. "I asked you to stay away. You didn't."

"Because he's dangerous, Adoncia. He could have hurt you."

Or he could have hurt you! I want to scream. *Why is my safety the only thing important here? What would become of me if something happened to* you?

But aloud I take a different tack, pulling myself away from him, crossing my arms protectively across my chest. "You could have blown everything!" I yell. "If he tells Travis that you stayed over here, where I *live*, Travis will become even more convinced that my feelings for you have grown and that my loyalty lies with you, not him! My entire advantage, *our* entire advantage could be blown!"

"Are you listening or are you being purposely obtuse? Micah is dangerous. We agreed that you should only meet him in public places. But you don't have as much control when you stay here alone, away from me or *anyone* else who might be willing to talk to the cops. You simply cannot be here by yourself."

"There are risks that we're going to have to take!"

"Not this risk."

"*Every risk!*" The wind whips through the streets. Empty soda cans and bits of garbage roll down the street like tumbleweeds in the desert. "I will take *every risk* that is necessary to beat them! Until I can make the people who destroyed my mother pay, I will stay on the front lines and I will fight! And in case you haven't noticed, I don't fight to live. I fight to *win*!"

But even as the words leave my mouth I realize they're not true anymore. I will take every risk I need to take with my own life. That's never been a big problem for me. But I'm not willing to risk *Lander's* life.

Lander is making me a weaker soldier. How can I be okay with that?

"And what is it you expect me to do?" His voice

is steady, there's no indication that he's ready to back down. "Leave you wounded on the field?"

"I'm not wounded."

"I beg to differ."

I cock my head to the side. "Are you here to heal me, Lander? Do you think you can piece me back together?"

"Maybe," he says. "Maybe I'm trying to keep you from tearing yourself apart."

I open my mouth to protest, but my voice gets caught in my throat. I feel a stinging in my eyes as I look away from him, down at the windswept streets.

"Why?" I ask softly. "Why do you care?"

"Because that's what people do." The sharp edges of anger shape his voice. "People care about other people. Life isn't supposed to be about revenge. It's supposed to be about being human."

"Ah," I say, my eyes still on the street. "You care because you're human."

"Adoncia . . ." But he stops. Whether he's stopping himself from saying something or he just doesn't know what else to say is anyone's guess. He takes a deep breath and blows it out slowly, as if calming himself. "You can't take these kinds of risks," he says quietly. "We're a team. We can't take joyrides with our opponents without consulting one another first."

"Of course, Lander," I hear myself saying. "We'll work as a team."

There's a silence, one filled with unspoken thoughts and unexpressed feelings . . . but I don't know if the emotion Lander is repressing has anything to do with love. It's entirely possible that what he's hiding is ambivalence.

"Spend the day with me," he says. "I'm going to be working on the encryption. We'll order in Chinese—"

"I have errands to do for Jessica today," I interrupt. "And then I'm going to meet her back at her place at four so we can go over what I've accomplished. If I'm lucky I'll have the opportunity to move the stepladder."

"I could help you with that."

"What?" I say, a little too sharply. "You don't think I can handle *Jessica* by myself?"

"Adoncia," Lander says, the exasperation thick in his voice.

"No, it's fine. I don't mean to be touchy," I say, waving away my words. "As far as I know the whole family will be there when I arrive, so the stepladder may have to wait. Still, if you come up with a plan for that, let me know." I glance up at the front door of my building. "I need to shower and get going. Feel free to hang out while you wait for your driver."

He nods and together we walk back inside. The dreariness of the building feels fitting now.

"One moment," I say, and unlock my mailbox. "I just need to—" I cut myself off with a sigh. The box is jammed, not an uncommon event. I try to pry it open with my fingernails but only end up breaking one of my nails down low. "Damn it!" I yell, jumping back and putting my finger in my mouth.

"Let me see." Lander quickly steps forward and

pulls my finger from my lips. There's only a small, thin line of blood but it stings like crazy.

"Do you have Band-Aids?" he asks.

"In the medicine cabinet."

I lead him up the stairs, my finger now firmly back in my mouth. And as my blood touches my tongue I wonder, *When did I lose my tolerance for pain?*

chapter eleven

I did everything I had been assigned to do. I went to the flower shop and checked to make sure that the arrangements were being done to Jessica's specifications. I went to the venue and checked in with the caterer and Robyn, the event manager, confirming that the seating arrangement and menu were set and ready to go. The linens are the ones that Jessica asked for. The photographer knows which kinds of pictures are wanted and which aren't.

I haven't told Lander that I invited Cathy. When she comes, and she *must* come, it will be a surprise to everyone. The chaos I think she'll cause will be my gift to Lander and to myself.

I also made copies of the keys I found in Travis's closet door, which are now snug in the small pocket of my purse while the magnet, stolen keys, and a new blank USB drive, identical to the one we've taken from

Travis's place, are in a zippered plastic bag. I've retaped the keys together and wiped my prints off them. I'm also carrying a pair of latex gloves. I doubt that Travis will ever do any kind of fingerprint sweep, but if he does he won't find my fingerprints to be anywhere that I can't explain. Eventually I'll need the original flash drive, but unfortunately I didn't think of that until after Lander left, and I've been so busy I haven't had the chance to swing by his place and collect it.

If I'm incredibly lucky I'll have the chance to put the keys, the dummy USB drive, *and* the stepladder back. How I'm going to do that is a mystery. Still, the opportunity has to come. It literally *has* to.

When I get to the right floor and knock on the door it's seven-year-old Braden who answers. He has his mother's strawberry blond hair and delicate bone structure and his father's mouth and eyes. Perhaps he has his father's temperament too, because rather than saying hello he just throws the door open and then stomps off, allowing me to follow. As I trail behind I sneak a peek at the master bedroom. No one's in there at the moment, but it's still not safe to go in. Not yet.

Patience, patience. I silently chant the word in my head as I walk into the living room, where I find Jessica arguing with a woman with brown skin, cat-eye glasses, and dark hair that falls just below her shoulders. She flashes me a quick *help-me!* look but then out of what I assume is obligation, turns her attention back to Jessica.

"Mrs. Gable," she says, pleading plaintively. "My shift is not over. I'm not supposed to leave."

"You mean *he* told you not to leave!" Jessica says in something that is almost approaching a shriek. "*He* told you not to leave me alone with them, is that right? Is that *right*, Lorella?"

Lorella, right. I've heard the name; she's their weekend nanny.

"They're my children! Mine!" Jessica puts her hands over her flat stomach as if to remind us all that she has a womb. "I carried them! They're part of me too! Me! Not just Travis, *me*!"

Mercedes is huddled in the corner clutching a doll, her lips pressed together as tears stream down her cheeks. Her brother stands sullenly by her side. I don't know that I've ever seen a three-year-old cry silently before. I reach into my purse and pull out some loose change before crouching down and holding up a quarter for Mercedes to see. Once I have her attention I perform a simple coin trick that a high school boyfriend taught me years ago. Mercedes watches the coin "disappear," only to reappear in a different hand than she thought I had dropped it in. Hesitantly she walks over to me as her tears begin to slow. Braden is close behind, his frown softening, if only a little.

"Mrs. Gable," Lorella is saying, "I'm just trying to do my job. Mr. Gable was very clear—"

"I haven't had anything to drink today," Jessica says desperately. "Not even a mimosa, I swear it. And no Valium this morning, surely you can see that? I just want some time with them. It's not like I've been regulated to supervised visitation! I'm entitled to that! I'm their mother! Not you, me! Do you hear me? You are nothing but a servant! Another one of Travis's sluts! You're nothing! I'm their mother!"

I can't speak for Lorella, but that little speech was enough to convince me that Jessica hasn't had her Valium. I hold up my quarter again, and again I make it disappear, only to retrieve it from Braden's ear. Both children erupt into giggles.

The sound of happiness is so jarring that Jessica seems to notice me for the first time. "*She's* here! Our personal assistant? You've heard both Travis and me speak of her, yes?" Jessica demands, pointing her finger in my direction.

"Yes, I've heard Mr. Gable speak of his PA, but—"

"Well, there you go then! I'm not alone. She's here, one of *Travis's* people! You see? You can leave now without disobeying your . . . your master," she says, pronouncing the last word with sarcastic acidity. "Everything's fine, you can go."

Lorella looks at me questioningly. I pull myself back up to standing. "I . . . um, I hadn't planned on staying very long, but if you need me—"

"There!" Jessica says triumphantly. "You can leave now!"

Lorella shakes her head. "Mr. Gable was very clear—"

"This is my home, Lorella. If you don't leave now I will call the police and have you arrested for trespassing!"

Lorella still looks uncertain but I can also tell how badly she wants to hightail it out of here. "You're really going to be here?" she asks. "You'll stay?"

"It's my job to be available when the Gables need me," I say, choosing my words carefully.

Lorella nods, both fear and gratitude radiating out of her in equal measure. She turns to the children. "Would you like to spend a little time with your mom and . . ." Lorella throws me an apologetic look. "I'm sorry, your name?"

"Ad—Bell," I say, quickly correcting myself. "My name's Bell."

It was a quick, muttered slip, and if anyone noticed, they show no sign of it. Still, the fact that I made it at all is alarming. I've never done that before. I've always been able to compartmentalize my different roles perfectly.

"It's fine," I hear Braden tell his nanny. It occurs to me that he sounds more world-weary than any seven-year-old should be.

"She can make things disappear!" Mercedes adds, the wonder in her voice an odd contrast to her tear-stained face.

"All right then," Lorella says, clearly relieved as she goes to collect her tote bag left by the side of the sofa. "I'll be going then, Mrs. Gable, if you're sure—"

"Get. Out!" Jessica cries, now visibly shaking.

Lorella nods again and quickly leaves the room.

"I'm just going to . . . I just need to ask her something," I say, and rush after her before Jessica or the kids can stop me.

"Look," I say, standing behind Lorella as she retrieves her coat from the hall closet. "I said I'd stay, but if she kicks *me* out I'll have to go. And when Travis finds out you left despite his specific instructions—"

"His specific instructions were to never even leave her alone in the same room with those kids," Lorella grumbled, impatiently pushing her hair out of her face. "If he thinks that little of her, why doesn't he just divorce her? Since she's an addict she probably *would* only get supervised visitation if that's what he wants! So what's he afraid of? Does he think she'll get half and he'll be knocked down a couple spots on *Forbes*'s wealthiest Americans list?"

"Well, to be fair that would bump him out of the top one hundred," I say dryly.

Lorella laughs ruefully.

"Like I said," I continue, now hopeful that she will hear me, "I will stay as long as I can. But if you leave despite Travis's instructions, he may fire you regardless of whether I'm here or not."

"You know what? If he fires me so be it." She leans on the door and stares down at her shoes. "I stay for the kids, I want to help them. Plus Mr. Gable pays me so much I can afford to work part-time, and *that* means I can take care of my own babies. But, you know, you can't work for the devil without expecting to catch a little hell."

"I like that," I laugh. "Where is the devil today, anyway?"

"He went off with his father and some other guy they work with. Think they're getting a late lunch or something."

"Some other guy?" I shift my weight back on my

heels. "I don't suppose the other guy was Mexican? Or maybe Russian?"

"Nope, not that I could tell." Lorella pauses as Braden enters the hall, pulling a willing Mercedes into his room before slamming the door behind them.

"God help those poor children," Lorella sighs as she opens the front door. "Good luck," she calls out as she hastens to the elevator.

I stand in the foyer for a full two minutes, waiting to see if Lorella will come back with a change of heart. But when she doesn't, I reluctantly walk back into the lion's den, throwing one more wistful glance toward the master bedroom as I do. Jessica is sitting in the armchair clutching a glass of clear liquid as she stares out the window.

"They went into Braden's room," she says dully as I sit down beside her. "Braden said he and his sister wanted to play by themselves. I was going to ask you to leave, just as I asked Lorella, but now . . . what's the point?"

I glance at the side table and realize that there's a pill bottle where there wasn't one before.

Jessica follows my gaze. "Please don't tell Travis. I told him that I had thrown them all out. I told him I did and he . . . he laughed at me and called me a liar. It will make him so happy to know that I failed. Please . . ." Her voice fades off as if she can't think of how to proceed with her entreaty.

"Tell him what?" I ask innocently. "That you took a moment to enjoy a glass of water? Because that's all I've seen."

Jessica's lips curl up into a wry smile as she reaches over and takes the pills in her hand. "I wanted to prove him wrong. I thought maybe if I had absolutely nothing today . . . maybe then I could prove that I could be a good mother. The kids would want to be with me and no one would have a good argument for why they shouldn't be. But these days, without help . . ." She shakes the pill bottle to indicate what kind of help she's referring to. "What did Mick Jagger call it? Mother's little helper?" She lets out a humorless laugh.

"Mrs. Gable—"

"I really don't blame them," she continues, as if I hadn't spoken. "How can Mercedes and Braden like me if they don't even know me? They haven't been *allowed* to know me. And I . . . I don't know how to fight him. Travis is too strong for me. And far too clever. My only recourse is to find ways to escape." She brings her glass to her lips, her eyes vacant and her shoulders slumped. "Why are you here, Bell?"

"Um, you asked me to come?" I remind her awkwardly, "You wanted updates on how things were shaping up for Tuesday's dinner. So . . . well, anyway, I sat down with Robyn and she has the seating arrangement—"

"I reworked that last night," she interrupts. "Will you be an angel and go over it and see if I've left anyone out? And of course you'll need to bring the new arrangements to Robyn. I prefer if you didn't just email it to her. I want to know that it was put into her hand and that she understands everything."

"Yes," I say with a forced smile, "of course."

"And I think I want different flower arrangements. Cherry blossoms are too delicate. Travis likes things bold. Maybe some hibiscus flowers? Or heliconia? You'll need to see if they have those flowers available. If not you'll find me a different florist who can rise to the occasion."

"Of course," I say again, my smile growing more saccharine by the second.

From Braden's bedroom there's a burst of laughter and a happy squeal. Jessica looks as if the sound has stabbed her in the heart. "I used to be good with children, back when I was young," she says quietly.

"You won't be thirty for another month," I point out. "You're still young."

"Only if you measure age by years," she retorts. "And that's really a silly way to do it, don't you think? Heartache will age you faster than time ever could."

I smile despite myself, marveling at how the most corrupt and drug-addled brain can still occasionally stumble upon bits of wisdom.

"I used to be good with children," Jessica says again. "You know how some people hear about a fatal car accident and they just shrug it off, but then if you tell them that there was a dog in the car they break down crying? That was me with children. I could always betray and manipulate the adults in my life. That's what adults *do*. But kids?" She shakes her head. "I wish I could apologize to every child I've inadvertently hurt. I wish I could hold them in my arms and tell them how sorry I am. How wrong I was. I wish I could just take the pain I gave them and throw it away."

"Do you think you've hurt children?" I ask, unsure if I'm following her very well.

"Yes, indirectly . . . you know how it is. You support a politician who ends up gutting an important school program. You invest in property development only to later learn that the playground that was built over was the only one around for miles. Or sometimes . . . sometimes you hurt a child's parent. Travis used to tell me that I should treat life like a chess game. Each person is a piece to be moved to your advantage. But in chess the pawns don't breed. In *chess*, when you knock a piece off the board you're not destroying an entire family." She pauses for a moment and then says, "I wish I could apologize to the child."

The child. Not *the children.* Is she talking about someone specific?

Is she talking about me?

It takes me a moment to realize that I'm holding my breath, and when I do, I try to exhale as silently as I can so I don't bring her out of her thoughts. "If you want to apologize," I finally whisper, "why don't you?"

"Because children grow up," she says with a harsh laugh. "I want to apologize to the child, but I'll be damned if I'll grovel at the feet of an adult who is as corrupt, manipulative, and deceitful as the rest of us. The adult doesn't deserve my apology. And the child is gone."

I'm not sure how many pills Jessica has taken, but

I have to assume they've screwed with her logic. But that's almost beside the point. I want to know specifically who and what she's talking about. I *need* to know. Was my mother this "pawn" who she helped knock from the board?

And most importantly of all, does Jessica know who I am?

"Mrs. Gable," I begin, drawing out the name as if an extra syllable or two will help me get a grasp on what's going on. "Are you—"

There's a knock at the door and Jessica is immediately on her feet. "I swear to God, if that's Lorella . . ." She stomps down the hall, leaving me frozen on the sofa.

I hear the door swing open and a surprised "Oh!" from Jessica.

And then I hear his voice. "Jessica, how are you? I hope you don't mind me popping by?"

Well, now, that's interesting. I get to my feet and walk into the hall.

"Travis isn't here," Jessica says, somewhat confused.

"No? I was sure I would catch him. No matter, how are *you*?" he asks, emphasizing the last word in a way that is meant to remind her of the state she was in last time he saw her. Jessica bows her head and Lander looks over her to make eye contact with me.

"I didn't expect to see you here on a weekend, Bell."

"We're getting some things ready for the dinner," I explain. "I'm really looking forward to it."

"I'll tell Travis you were here," Jessica interjects, clearly trying to get rid of him.

"Well, since I'm here," Lander says, pushing past her, "I might as well say hi to my beautiful niece and nephew. And you, Bell. You look gorgeous." He takes both my hands in his and at that moment I realize that he's secretly pressing a USB drive into my palm. Discreetly I slip it into my pocket without Jessica noticing. "Oh, speaking of the kids, Jessica," he says, turning back to his sister-in-law. "When I got here I noticed a guy making balloon animals for children. Think Braden and Mercedes would be into that?"

"A man making balloon animals . . . here? In the building?" Jessica asks, confused.

"No, no, just around the corner. About a block and a half away."

"Mercedes loves balloons," she says quietly.

"And Braden loves animals," Lander reminds her. "His favorite is an elephant, right?"

Jessica looks at him blankly. "Um, it might be . . . I mean, yes, I believe . . . or at least possibly . . . well, you know children. They change their minds about these things so frequently."

"They do." Lander pats her on the shoulder. "Where are the kids now?"

"In Braden's room."

"Right, well, why don't you call them and we'll go get them a whole balloon *zoo*. I'll lead you to where this guy has set up shop for the afternoon."

Jessica stares at Lander for a moment and then a

little light turns on in her eyes as she begins to realize that she might finally have something fun to offer her kids, something that might make them want to be with her, if only for a few minutes. She goes to Braden's room and knocks politely at his door.

After a moment the door's flung open and Braden, looking irritated, glares up at his mother. "We're *playing*!" he snaps, but then from the corner of his eye he sees who is down the hall. "Uncle Lander?"

As soon as the words leave his lips Mercedes pushes past him and looks left and then right, which is where Lander is. "Uncle Lander!" she cries, and runs toward him, arms outstretched. Braden is trying to play it a little cooler, but the bouncing on the balls of his feet gives away his excitement.

Lander laughs and swoops Mercedes up into his arms. "Happy to see me?"

"So happy!" She laughs. "We were just playing Wizard of Oz! I'm Dorothy and Braden's a flying monkey. Want to play? You could be Scarecrow! We need a Scarecrow!"

"Tempting," Lander admits, "but your mom was just telling me about an idea she had, and if you ask me, it sounds pretty good."

Both Braden and Mercedes cast skeptical looks over at their mother.

"Yes," Jessica says, wringing her hands as she plasters on a smile. "I was just telling Lander that there's . . . um . . . well, I suppose the term is a balloon artist just over a block away. You know, one of those men who can make balloons into animal shapes?"

"Fun!" Mercedes squeals, wriggling out of Lander's arms.

"Yes," Jessica says again, turning to Braden. "I thought perhaps you'd like an elephant?"

Braden blinks in surprise. "You remembered my favorite animal?"

"Don't be silly, Braden!" Jessica says, clearly elated by the assumption. "As if I could ever forget how much you love elephants! Uncle Lander thought it was an ostrich, if you can believe that. Everyone knows an elephant is much better than any ol' bird. But then I suppose I'm biased because elephants are my favorite animal too!"

"Since when?" Braden asks suspiciously.

Lander clears his throat, interrupting the moment before Jessica has a chance to screw it up. "Shall we go now? We wouldn't want to miss him."

Mercedes's and Braden's enthusiasm is unbridled as Jessica laughs and fetches her purse. "Oh, Bell, we'll be right back. Go ahead and take a look at the new seating chart. It's on my desk."

"Right away, Mrs. Gable."

"Yes, we'll be right back, Bell," Lander adds. "This really won't take more than fifteen minutes at the most."

As the door closes I pull out the USB stick and stare down at it in awe. Lander and I are on exactly the same page. More than that, we're on the same line of the same page! I pull on the latex gloves from my purse and then dash to the bedroom and drag out the stepladder from under the bed and up to Travis's closet door. I pull the magnet out of my pocket and then, pulling out the cigar tube, put in the flash drive and keys before carefully replacing it. Then in no time at all I'm carrying the stepladder through the penthouse and into the laundry room and putting the magnet back into the drawer.

And boom. Just like that, we're done.

It almost feels like the accomplishment deserves a little victory dance. But there isn't time. I run to Jessica's office and gather myself together so that when they all come back a few minutes later I'm seated at the desk, completely composed and looking over the new seating chart for the Highkin dinner.

And a little over ten minutes later, they're back.

"Look!" Mercedes says as she runs into the office, holding up what is clearly a lion. "Isn't it the best?"

"It's the king of the jungle," I say as I admire it. "And he's all yours." I look above her head to Lander, who is now leaning against the doorframe looking like a modern-day James Dean. "Every girl needs a lion of her own," I say, softer this time.

Lander just smiles.

chapter twelve

The balloon animals buy Jessica a few minutes of love from her children. She suggests Lander and I go off to get a late lunch, clearly hoping to finally spend some time alone with them. Initially I try to convince her to let us stay because I know what will happen to Lorella's job if Travis comes home and finds out that Jessica is the adult who has been left in charge of the kids. But Jessica is insistent and for once both Braden and Mercedes really do seem to want to spend time with their mother. So I send up a little apology to Lorella and let Lander lead me out. We don't say a word to each other until our feet hit the sidewalk, and even then we wait until we're half a city block away before breaking out into celebratory grins.

"Your timing was perfect!" I squeal. "I just had a copy of those keys made today so I was able to sneak *everything* back! There's no evidence we were ever even searching for anything!"

"Yes," Lander says, taking my hand. "It worked out well."

"Did you *know* that I would get the keys made?"

"I did."

"How?" I demand. "How did you know?"

He stops, making the New Yorkers and tourists flow around us like we're rocks in a stream. He lifts my hand and brings it to his lips for a kiss. "I know *you*, Adoncia."

"And I know you." My smile reaches all the way down to my heart. "You called in that balloon guy, didn't you?"

"I called Travis and he told me he was going to be out for the second half of the day. You already told me you were going over there. The idea just sort of came to me. And as it turns out, if you pay them enough, those kid party places will accommodate extremely last-minute requests."

"How much is enough?"

"More than most people's monthly salaries."

I laugh and shake my head. "Must be nice, getting everybody to do what you want when you want it."

"I'm not sure getting someone to make balloon animals at the last minute is a testament to my influence."

"I don't know about that. Those balloon artists are tough. They have highly inflated egos."

"Well, look at you, all carefree and making puns," Lander chuckles.

"I did," I say, pulling his hand, urging him forward. "I did make a pun. Come on, let's go back to your place. I'll come up with a few more while you work on the encryption."

"I'm afraid the encryption proved a little too difficult for me. But I have someone who is much more tech savvy than I am working on it now. I suspect he'll be able to crack the code in a few days."

"Oh." I slow my pace a little as I think this over. "You trust this . . . someone?"

"I trust his greed." He checks his watch. "He's being paid for both his skills and his discretion. Have you ever been in here?"

I stop and look at the store Lander has stopped in front of. Two stories of glass walls divided by one sign that spreads from one side of the establishment to the other, Callow's Rare Books.

"I've heard of it." And read about it and fantasized about it and dreamed about it. Callow's is a place where you can find the first edition of everything and anything ever written, from Dan Brown to Shakespeare. When I learned that there was a place right here in New York that had so many amazing books, so many signed by the author, it was like being told that God had moved Heaven to Manhattan, right on Columbus and Eighty-Seventh.

"Want to go in?"

The question is ridiculous in every way. He says it so casually, as if walking into this place doesn't take audacity of the highest order. Worming my way into Jessica and Travis's world, messing with the heads of gangsters, turning Lander's world upside down, these are the things I'm suited for. But to be in a room with *those* books?

I feel like I'm not good enough. Like I'm not *clean* enough.

"Come on," Lander says, apparently oblivious to my apprehensions. He takes my arm and pulls me through the door.

The place is designed to look like a cross between an old library and a fine antiques dealership. A few books are displayed, face out on the shelves, under careful lighting: a signed copy of *This Side of Paradise*, by F. Scott Fitzgerald; a first-edition collection of Emily Dickinson's poems; there, on the opposite wall, is a signed first-edition copy of *The Color Purple*; and behind glass is a first edition of *Robinson Crusoe*.

A woman walks out from one of the rooms toward the back of the store. Her hair is pure silver and worn in a stylishly short cut. The lines around her eyes look as if they were purposely drawn to make her look both wise and kind. Something about the way she carries herself and the way she so clearly belongs here tells me that she works here. I take a deep breath, waiting for her to ask me to leave, to tell me I don't belong.

"Mr. Gable, how are you!" she says warmly, her attention fully on Lander. "We haven't seen you in a while."

"I've been a little busy these days," he says amiably. "This is my friend . . ." He hesitates as he tries to decide which name to use.

"Adoncia," I say, extending my hand. "Adoncia Jiménez."

I don't even remember the last time I spoke my full name, my *real* full name aloud. I've lived by so many aliases you'd think I worked for the CIA. But I can't bring myself to lie while in a church such as this.

"Pleased to meet you, Adoncia. I'm Garda. I usually help Lander when he's in the market for a rare book."

"You're the *only* one who helps me when I'm in the market for a rare book," Lander corrects. "This is Adoncia's first time here. I was hoping you had something that might wow her."

"Well, we always have *something*," she says. "We just acquired *De la France et des États-Unis* and it's inscribed by Thomas Jefferson—"

"I think something less political might be of more interest."

"Of course." Garda smiles. "How about Alexander Pope's eighteenth-century first-edition translations of Homer's *Iliad* and *Odyssey*? Or perhaps you'd like to see a signed first edition of Robert Frost's work?"

"You have a signed copy of Frost?" I whisper.

"We do." She leads me over to a table and asks me to wait. In less than a minute she's back with a white hardcover. "*New Hampshire*," I say, reading the title. "The first collection of poems that Frost won a Pulitzer for."

"Very good!" Garda says, clearly impressed. But I can barely acknowledge the compliment. I'm too entranced with what's in my hands. There's a picture of a landscape on the cover, inked entirely in green. I touch it lightly and then slowly, reverently open it . . . and there it is. An inscription; no, more than an inscription, a handwritten poem by Robert Frost.

"He signed it for his friend," Garda explains. "That's not the complete poem; he added more stanzas once he decided to publish it."

I keep staring at the words, and when I feel Lander's hand on my shoulder, I cover it with my own. It's a moment of reverence.

I'm so glad I'm sharing it with him.

We spend another twenty minutes there, going over book after book, each more spectacular than the last. They have everything from Webster's first dictionary to signed first editions of Mark Twain to signed first editions of George R. R. Martin's Song of Ice and Fire series.

But it's not until Garda puts down a copy of a nineteenth-century collection of short stories titled *Fairy Tales Told for Children* that I find myself literally unable to breathe.

"This . . ." I say, barely daring to touch the cover. "It's a first edition?"

"It is," Garda says, opening it up to the title page. "The first English translation of his stories. Unfortunately it isn't autographed. Hans Christian Andersen wasn't big on that."

"Having authors sign their work was only beginning to become popular during his time," I note quietly, my eyes still glued to the book.

"That's true!" Garda says, clearly surprised by my knowledge. "Of course, if there is a signed copy, we can probably find it," she says as she looks up at Lander. "We can hunt down almost anything for the right collector."

I touch the page, feeling the delicate roughness of the aging paper. "The critics didn't like this," I whisper. "Not at first. They preferred his novels but . . . he had to write these stories. They must have called to him somehow, all those stories from his youth that he reimagined and made his own."

"Very good!" Garda says, clasping her hands in front of her. "Not many know that!"

I turn the page again. "The Princess and the Pea," "The Little Mermaid," "The Emperor's New Clothes." My mother read all these stories to me, and when she was gone I read them to myself. I never outgrew them. I was fascinated by their dark romance. The bloody brutality mixed with gentility and grace. The torturous sensitivity of a princess, the mermaid who gave up her voice and agreed to endure the pain of walking on knives just so she could be near the man she loved, the emperor who was arrogant and foolish enough to allow himself to be humiliated in front of those he would have worship him . . . it was irresistible. And now, here those stories are. In a book that was published when the author was still alive, still writing, creating magic.

"How much is it selling for?" Lander asks.

I look up at Lander, shocked by the question. Surely something like this can't be priced.

"One hundred eighteen thousand," Garda says smoothly. "It's extraordinarily rare. I've never seen a first edition of *any* of his works in truly good condition before."

"It's too cheap," I say as I turn the page again.

Garda looks down at me, a little taken aback, and then she breaks out laughing. "I couldn't agree more."

I linger over the book as long as possible, trying to touch every page, but eventually I realize that no amount of time will ever be enough.

I love this place.

I love that he's brought me here.

I love that he knows me.

When we leave I can't help but notice that New York looks a little prettier, the sound of the city seems muted, and I feel relaxed in a way that I haven't felt in . . . well, *ever*. I'm holding on to Lander's hand, I've touched books that I never even thought I'd get to see. I feel safe.

And I don't feel angry.

"I was impressed by how much you knew about each author and work," Lander says. "I can tell Garda was too. You're actually a bit of a literary scholar."

"No," I say, shaking my head, looking up at a billboard I haven't noticed before. "I'm a reader. It's different . . . it's better."

"You might be right." He gives my hand a squeeze. "I like seeing you like this. And I like that you can see those books for what they are. They're holy in a way."

"Not just in a way," I correct him as he comes to a stop. "Those are objects of worship. I mean, we saw a handwritten poem by Robert Frost. A poem he hadn't even published yet! And then there was . . . Lander? Lander, are you listening?"

But his eyes aren't on me. He's looking across the street. "That's interesting," he says under his breath. Pedestrians are walking by us, a man with a cigarette passes us, weaving a noxious smell into an otherwise pleasant breeze. For reasons I can't explain I'm hit by a subtle chill.

"What the hell are you staring at?" I ask as my eyes scan the street. And then I stop.

The *world* stops.

Standing outside of a restaurant are Travis, Edmund, and HGVB employee Sean White.

Former police detective Sean White. The man who arrested my mother.

Flashes of images explode like fireworks in my head. My mother on her knees while White stands over her, belittling her. My mother asking for help as he blames her, insults her . . . And then there's the sound. The sound of my mother screaming as he leads her away.

She screamed my name.

"Adoncia," Lander says slowly. "I think I'm going to try to catch up with my father. It'll be useful." He reaches into his pocket, pulls his house keys from his key chain, and hands them to me. "I'm going to call the front desk of my building and tell them you have permission to go up. I'll meet you there in a few hours, all right?"

He doesn't know. He doesn't know what effect this man has on me. He thinks that just because I can take on Travis and Jessica and Micah and yes, even Edmund, he thinks that means I can handle seeing White across the street and just go about my day. White, at least three hundred feet away and completely unaware of my presence.

But the thing is, Travis and Edmund may have been responsible for my mother's arrest, but White is the one who handcuffed her while she cried. White is the man who physically dragged her out of my life.

White is the man who made my mother scream.

"Adoncia?"

"Yes," I say, forcing myself to smile. "I'll meet you at your place."

"Do you need cab fare?"

"I got it," I assure him. "You go after your father. Let's see what you can find out."

Lander nods and stealthily moves down the street, several paces behind his father and Travis, following them, waiting for the right moment to accidentally bump into them.

But White doesn't follow them. He's walking in the other direction.

It's the direction I'll be going as well.

chapter thirteen

White doesn't go far. He finds a little bar that is advertising a Saturday happy hour. I wait a few minutes before following him in.

The place is dark, with cheesy diamond-patterned flooring. The bar is made of a decent dark wood and the tables look cheap but well cared for. It's a dive bar for the financially secure.

And sitting on a dark red bar stool is Sean White. The mustache he used to have is currently just a stubble. His hairline has receded since last I've seen him too, and there are heavy wrinkles lining his formidable brow. In his hand is a phone, not a gun.

But his physique is just as athletic and intimidating. And his lips, those haven't changed. They're the same thin, cruel lips I remember sneering at me when I was a kid.

And now he's here, twenty feet away, drinking a beer, chatting with the bartender like he doesn't have a care in the world.

I walk up to the bar, take a seat next to him. The bartender gives me a polite smile as White looks me over. For the first time I notice the two empty shot glasses by White's beer. Must have been a hard day.

"What can I get you?" the bartender asks.

"I'll have a Guinness," I start to say, but I stumble over the words and have to repeat myself.

White isn't staring right at me, but I can tell that he's paying attention. It's terrifying. Of all the people wrapped up in my mother's downfall, Sean is the most likely to recognize me. I was there, by my mother's side when he questioned her. He was the one who called over an officer to take me away to child services. Days later he met with me again, presumably to question me. But his questions were brief and lacked specificity. His main purpose seemed to be to explain. He explained why he knew my mother was guilty. He laid out "facts" and incriminating clues for me in a way that I could understand them.

I was ten.

There was no reason that I can think of for him to do that . . . unless he was trying to keep me from speaking up in my mother's defense. But again, I was a little girl with no father. A ten-year-old girl whose only family member had just been arrested. No one would have listened to me even if I had found my voice.

Perhaps White did it purely for the sake of sadism.

I glance up at a television mounted in a dusty corner as the Mets strike out in the final inning. I pound my fist on the bar as the hitter's shoulders slump with defeat.

"You a Mets fan?"

He's talking to me. That was my intent, to give him an opening to start a conversation, but to hear his voice, to know that he's looking at me . . .

I gather my courage and turn on my stool so that I'm angled toward him. Again I manage a smile. "Always have been. You?"

"I'm a Yankees man," White says as my beer is placed in front of me. "Hope you'll forgive me for it." He puts down some money for my beer, which the bartender quickly takes and makes himself scarce.

"There are greater sins than being a Yankees fan," I say sweetly.

White smiles and offers me his hand. "I'm Sean."

"Bell." I press my palm against his. This is the hand that handcuffed my mother. This is the hand that dragged her away.

"Belle, I like that." Not so much as a glimmer of recognition in his eyes. He lifts his glass, gulping his beer while he tastes the name. "That's French, right?" he asks. "Means beauty?"

"It's Latin, short for Bellona. It means war."

"War? Who names their kid after war?"

"I'm oversimplifying," I admit as I sip the froth off my Guinness. "It actually means goddess of war, which is essentially the same thing." I shrug, smile. "If you don't like it, blame my mother."

White chuckles, and lifts his drink in tribute. "I won't be too hard on her, seeing that she gave us all something pretty to look at when she made you."

"You're sweet." I lean in a little more, my hatred warming me, giving me strength, making me reckless. "You look kind of familiar. Have we met?"

"I would've remembered."

"Are you sure?" I cock my head to the side. "I would have sworn."

"Maybe from here?"

I shake my head no. "This is my first time here."

"Just as well," he says, leaning over conspiratorially. "I shouldn't tell you this, but they used to have a rat problem."

"Ew, you're kidding!" In the background the music changes from pop to something a little harder, a little darker.

"Yeah," he chuckles. "The owner is a pal of mine and he has a real phobia about rodents too. I mean the guy is always imagining little sounds or evidence of evil rats and mice hiding inside the walls or around the corner, so when he actually saw a live rat right here in the men's room after closing time he actually pissed his pants! I'm serious, I was sitting right at this bar waiting for him. He ran out of the bathroom, smelling like piss, and he was crying and shaking like a little girl!" Sean says, barely getting the words out through his laughter.

I manage a quiet laugh as well and shake my head. White may have aged since I last saw him, but he still has the emotional maturity of a frat boy. "I assume he took care of the problem."

"Oh yeah, there's not a live rat anywhere near here. He closed the place down for a week for *personal reasons*," he says, placing air quotation marks around the last two words. "He scattered those rat bait chunks everywhere then had the place completely scrubbed down. He still has a bunch of bait around the Dumpster out back. He probably killed a few stray cats and dogs while he was at it, maybe a Dumpster-diving bum or two." Again, White laughs. "He's a good guy, but nuts. Still, if you have a fear of rats you're at the right place at the right time. I doubt there's a live rat within five miles of this bar now."

"Oh, I don't know." I toy with the edges of my cocktail napkin. "Rats are pretty resilient. They find ways to live in the shadows, avoiding traps. Just when you think you've gotten rid of them"—I throw my hands up, smile—"they surprise you."

"Trust me." He pats my shoulder, letting his fingers linger on the place where my shirt exposes my skin. "There are no rats here."

"Mmm." I lift my glass to my lips. "How did we get onto this subject anyway? Oh yes, I was saying you look familiar . . . quite a detour there. Tell me, Sean." I take a moment to enjoy the taste of burned barley on my tongue. "What do you do?"

"A little this, a little that," he says, glancing down at his phone.

"Come now, what kind of this?" I replace my glass, rest my arm on the bar, and let my hair fall over my shoulder. "And what kind of that?"

"I work for a bank."

"Oh! Well, maybe that's how I know you! Maybe you work for my bank!"

"It's possible." White drinks more; his beer's almost gone. "But it wouldn't really matter. I work behind the scenes." He lowers his voice and raises his eyebrows. "High-level security stuff."

"Oh," I say, immediately putting on a disinterested face. "You mean you're an armed guard or something? In charge of getting the money on the trucks? Well, I guess we all have to make a living."

"No, no, I don't deal with any of that shit," White says quickly. "I'm up there with the big boys. Helping the law crack down on fraud, catching money launderers, the works."

"Wow, money laundering? Does that come up a lot at a bank?"

"You got no idea. But I'm good at my job. I got it under control."

"I bet you do." I tap my finger against his empty pint. "I think you need another drink. And this one's on me."

"I can't let a chick pay for the drinks," he says, shaking his head. "Not how I was raised."

"But I *want* to pay." I put my hand on his knee. "Every once in a while I like to indulge in a little role reversal. Just to mix things up."

He smiles, clearly encouraged by my audacity. "I do like a girl who can mix things up."

As he waves over the bartender I gently remove my hand and wipe it off on my jeans.

It goes on like that for a little while, with me peppering him with light questions, distracting him with the occasional batting of the eyelashes. He orders a plate of buffalo wings and I make sure his glass is never, ever empty. Every few minutes or so he checks his phone.

"Are you waiting for a call?" I finally ask.

"Yeah, I'm meeting someone here . . . not a chick," he says quickly, in case I was worried. "Just a guy who I referred to the bank."

"A guy who you referred to the bank?" I repeat, not understanding.

"Yeah, it's not really in my job description, but if I know someone who has some serious money to invest, sometimes I'll nudge them over to my bank. You know, explain why the bank I work for is the best choice. The money guys at the bank love me for it. But this guy, he's still a bit on the fence, so I was gonna nudge him some more." He looks me over again, his eyes becoming increasingly daring. "You know," he says, his words only slightly slurred, "I'm not usually into Latinas. But you're different."

"I am," I agree.

"I have learned to speak a little Spanish over the last few years. You speak Spanish, right?"

"I do."

"Tell you what, after we get out of here why don't we practice our Spanish, because I'm thinking"—he leans over, the beer heavy on his breath—"I'm in the mood for Mexican tonight."

"Mmm." I chew gently on my lip. "You know, you really do seem familiar to me. Our paths must have crossed somewhere. Tell me, how did you end up in money laundering—"

"*Anti*–money laundering." He reaches for a buffalo wing, his fingers already stained red . . .

✤

Red blood on my mother's pink shirt, on her knees crying as Detective White stands over her, jeering, insulting her with sexually suggestive taunts in front of her ten-year-old daughter.

✤

"Yes, yes, of course," I say, tucking the memory away. "How did you end up doing that? What did you do before?"

"I was a cop. Bullshit job. Doesn't pay shit. But, turns out I closed the right case. I put away some bitch who offed a bank executive and people noticed. The bank was impressed and grateful, one thing led to another, and"—he spreads open his hands—"here I am."

"Lucky you! And of course, you're sure you got the right person?"

Again he shrugs. "She got convicted by a jury."

"And juries . . . well, they usually get it right, don't they?"

"Sometimes they do," he says, grabbing the last buffalo wing with one hand, his beer in the other. "Sometimes they don't. But it's not a cop's job to worry about that. A smart cop knows that his one and only job is to bring cases to a close as quickly and efficiently as possible and to give the DA what he needs to make a conviction."

"But you do worry about a suspect's actual guilt or innocence, right?"

"Yeah, course," he says, suddenly looking bored with the conversation.

"Tell me." This time I let my hand run up and down his inner thigh. "Tell me about this career-making case! It sounds like something out of a movie with you as the hero, solving the mystery, catching the bad guy and everything!"

"Not much of a mystery." White laughs, and it's an ugly, drunken sound. "The shooter was a real piece of work. She was one of those anchor babies, you know? Born here, raised in Mexico? And then she comes back here, bad English, no skills, just making her living scrubbing brown floors and sucking white dick . . ." He flushes suddenly and shakes his head. "Look, I'm sorry. I've had a lot to drink and like I said, this woman was a killer, so I don't mind telling you she was also slutty, you know? Still, I know better than to talk like that in mixed company."

"Hey, no worries, I get it." I clink my glass against his. "You're the hero, she's the criminal. She's nothing."

"That's right, baby!" he says, perking up. "Anyway, one of the guys she was fucking was married. So she goes over to his house, her bastard kid in the car and everything, and then she just blows the poor bastard away! But she does have *some* brains, so she calls the cops and tries to tell us that she just happened to find the body."

"But you didn't buy it."

"Like I said, convicted by a jury."

"Wow." I shake my head, looking out into the bar as if contemplating it all. "So she expected people to believe that she just happened to find the body right after the guy had been shot? She must have been desperate to make up a story like that."

"You better believe it! I could have done anything I wanted to her and she wouldn't have said boo if she thought there was a sliver of a chance that I'd get her off . . . no pun intended. But of course I did it all by the book. I've always played it straight arrow."

As he lifts his glass again, I see his mouth twitch in amusement . . . perhaps remembering things that I don't want to know.

"You ever been with a cop, Bell?"

"No," I say. "I can't say I have. But then, you're not a cop. You work for a bank."

"Yeah, but I know how to play the part." He chuckles. "Look, this guy I'm waiting for, he's seriously late. He must have gotten hung up or somethin'. Normally I'd be pissed, but in this case I think his screwup is our opportunity. Why don't we get out of here?"

I shift slightly in my seat, bring my lips right up to his ear. "Stay right here. I'm going to go to the restroom, you're going to order us one more round, not beer this time, something stronger. And once we've finished our drinks . . . you can show this little Latina what an all-American boy can do."

His eyes widen and then, for the first time tonight I see a spark of wariness. "You're not . . . okay, sorry." White laughs and flushes. "But I gotta ask you this, are you going to be needing payment for this? It's just . . . I don't usually get *this* lucky, not with someone who looks like you. So if I gotta pay, that's cool, I'd just rather do the negotiating now."

"Oh, Sean, I'm almost flattered by that! But I don't want your money." I stroke his cheek sweetly. "I'm just one of those people who gets turned on by the razor's edge of life. A good girl probably wouldn't want to do what I want to do to you. But"—I get up from my seat, let my breasts brush his arm—"I'm not a good girl."

I slip away as Sean desperately waves the bartender over again to order our last round. In the meantime I walk into the ladies' room, and then, a moment later, sneak out. In fact I slink right out the back entrance, where the Dumpster is.

Rats have some of the best survival instincts in the animal kingdom. They don't just devour any ol' thing. No, before they eat something they sniff it, then take a teeny-tiny bite, and then they pause before continuing, waiting to see if their delicate palate and superior nose can detect even the slightest hint of poison.

The rats' survival instinct just shows their intelligence.

And, I think as I look at the many rat poison pellets that are all around the Dumpster, *man-made rat poison that is both odorless and tasteless just shows what clever killers humans can be.*

※

When I reenter the bar I have crushed rat poison in the very bag that I had used to store Travis's keys. Before going out to meet White I go back into the ladies' room, check to make sure all the stalls are empty, and then practice smiling into the mirror.

I study my reflection. My smile doesn't look forced; it looks relaxed, peaceful.

I'm really very calm. I don't even fully feel like I'm in my own body; it's as if I'm in some sort of meditative state. Of course the rat poison might not be enough to kill him, but once he's sick, incapacitated, anything could happen. With a little assistance he might "accidentally" bang his head into the edge of the bathtub or counter. He might choke on his own vomit.

Don't do this!

The voice in my head isn't my own. It's Lander's. But I can't listen to him. Not now. Because in the end, this has nothing to do with him.

"I dedicate this death to you, Mamá," I whisper.

And the woman in the mirror just keeps smiling.

I adjust the bag in my purse and step back out into the hall, my eyes trained on Sean, who is still sitting at the bar, waiting patiently. I'm about to go to him when the door to the bar opens and a new patron walks in.

The guy's wearing nice jeans, a black T-shirt, and an expensive jacket. Tattoos crawl all the way up his neck. He looks dangerous as hell.

And I know him. It's Javier. The man who Travis met with in the Bronx. The man who was with Micah the first time I was forced to take a joyride in Micah's limo. The man I'm trying to make Micah suspicious of.

He walks right up to Sean, gesturing toward his phone and then the door as he talks. I see White gesture behind him toward the bathroom. In a moment he'll come looking for me, either to introduce me to Javier or to ask if we can meet later tonight.

But he won't find me because once again I've exited through the back door and this time I just keep walking, away from the bar, away from White . . .

. . . away from my first murder.

It's only then that I check my phone and see that Lander has sent me a few text messages. He's still with his father, I shouldn't wait for him before eating, but he'll be back by ten. A perfectly mundane text, simple, friendly, and completely out of sync with my current emotional state.

❦

It's not until I'm back in Lander's empty penthouse, standing in his living room, that my legs begin to shake uncontrollably. I sink down into the sofa, my breathing shallow and ragged, my eyes on the window, looking out at the city but seeing nothing, my mind consumed with what might have been.

chapter fourteen

When Lander comes home I'm sitting in the same place. I haven't moved in an hour. But he doesn't know that. He doesn't know that the world has changed.

He leans down and places an innocent kiss on the top of my head. "I could get used to this," he muses, "coming home to find you here." He starts to sort through the mail he grabbed on the way up. "I had a very interesting evening with my father. It seems that Sean White just came back from Delaware, where he assisted in staffing the AML compliance department. Remember, AML is anti-money-laundering. They're boosting the staff because of a—how did my father phrase it?—a *request* from the FDIC that HGVB be more vigilant in its compliance." He starts to drop certain envelopes on the coffee table, separating the bills from the solicitations from the account state-ments. "Sean White is *not* qualified for that job. But he's definitely someone my father and Travis would trust with the execution of their dirty work. The fact that he's been moved into this position suggests that my father thinks Sean can find a way to game the system. Which means my father's complicit, and *that* means that once I can prove HGVB's love and actual solicitation of money launderers, I'll also be able to tie my father to the crimes. Now my father tried to ex-plain . . ." Lander's voice trails off as he finally realizes that I'm not talking, not looking at him, not moving. "Doncia?" When I don't answer he sits by my side, now clearly a little alarmed. "What's going on?"

"I almost killed someone tonight," I say quietly.

"Ah, well, I almost strangled my father, so I guess we're even. Wait." He places his fingers under my chin and guides my face toward his. "You're serious."

Again I don't answer.

"Adoncia, what the hell happened?"

"What happened," I say slowly, "is I had drinks with the man who arrested my mother."

Lander pauses and then slowly leans back against the armrest of the sofa, away from me.

"I followed him to a bar," I continue. "I spoke with him. I flirted with him. I was going to go home with him."

A flash of anger, but still he stays silent.

"I was going to pour him a drink, just like I poured you a drink the first time you took me home."

"The first time I took you home you drugged me," Lander notes. "You slipped me a sedative, and that was *after* you had sex with me."

"Yes, but this time I was going to give him the drink before he had the chance to touch me. And I wasn't going to use a sedative. I was going to use this."

I take the plastic bag out of my purse. Inside is crushed green powder.

"What's that?" Lander asks, genuinely bewildered.

"It's rat poison," I say, my voice hollow, even to my own ears. "To kill a rat."

Lander doesn't respond immediately. He just absorbs the meaning of my words as he stares at the bag. "Adoncia," he finally says, his voice steady but urgent. "What did you do?"

I finger the bag, making the green powder float this way and that. "Nothing," I say softly. "White left with Javier."

"Wait, Javier was there? Did he see you?"

"No."

"What the hell was he doing—"

"*White was supposed to die!*" The words come hurtling out of my mouth, bellowing through the room and ricocheting off the walls. I get to my feet and start pacing the bleached wood floors. "We play these stupid Scooby Doo games, trying to work out the mystery of who did what when and who knew, and in the meantime these people, these *murderers*, are out there living in the lap of luxury, literally destroying the world! I mean, drug cartels, Lander? Russian mafia? *Iran?* As far as we know they're funding terrorists!

And we're sitting here, twiddling our thumbs, talking about some Mickey Mouse operation in *Delaware*? Are you fucking kidding me? These people don't need to go to prison, they need to *die*! Don't you see that? They killed Nick Foley and when they did that they killed my mother. *My mother!*" I grab a vase worth God only knows how much and hurl it across the room, watching it shatter into a hundred pieces as it smashes against the wall. "They need to die, Lander," I say, softer this time, the tears slipping down my cheek. "I want these people to die."

Slowly, Lander stands up, walks behind me, and puts a hand on each of my arms. I wait for him to tell me to calm down, that I'm being unreasonable, but he says nothing, and the relief that comes from this gentle silence, from feeling understood, is so overwhelming I fall back into him, allowing him to hold me up as he kisses my hair.

"I shouldn't have called you when Jessica was on the verge of overdosing." The tears are flowing freely now and my words are staggered as I gulp for air. "I was supposed to just let her die. That's what I wanted. That was my *plan*. And then I was going to make it look like a murder and pin her death on Travis. I had it all set up. There's a paper trail that points to him . . . everything I needed to make it work. He would be on trial right now for murder, not fucking money laundering. And Jessica, that *bitch* who lied about my mother on the stand, she would be dead! And Sean White, he *should* be dead. But when the chips were down I was weak and I was slow and now they're winning. Every breath of air they take is another knife wound to my heart. I'm not even alive anymore. I mean how can I be, right? How can I be alive when every single fucking day I die just a little bit more?"

Slowly he turns me around; his eyes are so calm, so focused. He's hearing me. Somebody is finally hearing me.

And somebody cares.

I close my eyes as his kisses find my tears, pulling them away from my skin, warming me, centering me. I reach out and grab his shoulders, grateful to have something solid to hold on to.

"You're hurting," he says, whispering the words against my skin. "You're incredibly angry, but Adoncia . . ." He pulls away, holds my face in his hands. "You are more *alive* than any person I have ever met."

My lower lip trembles. If I move, if I so much as speak, I will weep.

"That's why you're hurting and it's why you're angry," Lander continues. "Because life was taken—from Nick Foley, from your mother. They lost their lives and you know what that *means*. And it's why Jessica is still alive and it's why you would never have gone through with your plan to poison Sean. Because you appreciate the value of life in a way that they never could."

"No," I say pulling away. "That's not true. That *can't* be true." I put my hand over my stomach as if trying to press back the pain that is knotted in my gut. "White talked about my mother tonight . . . If you had *heard* the things he said . . . Lander, he truly does deserve to die! I have to believe that . . . I can't . . . I . . . I *have to believe that*!"

"Adoncia—"

"Don't you understand? What you're saying, it means that they can hurt me in ways that I can never hurt them! And why? Because I value their life more than they value their own? That's not how I think! That can't be who I am!"

He's standing there, watching me, his eyes so kind, so sympathetic . . .

I shake my head fiercely, stepping farther back. "You're *wrong*! I don't value life for life's sake! Not for people like them! And not for people like me." The tears have started again; they're pouring down my face, blurring the room into some kind of abstract nightmare. "You've given me comfort, you've given me kindness and passion and I thank you for that, I *do*. It's why I'm here, right now, in your home, in this room with you . . . But the reason I'm still on this earth? The reason I'm *alive* is revenge. That's the only thing that keeps me here. That's all I care about. If I didn't have revenge I would've given up on my life years ago. I'd have no reason to go on."

"I believe you, to a degree," Lander says, his voice so soft, so tender it hurts. "But, Adoncia, when everything had been taken from you, when you had *nothing*—no money, no family, no real home, no *love*—did you give up?"

I open my mouth to answer but then shake my head when I can't find the words.

"No," Lander continues. "You never gave up. Instead you gave yourself the quest for revenge, you *gave* yourself a reason to live."

I'm trembling, the room is spinning, and I hold on to the back of an armchair for support. "But . . . but it's not like that," I plead. "Because when the revenge is gone, once I've made them all pay, then I can give up. I will, I'm sure I will."

"Just as you were sure you were going to let Jessica die?" he asks. "No, you'll just find another reason to go on. You won't let the world stop you. You may have your flaws, but a lack of tenacity isn't one of them."

I'm clutching the armchair, trying to breathe. Does he know what he's doing? I have trained myself to be ruthless, to be callous, to be a walking, talking weapon whose whole purpose is to destroy my enemies at all costs. But what Lander is saying . . . Does he know that he is challenging the very essence of how I define myself? Does he *get* that?

I close my eyes against the spinning room, trying to clear my head. *Another reason to live, another reason . . .* What could that possibly be?

Could it be him?

My eyes fly open and I try to see him through the tears. Could Lander be my reason to live? Could he give me that?

Because, I realize with a sad little jolt, I would like that. It's a gift that I covet. When my world of revenge is gone I'll be lost. But if he could just let me make him my world, if I could just make this man my home . . .

. . . if he could just love me.

In a moment of confessions these are the words I still cannot utter.

Pain, so much pain. For years all I've let myself feel is anger, but now he's weakened that armor, and all the hurt and confusion and fear that I've been suppressing for so long are flooding through me like a tsunami irreparably altering my internal landscape. My knees are weak, I can barely stand. I reach for him, extending my open hand toward him. "Help me," I whisper, "make me feel the things you say I am. Make . . . Make me feel alive."

In an instant he's holding me, wrapping me up in his arms, his scent, tickling me with his breath. My mouth finds his and I kiss him like I've never kissed him before. The kiss is so deep and so very urgent, like I'm going to consume him . . .

. . . like I want to be consumed.

His hands are moving under my shirt, up my back; I feel his skin against mine and I'm so grateful for that and so demanding of more.

I'm tearing off his shirt as he rips off mine. Nothing can be between us, this is my need, this is my life.

His hand weaves into my hair and pulls, forcing my head back so he can kiss my neck, and I welcome it, welcome the pleasure and the pain, welcome anything that can make me feel present, in this moment, anything that will force me to celebrate my own vitality while still being overwhelmed by his. I feel him loosen my bra and I desperately work on his pants. In seconds all our clothes are tossed about the room, discarded like the needless impediments that they are. He's so beautiful, every muscle so defined, so perfect, he's made his body his temple and I fall to my knees in worship, wrapping my lips around his erection, letting my tongue feel the shape of each vein, of his every detail. For over half my life revenge has been my church, but now he is my idol, golden and mystical. This has to be mine. *He* has to be mine. He has to give this to me . . .

. . . and I have to be his.

I hear him groan as I continue my ministrations, and for me that groan is like a Beethoven rhapsody, making me rejoice in the pleasure I can give him, celebrating the victory of being able to make him want me, to make him *need* me.

He pushes on my shoulder and I fall back, my legs bent under my thighs, my arms raised straight back behind my head as he lies on top of me, gripping my shoulders, his face just inches from mine as he thrusts inside of me, moving his hips in circular motions as he explores me. His lips find my ear, my cheek, and then my mouth again as his hands move to touch my breasts, which are now begging for his attention.

And as the kisses continue I realize . . .

. . . my idol is worshipping *me*.

Exhilarated, I arch my back a little more, bringing him in deeper, making the two of us one.

When he pulls away from me I almost cry again, the agony of losing our connection for even a moment too much to bear. I pull my legs out from underneath me, raise my knees to my breasts, crossing my ankles so I'm curled up in a ball, comforting myself for this temporary loss.

But Lander is far from done with me. He kneels before me, and grabbing my hips, pulls me onto his angled lap. My feet are now pressed against the hardness of his chest, giving me the leverage I need as he enters me, moving back and forth, testing and delighting in the tight friction we've created. He is so magnificent as he moves against me, such a tantalizing vision to behold.

I want this man to love me.

I uncurl my legs, placing them on either side of him, pressing down into his hard floor with the base of my feet. He leans over me, one hand right above each of my shoulders, but when he tries to press my hips down onto the ground I stop him. With a small hand gesture I motion for him to stay still as I lift and lower my hips, controlling our rhythm. With each small thrust I only take in half of his cock, knowing that I am creating a sweet torture of my own. Again he groans, his eyes wanting so much more from me, wanting everything.

I want this man to love me.

With one powerful thrust I push my hips all the way up, taking him in completely, and I can see the ecstasy play across his face as I continue. I know what I'm doing to him, know that he is on the verge of filling me with everything that makes him a man.

But when I bring my hands to his sides, making my body completely open to him, he finally pushes my hips down to the floor, pressing his pelvis against mine, entering me at a higher angle, moving inside of me in a slow, sensual, dancelike movement, forward around, back around, driving me crazy, while his pelvis massages my clit.

I'm going to come, there is no holding back anymore, and as the orgasm takes hold I feel him pulsating inside me, filling me, and I hear him calling out my name.

"Adoncia."

Lander, my lover, is the only one who calls me by my real name.

I want this man to love me.

chapter fifteen

The next few days blend together like raindrops in a puddle; not one is distinguishable from another. We don't talk about Sean White or what I might or might not have done to him. We don't talk about my anger, my pain, or my reason to live. Sometimes the more important parts of life have to be put aside just so you can get through the day. And these days there was a lot to get through.

Each day I call Micah and lie. I tell him I haven't seen Javier. I don't know if anyone associated with the Gables or HGVB has seen him either. Micah takes the news in stride. As far as I'm concerned the only thing that is important is that he thinks I'm spying for him.

And I do about a thousand little errands for Jessica in preparation for the party. Lander does whatever it is he does, talking to his mysterious detectives, conferring with his "man" who is working on the encryption, sharing little, promising everything. I imagine myself as the star of a dark version of *Annie*, always singing that the crimes will come out tomorrow.

Travis has little to do with me. I serve Jessica when I work on Monday, and on Tuesday there are so many last-minute details to take care of I almost forget that I'm not really there to be a personal assistant, that I'm not supposed to care how this dinner turns out. Because when every moment is about flower arrangements and seating charts and who's getting the vegetarian meal and when will the champagne be served . . . Well, it's hard not to get lost in that. It's almost as if Jessica is planning a wedding. But maybe this is what the rich do. They plan wedding after wedding, labeling them by different names (political fundraiser, Harvard alumni dinner, themed costume ball). These events don't end in marriages, but then the real weddings—the big ones with the tiered cakes and the ten-thousand-dollar gowns—those aren't really about marriage anyway. They're about the production. And by those standards, this dinner Jessica has orchestrated for Sam Highkin is one spectacular ceremony.

Jessica sends me down to the venue early, to make sure that all her last-minute requests are being carried out. Robyn, the event manager, a fortysomething woman with narrow eyes and a neck like a giraffe, is frantic with all the adjustments, and the two of us decide to partner up and make it happen. Jessica shows up only minutes before Sam Highkin's campaign staff, and there's no denying that she looks positively lovely.

Her high-waisted, short-sleeved silk dress hovers between a pale yellow and nude, with a keyhole neckline and embroidered gold flowers on the shoulders. It's a tailored cut that flares, just slightly, midthigh. The whole thing seems to be a nod to the 1940s styles that might have been worn by Lauren Bacall or Ingrid Bergman. Nothing racy, but figure flattering and literally dripping with sophistication.

And the funny thing is, Jessica looks comfortable wearing it. More than that, she looks confident. As members of Sam Highkin's campaign team trickle in, she greets them with a balance of grace and aloofness. Her eyes are a little glassy, but other than that you can't tell that she's a regular pill popper. If anything, she comes across as a quintessential old-money socialite.

But it's not until Travis shows up a half hour later that I realize that for tonight, the rules of the game have changed. For when Jessica spots him walking through the door, her shoulders remain relaxed; she doesn't cower or fold into herself as she so often does in his presence.

No, tonight she simply curls her lips into a benign smile. And when he approaches her he does the unthinkable.

He gives her a kiss on the cheek.

To say this is out of character is an understatement. Before this moment the kindest thing I've ever seen Travis do for Jessica is refuse to talk to her.

But tonight? Tonight they seem like a perfectly normal, if not overly affectionate, married couple.

Travis addresses the campaign staff, shaking hands, saying a few words to this one, then to that one as Jessica stands by his side looking like the model political wife.

They're wearing their game face, I realize. The way Travis treats her in the privacy of his home is one thing, but he won't make a spectacle here. Here he is a figure to be feared, but also to be admired. He's an actor . . . like me.

It's tempting to just sit back and watch the performance art, but there's too much to do, and so as their play continues I run around with Robyn, making sure that all of Jessica's whims are being realized to perfection.

At some point the event manager taps me on the shoulder and points to her watch. "The guests will be here soon; you have to change," she says.

"Right." I glance over at Jessica, who clearly had all the time in the world to put herself together perfectly. I would have liked to have gotten dressed at Lander's, or even at my apartment, but Jessica had no interest in allowing me that luxury.

"I moved your dress and other things out of my office," Robyn continues as she straightens out a place setting.

"All right." I sigh. "I'll change in the ladies' room."

"Um, no, that's not what I meant." Robyn laughs as she steps away from the table to examine her work. "I moved you into our bride's dressing room. You deserve at least that much."

"Oh, that's not necessary."

Robyn turns to me and gives me a look. "Your boss is extremely particular and she seems to have a hard time making up her mind. If you hadn't helped me I'm not sure I would have been able to pull all this off. So yeah, I think providing you with a decent room for you to change your clothes in is absolutely necessary."

I smile my gratitude. I like Robyn, and to be honest I like being appreciated by a person for whom I'm not bending over backward to please or destroy. I follow her out of the room as she leads me through wood-paneled corridors, past doors leading to ballrooms and smaller private dining rooms. "We only have one other event tonight," Robyn says as we pass an open door with people mingling inside. "A retirement dinner, and that will be wrapping up in about an hour, so then it'll just be you guys. It's a good thing because I suspect Jessica is going to demand all our attention, and I really can't afford to get on a Gable's bad side. I hear that after Jessica hosted a fund-raiser last year at The Orchid she managed to get six people fired for not refolding the napkins of the guests who got up to use the restroom."

"I can see her doing that," I say as Robyn stops in front of a plain brown door labeled Bride's Room. She pushes it open and I stand there for a moment, feeling honestly confused. The room is huge. It's clearly not meant for one person, it's meant for a bride and an entourage of bridesmaids. In the center there's a table holding a single champagne flute, which has already been filled to the brim, along with a small fruit bowl and a dish full of mixed nuts. The walls are painted a quiet blue, the makeup counters are expansive, and there's an oversized mirror mounted on the wall and storage bins for personal items.

And there is my silk chiffon Badgley Mischka dress, hanging from a single cast-iron hook designed to look like a Victorian skeleton key in a door lock. The light pink shoes have been placed next to it on a small pedestal. Lander paid for these weeks ago, although he's yet to see them. He just handed over his credit card number and blindly bought me a little magic.

It's right out of a fairy tale.

"Enjoy it," Robyn says with a smile. "You earned it. The champagne was just poured a few minutes ago so it's cold. Figured you might need a drink before you share a table with the Gables."

I laugh politely and thank her as she rushes off to get back to the preparations.

This is a bride's dressing room. A princess room. I try to imagine myself as the kind of woman who belongs here. If I was that woman I would have at least ten, no, twelve bridesmaids. All of them would be good friends from school, people who really cared about me. And there would be a flower girl who was . . . a cousin? Is that who flower girls usually are? She'd definitely be some kind of family member; a bride who would get dressed in here would definitely have a big family.

My groom would be extraordinarily handsome, impressively daring, and ridiculously rich, like Lander. Yes, Lander would be perfect! And my father . . . my father who . . . who always calls me princess, but not in a condescending way, he would escort me down the aisle, while my beautiful mother would weep with pride from her front-row seat.

It's with that final detail that the fun of my little fantasy goes up in smoke. I sit down in the middle of this cavernous room as my spirit crashes down to reality. My mother will never see me get married. And when she died she certainly wasn't proud of me. I gave her no reason to be.

I don't have a father to walk me down the aisle. I have no little cousins that I know of, no friends who would want to attend to me on my special day.

All I have is the man, Lander, my imaginary groom. I can't lose him.

I take a deep breath and then a sip of my champagne before pushing myself to my feet. I pull off my clothes, *my muggle clothes*, I think with a smile, and then I reach for my dress and slip into magic.

That's what the dress feels like, like a bunch of pixies took wisps of a cloud at sunrise and then used their magical talents to weave the ethereal fabric into a gown. The silk chiffon is the lightest shade of pink. Artfully draped ruffles adorn the bodice and fall along my left leg from where the dress gathers at the waist. The straps themselves are beaded and delicate, so delicate they can barely be seen. The shoes are patent leather heeled platforms in a slightly darker shade of pink.

I take a moment to examine myself in the mirror. I stare hard, waiting for the illusion to dissipate the way my last fantasy did, but it doesn't happen. While Jessica's dress has the glamour and sophistication of the old Hollywood movie stars, this dress isn't about sophistication at all. It's about innocence, femininity, romance.

Staring into the mirror I can almost see my fantasy family and friends behind me, all smiling approvingly except for one, the only one I recognize: my mother. She's wearing her prison uniform and she looks so tired, so very disappointed.

Because she knows I'm not an innocent. I'm certainly not some kind of fairy-tale princess. No, tonight I am Bellona Dantès. I'm here for revenge. This dress is just a nod of respect to something that has gone. It's a quiet tribute to the woman I once thought I could be.

"I'm sorry, Mamá," I whisper. "I can't make you proud. But . . ." I inhale deeply, forcing myself to absorb a new energy as I reach for my champagne and hold up my glass. "I *can* make them pay."

I pick up my evening bag and walk back out to the dinner.

When I get there Travis and Jessica are talking to an elderly man with starkly white hair and the blotchy skin that comes with age and too much Scotch. Jessica spots me first and her mouth opens slightly in a rather unflattering manner. Then it's Travis's turn, and for a moment his expression is one of complete surprise, and then confusion. It's as if he's not entirely able to make sense of what he's seeing. The old man, on the other hand, appears to be very happy to see me coming his way.

"Mrs. Gable," I say once I'm in their little circle. "Robyn has everything under control now. Things are ready to go."

"Good," Jessica says after she closes her mouth and collects herself. "Jeremy, this is Bell, our personal assistant. Bell, this is Mr. Dixon. He's the CEO of Portrait Electric and a major backer of some of our most respected political leaders."

"A personal assistant, really?" he says, shooting Travis a bemused look. "I would never have guessed. Where are you from, young lady?"

"Right here. I was born in Brooklyn, sir."

"Well, I wouldn't have guessed that either. I would have thought you grew up in Connecticut or some such place and that you worked in a gallery somewhere, giving the old coots like me something to look at when the art isn't enough."

I can see that this is meant to be a compliment, so I manage a smile and give a deferential nod.

"You're hardly an old coot!" Jessica laughs, resting her hand on his arm. "You're a gentleman of culture and intellect. Highkin can't wait to hear your thoughts on how best to restructure the tax laws, isn't that right, Travis?"

"Absolutely," Travis agrees, jerking his eyes away from me. "I think you'll find him to be a very impressive candidate. He can win this thing, and more importantly, he has a good memory. He never forgets a friend."

"Mr. Dixon, have you met Jon Gilmour?" Jessica interjects. "He starred in that film *Projections*? You simply have to meet him." She leads Mr. Dixon away as Travis nods his approval.

"You look different," he says once we're alone.

"Well, I should hope so." I laugh. "It's a formal event. I wouldn't wear something like this to work."

"That's not what I mean, and you know it. The look's all wrong for you. You *seem* different in that dress."

"Is that so bad?"

He shrugs, a little annoyed. "It's not what I'm paying for, that's all. Innocence and romance bore me. Then again, it doesn't really matter what dress you wear tonight," he notes, a cool smile playing on his lips. "You'll be taking it off for me later anyway."

I smile coyly but bristle inside and scan the crowd for Cathy. She's not here. That could be a huge problem.

"When I'm done with you you'll be going to Lander's, correct?"

"Correct," I say tersely.

"Good." He reaches into his breast pocket and pulls out a USB flash drive.

My heart slams to a stop. "What, um, what is that?" I'm trying so hard to make my voice sound calm, but it's just a little too high, a little too strained.

"What do you mean, 'what is that?'" Travis asks,

irritated. "Obviously it's a flash drive. Here, put it in your purse."

Somehow I manage to keep my hand steady as I follow his instructions.

"I want a copy of every file on his computer. I want every email that looks even remotely interesting. I want his calendar. I want—"

"This USB is blank?" I interrupt.

Travis gives me an odd look. "Why would you think otherwise? Your job is to give me information, not the other way around."

"I'm . . . I'm sorry . . ." I say, once again glancing at the door, trying to will Cathy into the room. "You gave me a flash drive, I . . . I just got confused. But," I say, finally pulling it together, "I don't know the password for Lander's computer."

Travis gives me a withering look. "Have him look something up on the Internet and stand behind him while he logs on. Use your eyes."

"What would I have him look up on the Internet for me?"

"Stock trends, porn, a YouTube cat video, I don't care. Just get this done. If you can't be cunning you're of no use to me."

If I can't be cunning? It's almost funny considering the circumstances.

"Travis, how long has it been!" A woman in her late forties with a helmet of platinum-blond hair approaches Travis with arms outstretched before grasping his shoulders and leaning in to kiss him on both cheeks. "It's been eons, no?" she says, then continues without waiting for a response. "Probably at one of these ghastly dinners. Now I have to ask you, are you sure about this Highkin fellow? He's rather wet behind the ears, don't you think?"

I quietly excuse myself as the woman continues to ramble. I stare pointedly at the door. *Please, please, please, Cathy, show up!*

But it's just more guests, all with similar looks. Sophisticated, pretentious, wealthy. I'm surrounded by them. I feel like a shiny penny in a suitcase full of hundreds.

And that's when Lander walks in.

He looks in my direction and stops in his tracks. I look around me to see what has him frozen, but then I realize he really is just looking at me. I turn back to him and now he's smiling, his hand pressed firmly over his heart.

The smile that comes over me is one of those smiles that's rooted so deep it radiates throughout your whole body. The walking, talking hundred-dollar bills in the room become a blur, nothing more than background noise as Lander moves through them easily, not stopping to talk to any of the many people who are clearly trying to get his attention. When he reaches me, he strokes my cheek with the back of his hand and I find myself closing my eyes and leaning into it like a kitten.

"You look," he breathes, and then stops as if he can't find the words.

"I look?" I ask, egging him on. "I look like what?

Like I'm in costume? Like I'm playing dress-up? Like I'm—"

"Beautiful," he says.

In my entire life I've never heard anyone say the word *beautiful* quite like that, not unless they were talking about God, or a Fourth of July fireworks display, or a Van Gogh masterpiece. Never about a person. *Never* about me. I feel the warmth spread to my cheeks. "It's just a dress, Lander."

"No," he says quietly, his eyes still holding me, "it's you."

The comment makes me happy, and then incredibly sad. It's the same kind of sadness that hit me when I lost hold of my bridal fantasy. "You're wrong," I say solemnly, taking his hand. "I don't know who I am tonight, but it can't be me."

"Here he is!" Edmund Gable's hands are on Lander before we even fully register his presence. He grips Lander's shoulder firmly, jovially demanding his attention. "So glad you decided to come, my boy!" Edmund says, giving Lander a little shake. "And Bell." His eyes rest on me a little longer than I'm comfortable with. It's not an entirely approving look. "I haven't seen you since we met in Travis's office. What a wonderful coincidence that you met my other son as well."

"It wasn't a coincidence," Lander says smoothly. "We met at Travis's."

"Yes, yes, so I hear." He's still looking at me. More than that, he's studying me . . . almost like a poker player looking for a tell.

It's amazing how much danger can be hidden behind a hearty smile.

"Serendipity aside," Edmund continues, "you really do look exquisite." He tilts his head to the side, just a little. "Last time we met you swore it was for the first time, that we had never met before."

"That's right, Mr. Gable," I say, hiding behind a smile of my own.

"It's odd. There's something so familiar about you."

It's very close to what I said to White.

A man with thinning hair and impressive girth moves over to us. "Edmund, how the hell are you?"

"Not too bad, not too bad at all. Lander, allow me to introduce you to Peter Turan, CEO of Wonder Nation. Pete, this is my youngest son, Lander, and Bell Dantès, his date for the evening."

It's a telling introduction.

Edmund continues to drone on—about Highkin, about the market, about the ineptitude of Washington—all the while carefully excluding me without ever being overtly rude. It doesn't bother me. I listen carefully, trying hard to pull out bits of information that might be useful, but there's nothing. When Edmund finally goes off to chat with the other donors, Lander lets his irritation show. "I can't wait to bring that son of a bitch down."

His voice is so low, so serious. We have the same goal, of course, but looking at him now makes me wonder. Did I ever look that angry when I was talking about my mother? Back when I thought she was guilty? When I visited her in the prison, did she look into my eyes and see that kind of disgust?

The thought gives me a chill. "Come," I say, pulling gently on his arm. "Let's get a drink."

We only get through half a glass of wine each before it's time for us to be seated. I lead Lander to our table (I know the seating chart by heart at this point) while scanning the faces in the room, only looking for one person. One person who needs to be here, and isn't.

Our table is in front, near where Highkin will be speaking. Edmund is already there. He has no date for the evening. Travis and Jessica are making their way to the table now from the opposite side of the room.

I crane my head to look toward the table where *she* should be. But her seat is empty.

This could be it. Without Cathy I may have no option but to be up-front with Travis, tell him the deal's off. He'll fire me; my advantage will be destroyed.

Jessica and Travis reach the table first, although they continue to stand, hovering around Edmund as if they need his permission to sit. Lander apparently doesn't think that we do. He pulls a chair out for me, and when he does, I think I see the momentary flash of disapproval cross Edmund's face. But it's so fleeting I could be wrong.

Besides, it's hard for me to really worry about whether or not Edmund dislikes me. Cathy's not here. By the end of this night I will have lost Travis's trust, unless of course I do the unthinkable . . . which I can't, because it's *unthinkable*. But to throw all my work away . . . How can I do that? What if . . .

"Oh my God."

This from Jessica. The words come out a little louder than I think she intended, because not only did everyone at our table hear her, a few people at the next table did as well.

Confused, Travis follows her gaze to the door.

And then, in a moment of *true* beauty, all the color leaves his face. His eyes grow to a different size and his whole body seems to almost weaken . . . the way Jessica's does when she's anticipating his abuse.

Lander and I, Edmund, *everyone* around us looks to the door. And there she is. Cathy Earnest Lind, walking right into the banquet room with an odd mixture of defiance and trepidation. By her side, Robyn is gently directing her to her table.

Cathy doesn't look like the other guests. She's wearing a cocktail dress, not an evening gown . . . and it's a showstopper. Sporadically placed silver beads spin a sparkling and delicate web from the illusion neckline to the above-the-knee skirt. Under the beading the fabric is a perfect shade of nude, so perfect that it's hard to tell from a distance that there's anything at all beneath those beads . . . particularly when she walks near certain lights and you can see how very sheer the fabric is. If you look very closely (which we all do), you can make out the faint silhouette of her legs as she walks across the room. Her hair is slicked back and pulled tight into a bun at the nape of her neck. She could be a model; she could be a guest at the Great Gatsby's party.

Or she could just be Cathy, the woman who is already bringing Travis to his knees.

Robyn finally gets Cathy to her seat and I watch as three men jump up to pull her chair out for her. She rewards them with a flirtatious smile as she lowers herself into her seat.

"Sit down, Travis," I hear Edmund hiss. Edmund's lost his happy exterior. He looks like he's about to go on a shooting spree. But as Travis looks down at him he doesn't seem to register that. He simply looks back up at Cathy and then finally he falls back to his seat, next to his wife.

How many times have I seen Jessica in ruins because of her husband's actions? But I've never seen her quite like this. She looks utterly and completely defeated.

Tonight is going to be fun.

chapter sixteen

The politician's speech is by far the least consequential part of the evening.

As Highkin drones on and on about financial policy, regulatory agencies, and the "people who are destroying this country," Travis looks like he is about to jump out of his skin. He cannot take his eyes off Cathy. Jessica, on the other hand, is no longer the elegant, sophisticated socialite. She is now the depressed, desperate, browbeaten wife . . . who has been drinking an impressive amount of wine.

When Highkin starts to talk about domestic energy production, Jessica finishes her fifth glass. "Travis," she says quietly. "What does this mean?"

"I don't know," Travis replies as his father simultaneously shushes her.

Lander waves over the busser and asks him to fill Jessica's water goblet.

"I'm serious, Travis," Jessica continues. She's holding on to the edge of the table so tightly her fingertips have gone white. "I have to know what this means."

"I just told you," he snaps, although his voice remains hushed. "I don't *know*. I didn't even invite her!"

Highkin moves on to another subject, although it doesn't appear that anyone at our table is paying enough attention to actually know what that subject is.

From the corner of my eye I can see Cathy leaning into another man at her table, bending her head so she can catch whatever whispered words he wants to share.

Travis sees it too.

"You have to tell me," Jessica pushes. "I simply can't take another—"

"I. Don't. *Know!*"

The entire room falls silent. Everyone turns to our table. Edmund's smile is frozen on his face as Lander leans back casually in his chair, clearly amused.

"Yes," Sam Highkin says with a light laugh. "That's what I was saying. None of us really know what the long-term effects of this new regulation will be. Thank you, Travis, for being so passionate about the subject."

The room bursts out into uncomfortable laughter. They're laughing.

They're laughing at Travis.

And now Travis is positively red.

It's sorta hard not to rub my hands together in glee. Instead I satisfy myself by studying Travis's face, relishing the idea that he might be turning red with humiliation. Although now that I look closer I can see that he's red with rage.

That's good too.

It's also true that Cathy has looked over to our table for the first time. And when Travis sees *that* he goes from red to white. It's odd, Travis is always so composed, but tonight his face is like one giant mood ring. Whatever effect this woman has on him, it's powerful.

Edmund, on the other hand, has remained one color. He's also remained in one position. Since Cathy walked in he's barely moved a muscle. Unlike Travis, he hasn't had an outburst, but you can tell that he's seriously pissed.

I'm having *such* a good time.

As Highkin launches into another long-winded answer to another overly simplistic question, Edmund leans forward, toward Jessica and Travis, and says in a voice that's quiet but absolutely impossible to miss, "Pull it *together*."

Jessica is staring down into her empty wineglass, her water still untouched. "I can't take this," she sobs.

"You will take whatever you need to take!" Edmund replies in the same low voice. "You are the wife of a Gable and you will do what is necessary to keep up appearances."

"I'm his wife?" Jessica asks as the rest of the room bursts into applause for whatever Highkin just said. "Really? How long will that last? Am I on my way out? Is that what this is about?"

"Shut your fucking mouth," Travis growls.

This is *not* how Travis talks. He's losing his cool.

"Is that my replacement?" Jessica asks, the hysteria rising in her voice. "So will you be sending me to the guillotine or will you skip the formalities and go with a sniper?"

"Get your wife in line, Travis."

"And what line would that be, Edmund?" Jessica demands. "Have I made the Gable family assassination list? Or are you going to have me locked up on trumped-up charges? Or do you have something *new* planned for me?"

In the background, Highkin is walking away from the podium, and people are getting up from their seats to approach him and mingle.

But at *our* table the world has stopped.

"You're being ridiculous, Jessica," Edmund says, looking surreptitiously over his shoulder.

"Ridiculous? *That's* a ridiculous concern? Have you forgotten—"

Edmund slams his hand on the table so hard all our silverware jumps. Again there are looks and whispers around the room, but no one dares get close enough to eavesdrop.

A single sob escapes Jessica's lips as she grabs her purse. "I can't take this. I really can't." Jumping to her feet, she rushes out of the room. A hundred curious eyes follow her, all wondering what has spurred this rare meltdown of the Gables.

chapter seventeen

"Travis, I demand that you go after her right now and deal with this," Edmund hisses.

"She'll be fine," Travis says distractedly, his eyes on Cathy. "She'll go to the ladies' room and take a few Valium to calm herself. Jessica is well versed in the ways of self-medication."

"People are *looking*!" Edmund snaps. His hand is shaking and his jaw is tense. "Go *after her*!"

"I can't very well follow her into the ladies' room."

The look Edmund gives Travis is so vicious it actually pulls his attention away from Cathy.

Slowly and very reluctantly, Travis stands. "Bell," he says, snapping his fingers in my direction, "I'm going to need your assistance with this."

"She's not a dog," Lander says coolly. "You can't summon her with the snap of your fingers."

I turn to look at Lander. He has been enjoying this

show every bit as much as I have. I can just sense it. But he hasn't added his voice to the conversation, until now.

"She's my employee," Travis replies, as if that gives him the right to summon me any way he likes.

"Ah." Lander bows his head and puts his forearms on the table, pretending to ponder his brother's logic. "Perhaps I should rephrase. If you snap your fingers at her again I will break them." He looks up at Travis, his gaze unwavering. "I will hold down your hand and pulverize each digit with the pounding of my fist, crushing the bones—"

"*Enough!*" Edmund growls. "You are men! Stop squabbling like little boys and hysterical women!"

Lander opens his mouth to address his father, but I put my hand over his, gently, calmingly, like a wife. "It's all right," I say. "I want to help with Jessica."

"Then you should do that," Lander says kindly, raising my hand to his lips for a kiss. "After he apologizes."

Travis gives him a withering look. "You must be joking."

"She is not your assistant tonight," Lander says, turning his attention back to his brother. "She's my date. If you insult my date, you insult me. An apology is called for."

"Ah, so long as we know this is about you," Travis notes, his eyes traveling back to Cathy's table. "I'm not in an apologetic mood so I suggest you withdraw your request. After all, you should never ask for more than you can get. It makes you look weak."

"For God's sake, apologize, Travis, and get your damned wife in hand before she does something even more idiotic than usual!" Edmund demands.

Travis gives his father a poisonous look. "You're siding with him?"

I press my lips together. He *is* acting a bit like a little boy.

"I am *siding* with the Gable name!" Edmund's voice is trembling slightly as he strains to control his volume. "Considering what the name has done for you, I'd think you would appreciate that!"

Travis stares at him for a beat and then inhales sharply and gives his father an almost imperceptible nod. "Bell, for the sake of my family's name, I apologize."

I immediately get to my feet, not wanting to give anyone time to weigh in on whether or not the apology was adequate. "Be back soon," I call over my shoulder while following Travis as he strides out of the banquet hall.

Once we're in the wide corridor he stops short in front of the ladies' room. "She's in there," Travis says, with both certainty and irritation. "Get her out and bring her back to the table."

"You're not going to wait here?"

"You have your instructions," he snaps.

I smile obligingly and walk through the door.

Once inside I walk through what is truly a "ladies' lounge," crossing the sitting area and heading straight to the sinks and mirrors. That's where Jessica is, one hand on the counter, an open pill case in the other. My guess is that she's already taken three or four of whatever those are and is now just waiting for them to kick in.

But what strikes me is the way she's looking at her reflection. You would think that she was looking at a stranger. I know she's aware of my presence; my reflection is right there in front of her. But she makes no indication of it.

And then, she smiles. It's the slow, despairing smile of a woman who knows her fate has been decided and there isn't a damn thing she can do about it.

"You see," she says as if we're picking up in the middle of a conversation, "Travis has always been respectful toward me in public. That was important to him. He doesn't care if he humiliates me in front of the help. But he recognized that our behavior at social gatherings had professional implications." She reaches for her purse on the counter and starts looking through its contents. "I've always liked going out with Travis to these kinds of events, even when things are bad between us. And really, when are they *not* bad between us? But when we go to these dinners and parties, for the space of a few hours, I can pretend that my life is okay. Can you imagine?"

I don't respond; I'm not meant to. It's clear that my role now is to listen.

"At these parties I can pretend that I'm married to a man who values me," she continues, pausing long enough to drag a lipstick across her mouth. "I can pretend that our marriage is comfortable and decent. And for those few hours I can almost forget that I am, in fact, a prisoner."

"You're *not* a prisoner—"

"If Cathy's here, it's because he invited her. He knows how humiliating that is for me. He knew how I would react. And he did it anyway. He has tossed aside the rules of our little game and suddenly he's willing to humiliate me in front of everyone. Now, you tell me, *why*?" She leans closer to the mirror as if the reflection could give her an answer. "Why would he risk a scene? He must have *known* there would be a scene!" She squeezes her eyes closed, shakes her head. "He's planning something, that's why. This is part of a plot. This won't work out well for me. It never does, you know."

If Jessica were to say all this to a psychiatrist he might diagnose her as a paranoid schizophrenic. But when you're married to a Gable, paranoid is just another word for rational.

"Maybe he simply wants to see this woman," I suggest. "Maybe it's just an affair, just like any other affair. You said you could withstand that, remember?" I ask, unable to resist throwing that conversation back in her face.

"I *can* handle him sleeping with other women," she says steadily. "I've made my peace with that. But that is *not* what this is." She pauses a moment, then she slips the pill case and the lipstick back into her evening bag, shifts her weight, and makes eye contact with me through the mirror. She smiles a light, casual smile. "You know," she says, "I once read a news story about this interesting little man from Colombia."

I blink, momentarily thrown by the non sequitur.

"From what I understand, Colombia is a horrible place, filled with crime and corruption. But this man, he wasn't corrupt. He served in the army, did all the things he was supposed to do, and then one day, he was approached by members of a notorious and powerful cartel. They had heard about his army training and they wanted him to commit a murder for them. And this man, who had never had any criminal ambitions, realized that now that the cartel had told him what they wanted him to do, he simply had to do it. He had no choice, you see. By asking for his services the cartel had given him information that no one outside of their organization was allowed to have. He was trapped."

I suck in a deep breath, cross my arms over my chest. "What did he do?"

"He committed the murder, of course!" Jessica retorts. "The man they wanted him to murder wasn't exactly a pinnacle of morality anyway. He had certainly hurt his share of people. So this man killed him thinking that was it, he was done!"

"Was he?"

Jessica laughs. "Silly! Of course not! Because he would *always* know too much. The cartel was never going to let him walk away. The little man had no choice, he had to become a member of the cartel *family*."

Finally she turns to me. That same sad smile on her face. "It's a story I relate to."

"I don't think I understand."

"Bell, you understand perfectly."

The room goes silent as we hold each other's gaze.

"You hate me," she says. "And you have every right to. I've insulted you, demeaned you . . . I've truly enjoyed the power I've had over you. It's the only power I'm allowed, really. Like I said, I'm not a good person. But still," she says, stepping forward and putting her lips to my ear, "I may not be guilty in the ways you think I am."

I don't move. I can't. All my muscles have tensed and frozen. Slowly, Jessica pulls away, smiles down at me pityingly. "Depressed, desperate women aren't fools, *Bell*," she says, pronouncing that name with sarcasm. "We're depressed and desperate because we pay attention."

I meet her eyes and then, as she moves away from me, through the ladies' lounge and back out into the outside corridor, I continue to stand there, staring at nothing but my own reflection.

chapter eighteen

At least two minutes pass before I can move again, and even then I'm only able to slump into one of the overstuffed lounge chairs as I make sense of what just happened. *Does* Jessica know who I am? It's certainly not the first time she's caused me to ask myself that question. It's funny, but of all the Gables, she's the one I keep underestimating again and again. Maybe it's because she allows Travis to treat her the way he does. But then, perhaps she sees that as her penance.

Or, more likely, she truly doesn't believe that she has a choice. Once the cartel shares its secrets with you, you're theirs for life.

But if Jessica knows *my* secret, why hasn't she told Travis or Edmund? Is she simply biding her time? Waiting to cause maximum damage? I can almost respect that. And as she said, she's depressed and desperate. She could do anything.

I look down at my silk chiffon dress. I look like an ingenue. It's laughable really. There are no innocents in this dark fairy tale I seem to be living in.

I take a deep breath, pull myself to my feet, and check my reflection again.

Beautiful.

Just the memory of Lander saying that word is enough to give me a little strength. The truth is that at this moment everything, and I mean pretty much *everything*, is going my way. Jessica can hint around all she likes, but at this moment Lander and I are still five steps ahead.

With partially rebuilt confidence I leave the ladies' room and am about to head back into the banquet hall when I hear murmured voices around the corner, not far from the bride's dressing room. One of the voices sounds like Travis's.

Quietly I follow the sound, reaching the dressing room and then turning the corner only to find them tucked into an alcove, partially hidden in shadows. Travis and Cathy. I duck back behind the corner and try to quiet my breath, straining to catch every word.

"You're magnificent," I hear him say.

"Am I?" she retorts. Even without looking I can tell that she's preening.

"I can't believe I'm seeing you again. I didn't know you were coming."

"Oh, am I supposed to pretend not to know you wanted me here?"

At this I crouch down and dare a peek, praying that the truth of how she got her invitation isn't revealed.

"No," Travis says, in a voice that is much too gentle for him. His eyes are on her but she's turned partially away, staring stubbornly at the wall. "I always want you here." He reaches forward and takes her hand. "I just can't believe . . . or I simply didn't think . . . that is—" He breaks off and laughs ruefully at his own clumsiness. "It's been hell, Cathy. Not seeing you, not being able to talk to you." He looks down at her hand in his. "People have always said that I'm heartless and they're right, but when I lost you . . ." He hesitates and then shakes his head. "Jesus, Cathy, when I lost you I lost my soul."

Cathy's body language visibly changes. She seems to sway just slightly, and although I can't be sure from where I stand, it looks as if she might be holding back tears. He leans in, reaching to pull her closer, but then she suddenly jerks her hand away and takes a step back. "You didn't lose me," she says, wiping impatiently at what must be a tear. "You threw me away. It was you who decided that family loyalty was more important than your soul."

"It didn't have to be like this," Travis says. "I offered—"

"You offered me the chance to be your official mistress. Your kept woman. This is the twenty-first century, Travis. Women are no longer the property of their men. You can't *keep* me. You can't lock me up in some stupid gilded cage and expect me to twiddle my thumbs until you have time for me. I was supposed to be your *partner*. Do you remember that? Do you remember *any* of the promises you made to me?"

"Every one." Travis steps forward again. "Cathy, look at me." But when she refuses to he sighs and continues. "If there had been a way for me to keep those promises, any way at all, I would have done it. There were no good options. Not for me, not for us."

"You're unbelievable."

"I told you, one of the main reasons I did what I did was to protect you. To keep you safe."

"To keep me safe?" Cathy scoffs. "What was it that was supposed to keep me safe? The heartbreak? The loneliness? Watching that bitch get everything that was promised to me? If that's safety, then no wonder I've always craved danger."

"Cathy." Travis's voice has taken on a slightly different tone, one that actually hints at a budding concern. "Look at me." Her face remains turned toward the wall.

"Cathy," he says again, a bit more urgently. He reaches forward and takes her chin in his hand, turning her face toward his. "Cathy," this time with a note of panic, "is there something wrong with your eyes?"

For a moment Cathy seems as thrown as I am. I have no idea what he's talking about. There is no quick comeback from her. Instead she slowly reaches forward and places her hand gently against his cheek, only to then quickly pull away and turn her back on him. "My eyes are none of your concern," she snaps, then adds with a bitter laugh, "After all, I only have eyes for my husband now."

"Cathy." It's as if he can't get enough of saying her name. He's chanting it like a prayer.

She whirls around, this time reaching forward and grabbing his lapel. "Are you leaving her?" she asks, all sarcasm gone. "It's been so many years. Surely by now—"

"Nothing's changed," Travis says dully. "I can't divorce her. The risks are too great."

"The risks?" she asks weakly, and then, with building frustration, "You're afraid of the risks. And to think that I once thought you were fearless." She straightens her posture, rolls her shoulders back. "Well, then, I suppose our personal business has come to a close."

"If you could just listen—"

"No, I'm done listening. I'm done with the subject of *us*." She puts her hands on her hips and holds her chin high like a comic book queen. "Your candidate?" she says. "Sam Highkin? He's nothing more than a pathetic puppet for you and your Wall Street buddies. I'm going to support his opponent. And that's no small thing, Travis. I've been known to raise an obscene amount of money for candidates, and the supporters I can bring to the table will have the moral high ground. The supporters you can bring to Highkin represent everything people hate about the one percent. I know how to exploit that. I don't know or care what this man has promised you in exchange for getting him into office, but it's a moot point because you're not going to be able to get him there. Let's see how *you* deal with disappointment for a change."

"Fine," Travis says, sounding more tired than I've ever heard him. "If that's the battle you want."

She turns to leave and I quickly get the door open to the bride's room, jumping inside, but before I can close the door I hear Travis's voice again. "Cathy, I want you to know that I can forgive you for anything, do you understand?"

The click of Cathy's heels stops. "Really, Travis, I don't see the point—"

"Anything," he interrupts, "save one thing. I cannot forgive you for not taking care of yourself."

There's silence. In my mind I imagine her pivoting toward him, perhaps reaching for him again.

"What's wrong with your eyes, Cathy?" he asks, his tone even, insistent.

"Well, he has to be around here somewhere!" The sound of his father's voice coming from a minor distance (perhaps moving from the men's lounge back to the banquet room) ends the conversation immediately. In an instant I hear Cathy's heels start to click again. I don't get the dressing room door closed in time but it doesn't matter, she just hurries past without ever noticing me. Rushing not toward the banquet hall but toward one of the exits. As soon as she's out of sight I quickly pull myself up, count to five, and then walk to Travis.

"There you are," I say with a relieved sigh. "Jessica

is out of the ladies' room. She's taken a few Valium so I think she's okay now."

Travis doesn't even look at me; his gaze is still where Cathy was.

"Of course," I say, casting my eyes down to the floor, wringing my hands, "she doesn't know what . . . what you and I are going to do tonight." I bite my lip, bashful, timid, everything that Cathy is not. "Where shall I meet you tonight?" I ask softly. "To . . . well . . ."

"Not tonight," Travis says.

"But I thought—"

"I didn't hire you to question me, Bell," he snaps.

"Oh."

Just then Edmund appears with Lander by his side. They're both striding toward us, practically in lockstep. Even from a short distance I can see something that almost looks like camaraderie between the two of them.

It's disconcerting.

"Where the hell have you been?" demands Edmund. "Your wife is back at the event. She seems better now, but it's your job to control her and smooth things out with the donors, or have you forgotten your family obligations?"

"No, I have never been able to forget my family obligations." He glares at Lander, who responds with a winning smile.

"There was something I needed to handle," Travis continues. "That's done now. And the Valium will handle Jessica. We can get back to the festivities. After all," he adds as he starts walking briskly back toward the banquet hall, taking the lead, "we have to reassure Highkin that we're a family he can rely on. I'm going to get this man a victory even if it means stuffing every damn ballot box myself."

I glance at Lander as we follow Travis back. He's still walking right by his father's side. He doesn't say anything to me, but I recognize his smile. It's a smile of triumph.

chapter nineteen

When Lander and I get back to his place he's radiating a new kind of energy. "Genius," Lander says as he takes off his jacket and tie, dropping them over the back of his sofa. "Inviting Cathy Earnest was pure genius."

"She's Cathy Lind now," I remind him, "and I thought you'd like it. The opportunity to get her there sort of fell into my lap." I find a place on the sofa and sink into it, my mind whirling at a hundred miles an hour.

"Perfect, and the fact that she's married makes it all the better," Lander replies. "And in the face of Travis's meltdown, I was able to gain a little more of my father's trust. To listen to him for a moment there you would have thought that *I* was the favored son." Lander laughs in a way that implies the idea is both ridiculous and delightful. "I didn't realize the woman had that kind of hold on Travis! I was away at college for the bulk of that relationship. I would have thought after all this time things would have faded . . ." His expression grows a little more serious as he ponders this. "It's odd. I know my father wasn't a fan of hers, but if Travis wanted her *that* much I would have thought he would have found a way to have her."

"Oh, he definitely tried," I reply, thinking about his rejected offer to make Cathy a mistress. "Why didn't your father approve of Cathy?"

Lander sighs and waves his hand in the air dismissively. "She doesn't come from a family of influence or money and she's strong willed, so she can't easily be controlled. As far as my father is concerned, a woman who can't be controlled is barely a woman at all. It's something he always takes into account before approving someone's admittance into the family."

I look up at Lander, wondering if he's aware of what he's suggesting about his mother. But if he is, he doesn't appear to be bothered by it. He's currently pacing around the room, like a lion itching to hunt.

"That's it?" I press. "That's why your father didn't want Travis with Cathy?"

"As far as I know."

"And what about Jessica?"

Lander pauses, takes a moment to study me. "You think that Travis married her in exchange for her testimony against your mother."

"Don't you?"

"It's possible," Lander admits, some of his excitation fading into a reassuring calm. "But that's not a definite, Adoncia. My father had me believing that your mother was guilty, that testifying against her was a good thing. Jessica was even younger than I was at the time. It's not a stretch to believe that they convinced her of your mother's guilt too."

"Jessica lied about when she heard the gunshot."

"That, or someone manipulated her memory," Lander counters.

"Are you defending her?"

"No." He holds my gaze for a moment and then looks toward the window, although I suspect he's really looking into the past. "I've made mistakes, Adoncia. I trusted my father and my brother. My mother paid a price for that."

"My mother did too."

"She certainly did." He takes a deep breath and shakes his head. "There has never been a woman who has loved a Gable man who hasn't lived to regret it. Even when we don't mean to, we always end up crushing whatever heart has been handed to us."

The words hover in the air, dense and ugly like toxic smog. I hold my breath, trying not to breathe it in.

"Maybe it's not just women," Lander continues thoughtfully. "Maybe the only reason Travis, my father, and I are still standing is because there isn't enough love between the three of us to be used effectively as a weapon."

"You don't think your father loves you and Travis."

"No, no, he does . . . But it's not the kind of love

you think of existing between a father and his children. He loves Travis and me the way some men love their sports cars. When tended to and polished correctly we make good status symbols. And when properly managed and properly driven we can take him where he wants to go."

I think of Jessica and how she likes to pretend every once in a while that Travis values her. I think of Cathy and how she railed against the suggestion that she could be kept. "If you think of someone as a possession . . . that's not a different kind of love. It's not love at all," I say slowly. "At best you can value them, but again, that really isn't love."

Lander turns back to look at me, his eyebrows slightly raised. Apparently this is a revelation for him. It's funny, there are probably more songs, books, and movies written about love than about any other subject, yet despite being inundated with information on the topic, most of us still have a hard time distinguishing love from its many imitators.

He sighs, looks back to the window. "Look at us, we had a successful night. Things actually went the way we wanted them to, and yet even now we keep coming back to our sad little stories." He shakes his head. "There will be no more of that tonight. Tonight isn't about that."

"It's about victory?" I offer.

"And other things." He turns to me again, studying me for a moment. "Stand up," he says softly.

I smile, sensing where this is going. I slowly get to my feet. Lander's eyes fall to my shoes, traveling up my body with a slow and sensual appreciation. "In that dress you are the essence of femininity and beauty. You say that this isn't *you*, but you're wrong. It isn't just another costume. This is part of you, the part of you that is a princess."

I drop my gaze to the carpet, suddenly self-conscious. "I'm not a princess, Lander."

"If you insist. But *if* America had a princess, the title would go to someone like you. And . . ." He steps forward, slides his hands on either side of my waist. "There *is* no one else like you. You shouldn't have been at a dinner tonight, not looking like that. You should have been at a ball."

I peer up at him, unsure of how to respond.

"Perhaps," he says slowly, mischief lighting up his eyes, "I can make up for that error."

"What . . ." But Lander pulls away before I can get in a question, disappearing from the room. I stand there, looking out at the sparkling view, wondering what he could possibly be up to.

And then, out of nowhere, music fills the air.

I didn't even know there were speakers in this room, but now I'm surrounded by the soft sound of a piano, followed by a slightly rough woman's voice singing a haunting, bittersweet love song.

"Adoncia," he whispers in my ear, and I whirl around, startled. I hadn't heard him reenter the room. He smiles and gently takes my hand. "My beautiful warrior princess," he says softly, "may I have this dance?"

I look down at the hardwood floors, then at my

feet, still strapped into my patent leather heels. "I . . . I haven't danced in a very long time."

"Well, then," he says softly, "I think it's time."

With hesitant, self-conscious movements I position myself a little closer to him and put my hand on his shoulder as he lifts the hand he holds as if we're about to begin a waltz.

"Really, I don't know how to do this," I say, as his other hand slides to the small of my back. "The last time I danced with a boy I was still a teenager . . . and drunk. Very, very drunk."

Again Lander laughs. "Don't worry." He brings his lips right to my ear and whispers, "I'll lead."

And as the music slowly builds we begin to move. I shuffle my shoes against the floor, giggling as I keep my eyes on my feet, trying to keep myself from stepping on his. This is how I am, always limber, never graceful. But Lander puts his hand gently under my chin, lifts my gaze to his. And something in the way he's looking at me stops the giggles. We stop too for a moment . . . and then we move. His hold on me is now firm as we glide across the floor. He's urging me on, his body leading mine, coaxing it to respond to his wishes.

This isn't like the comical attempts I've made at dancing at raves or bars where everyone is too inebriated or high to notice how ridiculous they look. It's not like the school dances where the boys clumsily try to cop a feel while slow dancing in the center of the dance floor. This is something new. Lander is speaking to me with an exotic and silent new language as we increase our speed. For a moment it doesn't even feel like my feet are touching the ground as he leads me, brings me to this new place . . . the place of being a princess.

And his eyes stay with mine. We whirl across the floor with the lights of the city behind us, blurring together until they're nothing but streaks of white, like a thousand shooting stars.

And I laugh again. But it's a different kind of laughter now. He's making me feel joy.

And as I spin under his arm I think I might lose my balance, that I might fall, but then Lander has me in his arms again, holding me up as he continues to move me, allowing me to fall into a dip, only to pull me back up so quickly that some of my hair comes loose and falls over my shoulders.

I'm Cinderella. For this unlikely sliver of time I've truly been transformed from a dark angel to a perfect princess, my glass slippers filled with magic and enchantment as my prince looks at me and sees not the neglected scullery maid, but a woman, a good woman . . . the woman who will be his wife.

And when he lifts me into his arms, it feels right.

More than that, it feels perfect.

With a steady gait he brings me through the hall, to his bedroom, and there's music here too. And candles—on the nightstands, the dresser—and a fire burns in the fireplace. All of it here, waiting for us. Waiting for me.

It's all a gift for *me*! The room blurs and I realize that for the first time in my life I'm crying tears that have nothing to do with sadness or anger. I didn't know I could.

And before I know it, Lander is spinning me again as fire dances around us. I hold on to him tightly, laughing through these wonderful tears as he picks me up again and swings me around before gently bringing me back down onto my feet.

As he lowers his head and touches his mouth to mine, I wonder if he knows what he's done to me, that he's changed me. I close my eyes and try to hear his thoughts.

But I only hear music. I hear a bass that beats only a little slower than his heart.

And as the kiss grows deeper, his tongue parting my lips, as his arms hold me tighter, so that there isn't room for even a sliver of light between us . . . it *feels* like love.

My hands move from his neck to his shirt. A little frantically they work on the buttons, opening his shirt, placing my hand on his heart, trying to read it as if it was tapping out some Morse code. I close my eyes as he measures the length of my neck with his mouth, sucking gently on the skin that dips subtly below the collarbone.

He's made me a princess.

I pull his shirt from him completely, looking at him the way he has so frequently looked at me, drinking him in, honoring him with my eyes. I step forward, my hands fumbling with the button on his pants, and then I step back as he removes them. He looks almost savage as he stands before me, wearing nothing but the thin cotton of his boxer briefs. This man who was raised with caviar and opera looks like he could tear the world apart with his bare hands. Everything about his body speaks of dominance and strength.

Then he takes those powerful hands and places them gently against me. And then, there, in the light of the primal fire, the silk of my gown pressed against his bare skin, we begin to dance again.

I have never felt so feminine or delicate as I do now, whirling around being held by this graceful, gorgeous beast.

The music changes. This time it's a man's voice, a little more urgent, the melody a little more poignant. Again he kisses me. His fingers lace into my hair as my grip on his shoulders tightens. His heartbeat is so strong now, strong enough for both of us. He turns my back to his chest, finds the hidden zipper of my dress, and slowly lowers the fabric to the ground, then carefully helps me out of each of my shoes. It feels as if we're still caught up in the music. And when he picks me up in his arms and lays me on the bed while kneeling by my side, I know what it means to be royalty. The fire flickers and crackles as he removes my bra and then leans down to kiss my calves and the soft skin of my inner thigh.

The music is building.

His fingers move up and pull my panties down, exposing me to his gaze and then to his tongue as he makes delicate circles around my clit, causing me to shudder. My hands are in his hair as he tastes me, as his finger finds my core, sliding inside. The aching in the singer's voice matches the ache of my body. His tongue moves back and forth quickly now as I arch my back, giving in to this passion. His finger continues to move, one, then two, and the pleasure shoots from my core down to my toes, up, up through my lungs so that every breath is marked by desire.

He pulls away from me and removes what little is left of his clothes. But there is no recovery time. The music keeps building as I turn my head toward the window and see the artificial stars of the city slide as Lander drags me along the mattress, lifting my hips so they meet his. Desperate to hold him, to keep him, I lift my legs and wrap them around his back even as I prop myself up so I can see him, supporting my weight with my arms, which are stretched behind me.

He's watching me, holding me firmly in place with his eyes, as he grabs hold of my thighs and thrusts inside me.

We're still dancing.

But this dance is about anticipation. He's not going too deep, just letting me feel the contours of him, the strength and warmth of his erection, touching the nerve endings near the surface as I shudder. I want him, I ache to be filled by him. I want every part of him.

I want his heart.

With three little words you could have me completely. You could connect me to the world.

He continues to tease, giving me a taste, driving me wild and holding off complete satisfaction.

"Lander," I whisper as the music changes again.

I don't know if he heard me; perhaps he just saw my lips move, perhaps he thought I was echoing the words of the song. The words themselves slowly break through the haze of ecstasy that I'm enveloped in as a man sings:

> *The rage of love turns inward*
> *To prayers of devotion*

Yes, I think, *rage and love. I understand now, I understand how close they are. I understand that my rage can be used for something other than anger.*

Lander releases me, and as I reach for him, almost weak with yearning, he answers by covering my body with his and the song changes to another. The lyrics now give new wisdom . . .

> *And it feels like I've come home*

He enters me again, filling me completely now, and the consummation is so intense I let out a small cry, gripping the sheets beneath me. And as he pushes farther and farther inside me the cry builds, adding a new element to the music, making it ours. I can't hold back. I see how close he is, see it in the way he's looking at me.

"Lander," I whisper again, and this time I know he hears me because he leans in by my ear and whispers, "My queen."

From his lips the words have a musicality all their

own. It hints at all the things I want. Passion, understanding, and yes . . . love.

All control is gone. He rocks us with his rhythm, pushing us forward. My head and shoulders, no longer supported by the mattress, dangle over the edge.

And we're dancing.

"Sweet warrior," he whispers, and the orgasm rolls through me as it rolls through him. The blood rushes to my head, sending tingles throughout my upper body, making this climax an otherworldly experience.

He pulls me up and we lie there in the tangled sheets, our breathing uneven and our pulses pounding. He turns onto his side, propping himself up on one arm so he can look down at me. And for several seconds that's all he does. I know he's thinking, contemplating, and . . . and there's something else. Something in his eyes that I dare not name but I hope I understand.

I just want it to be real.

chapter twenty

The next morning starts early. I go straight to Travis and Jessica's, long before either of them are expecting me and over an hour before Travis will have to leave for HGVB. But that's the point. I don't want anyone to have time to prepare for me. I don't want them to be composed. And most importantly, I want to see Travis and Jessica together. I want to get a sense of the dynamic between the two of them now, after Cathy.

But above all, I want to see if I'm in trouble. If Jessica talks to Travis about what she knows—or at least what she suspects—yesterday's progress will be buried under the avalanche of that reveal.

My cab is almost at the building when I see Travis walk out. He immediately gets into his waiting limo.

My hopes of seeing Travis and Jessica together have gone out the window. *Damn it!* Why is he leaving for work so early anyway?

But when he pulls away, his limo turns left instead of right. It's driving *away* from his office.

He could be going on a minor errand. Really, it could be nothing.

But what if it's not?

I lean forward to speak to the cabbie through the glass. "I know how this is going to sound, but I need you to follow that limo."

He looks back at me with an are-you-*serious*? look, but then when he sees that I am he breaks into a big toothy grin and goes right into espionage mode, mimicking the limo's every turn while following at a discreet distance.

I'm probably going to end up following Travis to the dentist or something. He's leaving early enough that he's not really risking being late for work as long as whatever he needs to do lasts for less than an hour. But I have this *feeling*.

Travis's limo takes him into the heart of the Village. Not his normal hangout place. The limo drops him off at Bleecker and Sixth. I get out half a block behind him and stay on the opposite side of the street as I follow him. He walks for some time, one city block, then two, then three . . . What on earth is he doing? Travis doesn't take walks. And what's the point of a limo if you have it drop you off half a mile from your destination? You can take the bus for that.

But yes, finally, he does slow his step, in front of a small apartment building. It looks nice, but it's not a doorman building, which should make it beneath anything Travis would be willing to step foot into. But to my surprise he walks right in. In fact—and I can't be sure about this because I'm watching from a distance—but I think he has a key to this place.

Does Travis already have a kept mistress? I know he has no interest in being faithful to Jessica and I know there have been women. I just can't believe that there were any women he cared enough about to spend that kind of money on . . . with Cathy being the exception, and as she's made it abundantly clear, she's not interested in that arrangement.

I wait outside, across the street, kitty-corner to the apartment building. He's in there for a good twenty minutes. When he finally comes out his shoulders are slumped and his phone is pressed to his ear. I watch as he starts to walk back in the direction he came from. I consider following him but then I see his limo pull up beside him as he puts away his phone. Perhaps that's who he was calling.

It's only after the limo's gone that I approach the building. I look at the names on the resident list, and they're all labeled except for one. Just one empty space next to a buzzer. Gingerly I press the button, unsure of what to expect. But no one responds to my summons. It's probably just an empty apartment. Again I study the names. Which one was Travis visiting? There's not much to go on, a first initial and a last name at most. I'm about to randomly start pressing buttons when a new idea occurs to me. It's silly, probably. I certainly can't expect to be *this* lucky. Still . . .

Opening my purse, I fish out the keys I found at Travis's. They're gold, nondescript, could be the keys to anything.

I slip one into the lock and . . . nope. Doesn't fit. Figures. I take the second key and try my luck with that.

And it works.

The key works.

Holding my breath, I push the door open and step into the lobby. It's actually rather nice. Nowhere near as nice as the ones in either Travis's or Lander's building, but that's a high bar. I go to the wall of mailboxes. All identical, revealing nothing but the numbers that identify them.

Still, it's the apartment without a name that interests me most. I walk up to the fifth floor, which is the top level of this building. There are only four apartments on this floor. Three of them have welcome mats. I go to the one that doesn't and knock. No answer. I try again, and when nothing happens I take out the other key. I open the door and then step inside.

What I see is positively shocking.

It's an adorable little apartment. Travis Gable has the key to something that is *adorable*. How the hell is that possible? There's lots of light, and the furnishings have a nod to deconstructionism with the purposely unevenly painted coffee table. There are throw pillows on the green sofa and a collection of white candles on the fireplace mantel. Framed photos hang on the wall and are strategically placed on various surfaces around the room.

Every photo is of Cathy and Travis.

And no one lives here. I know that with every fiber of my being. Not a thing is out of place, but dust covers everything. There are cobwebs by the window. There are no ashes in the fireplace. I walk into the kitchen, then the bathroom, then the bedroom, and find more of the same. The bookcase is filled with books on the Tudors and a few modern political books that Travis would be interested in. The bed is made, and the pillows are so well plumped I have to assume that no one has *ever* rested their head on them. I flip the light switch on and off and realize that the electricity isn't connected. In the kitchen I open the refrigerator and find it empty except for one very expensive, warm bottle of champagne.

This was supposed to be the place where he would keep Cathy.

Once, Micah had told me that if Nick Foley had been a decent man he would have set my mother up in a nice place after making her his mistress. As far as Micah was concerned, that was a sign of respect. Had Micah advised Travis on this? Or is that just the way men like Travis and Micah think?

And did Travis really think that Cathy would be satisfied with this? I look around the apartment again. It probably cost Travis more than a million dollars just to buy the place. Furnishing it could have cost him a hundred thousand more. Still, where Cathy lives now is worth eight times as much. Which raises the question, did she really turn Travis down out of morality or did she just get a better offer?

Probably a little of both, I decide as I close the refrigerator. Still, he had to have gotten this place at least ten years ago. And he hasn't sold it.

He's obsessed with her.

Or maybe, maybe it really is love.

The thought hits me like a punch to the gut. I lower myself onto a kitchen chair and stare out the cobwebbed windows. I'm not sure what's more terrifying, that Travis might really know what love is or that I don't. And what about Lander? Would he miss me if I disappeared from his life? Would he cherish a memory, holding on to it despite all expense the way Travis has held on to this place?

There are few things that I find heartening in this world. Being in Lander's arms, a decent glass of wine, a good book—these are the things that comfort me. But when the book is finished, the glass drained, and the arms removed, the comfort is gone. So what's left? A clear worldview, that's what. I believe in a world that is filled with good guys and bad guys and people like me who may be closer to the latter group but motivated by the former. Travis, Jessica, Edmund, they're the bad guys. My mother had been a good guy; at least that's how I saw her. I know that other people could claim otherwise, and they would have plenty of facts to back them up. My mother had an affair with at least one married man that I know of. If I was Mrs. Nick Foley I might see Julieta Jiménez as a villain.

But I'm not Mrs. Foley. To me Julieta Jiménez was the woman who raised me in poverty but made sure that when healthy food and warm clothing were scarce, hope was available in abundance. My mother and I gobbled up hope like it was ice cream and drank it like it was ice-cold water in the desert. And we only supplemented our highly specialized diet with love, love that we shared for one another.

And when the bad guys took her away from me they also took away the *idea* of her. I loved my mother not just because she loved me, not just because she was my mom. I loved her because she was *good*. The landlord who was always threatening us with eviction when our rent was late, he wasn't good. The drug dealers and gang members in our building weren't good. My teachers at the local public school were always so overwhelmed or dejected that I couldn't really tell if they were good or bad. But my mom was *good*. And if she could be good then there had to be good in the world.

When I discovered her affair my faith in her goodness was shaken, but not lost. But when she was convicted of murder? I lost her, I lost the idea of her . . .

. . . I lost hope.

Only truly evil people would ever steal someone else's hope. So when I say that Travis, Edmund, Jessica, and Sean White are bad guys, that's not just my assumption, it's part of my religious belief. Those people are to me what the devil and demons are to pious Christians. Travis is my devil, and no one wants to discover that the devil has a soft side. The devil is not supposed to be a nuanced character.

I sigh and pull myself to my feet. Jessica will be expecting me in an hour. I need to search this place and see if there's anything useful here. Maybe there's a way to turn my knowledge of the apartment's very existence to my advantage, although I'm not sure how. Surely Cathy already knows about it, although she may not know he still has it. I start snooping around, but other than a few dead spiders and several live ones, there just isn't much here. Again I start pulling out the books to see if there's anything hiding inside the pages. As I go through them, one thing that jumps out is that not all of these books are as dusty as the others. Some of them are newer. Travis has been collecting books on Cathy's favorite subject over the years. Here's Alison Weir's latest on Queen Elizabeth, and he's stocked both of Hilary Mantel's bestselling novels featuring Thomas Cromwell. Was Travis hoping that Cathy would come back here? Was he reading them himself so he would be well versed if he should ever have the opportunity to speak to her again?

But then what does it matter? I pull each book out, flip through the pages, and then carefully replace it. Eventually I get to the bottom shelf, which is where Travis has lined up several coffee table books. Some of them are on the Tudors, others are on art. I assume this too is a nod to Cathy's interests. I pull out one by Susan Doran and start flipping through the pages when my attention is drawn to the wall behind that book. There's something there. Something in the wall. Something metal.

I start pulling out several more books and I see it. There's the wall safe.

I can feel my heart pounding against my chest as I

press my fingers against it. This is what Lander wanted me to look for. His instincts told him that there would be something valuable in here. Something that could do an enormous amount of damage.

And it's a combination safe. I know how to break into combination safes.

Immediately I try the try-out combination. That's the combination that actually comes with the safe. The try-out combo is an industry standard, the same numbers for everyone. Obviously you're supposed to change the combination after you get the safe, yet most people don't.

But Travis did.

The other thing that most people who have a safe do is write down the combination and place it somewhere, usually somewhere near the safe. But considering who I'm dealing with, that too seems unlikely. Which means that opening this safe is going to be a very time-consuming job.

But then, I've been waiting for more than ten years to get my revenge. Time is relative.

Lying on the floor, getting my ear as close to the lock as possible, I start turning the dial *very* slowly. I'm listening for the clicks. There will be two. They won't tell me the combination, but they will tell me where the contact points in the lock are. Again, it's a slow, technical process.

It takes about ten minutes, but I finally hear the clicks.

Okay, step one done.

My cell phone rings. I consider not getting it, but if

I'm going to do this, at the very least I need to turn the sound off. I climb to my feet and fish the phone out of my bag. It's Lander's name on the screen.

"Hey," I say as I pick up. "You will not believe—"

"Adoncia," he says, cutting me off, "my man cracked the encryption."

My heart, which was beating so rapidly a few minutes ago, slams to a stop. "And?" I whisper.

"We got them."

Three more beautiful words have never been spoken.

chapter twenty-one

I race back to Lander's place. Jessica can wait. When I get there the front door is unlocked and I find him in his home office, sitting in front of his computer, staring unblinkingly at the screen, frantically making notes as he scrolls through file after file.

"Tell me," I insist.

"It's all here," Lander says, his voice edged with excitement. "Reports, emails. Here's an email sent to my father by Sean White, referring to how HGVB has been scrubbing wire transfers from Iran of any mention of the country of origin so federal regulators couldn't catch them or investigate them. Here, right here"—Lander urgently taps his finger against the screen—"in an email Sean White informs my father that, '*The knowledge that Iranian money is passing through our American branches has been contained to only a handful of top preapproved executives.*'"

"He . . . oh my God, Lander." I stare down at the monitor but I'm just looking at a bunch of little black letters strung together; it's as if I've forgotten how to read. "He wrote that," I finally manage, "to your *father*?"

"And it gets better. Here's a memo written *by* my father stating, '*Our clients in Iran are willing to increase their investments if we can find creative ways to overcome existing challenges and impediments.*' Those challenges are our *laws*, Adoncia. The *impediments* are America's foreign policy!"

"Who was the memo sent to?" I ask urgently.

"You mean was Travis one of the people this was emailed to?"

I stare at him, nodding, unable to speak, hoping against hope.

"It's there," Lander says, reaching out and giving my hand a quick squeeze without taking his eyes from the screen. "Travis's name is on the email list."

"Oh my God," I whisper. It occurs to me that this time I'm not just using those words as an exclamation, I'm actually praying. For *years* I've been praying.

And now, for the first time, I'm beginning to believe that someone has been listening. And this room, this little office tucked in the corner of a penthouse, this now feels more like a church. I should lower myself, crash my knees against the hard surface of this pretty wood floor, and bask in the glory of this bloody victory that is now, for the first time, truly within my reach.

"There's more," Lander says, his fingers back on

his keyboard as he pulls up another file. "In Mexico we have an account for Primo Calles. Do you know who that is?"

"I . . . I'm not sure . . ."

"He's a major drug lord. People *know* this guy. And here, do you see this?" Again he taps his finger against the screen impatiently. "See the name of this bank? This Saudi bank?"

"Um . . ." I shake my head. He's moving too fast and I certainly am not well versed on Saudi banks. For a moment I let my eyes wander to the rest of the desk as I wonder if I should find a pen and paper to write this all down with.

"We're doing business with them, we've opened accounts for them. This bank has been tied to terrorism, a conduit for extremist financing. No one in the Western world is supposed to be working with these guys, but we are!"

My hand slowly rises to my mouth as I stare fixedly at the screen.

"And that subsidiary in the Cayman Islands, I told you I found a few highly irregular accounts that had been opened there."

Highly irregular seems like a pretty big euphemism.

"One of the reasons I didn't find more is that at least fifteen percent of customers there don't even *have* a file. And the files that are opened there, Adoncia, almost half of them don't have complete information. The whole Cayman Islands branch is a shell company that accommodates wealthy criminals. They take their dirty money to the bank and get US dollars back and no one in the US government *or* the Mexican government is aware of it at all!"

"Lander, this is . . . I don't . . . I mean, it's too big, isn't it?" I whisper. "They can't have gotten away with all this. There has to be something wrong. Or the accounts must be small . . . Are they small?"

"Adoncia, this branch holds over two billion in assets."

I step back, leaning against the wall for support. "This kind of thing . . . I mean the kind of transactions you're talking about should have triggered automatic alerts."

"Yes," Lander says. He looks up at me for the first time. There's a vicious glint in his eyes and his jaw is tense, his smile small, contained, anticipatory. He's the perfect predator and he's zeroing in on his prey. "This is the fun part."

He taps a few more keys and pulls up another file. "Alerts were generated. And they've been handled by our compliance department, in Delaware."

"The one White just helped staff."

"Mmm, yes. It was barely staffed at all before."

Lander is practically bouncing out of his chair with excitement. I've never seen him like this . . . this giddy. The tools of destruction make him giddy.

He's like me.

"As far as I can tell, the four or five people who were working there weren't even trained on what money laundering *is* let alone how to handle these alerts," he continues. "And here we have an email from my father asking Sean White to increase the staffing at the compliance center in order to appease the FDIC. Sean White was charged with hiring the people who would be handling these alerts, and here, here's an email from White to the new supervisor of the Delaware department. Sean is explaining that this supervisor should consider awarding his employees for clearing seventy-two alerts a week."

"Clearing?" I shake my head, again. "I don't understand."

"Clearing, giving them a stamp of approval so they don't have to be reported to the FDIC or any other government agency. According to this email, if the parties whose transactions are being questioned have so much as a website, that's good enough for HGVB. We don't report it. They've rigged the whole system."

"But . . . why? HGVB is a huge institution. They don't need to do this, do they?" I ask. "Why would they risk this?"

"Adoncia, what we're doing is providing these criminals and terrorists financiers' *specialty services*. Services they literally can't get anywhere else. We can charge anything we like for specialty services. The margin on money laundering is roughly twenty per- cent . . . and we're talking about billions of dollars in money laundering."

Billions of dollars. The figures don't make sense to me. I had known there were secrets, I had even known that HGVB had to be doing things that were seriously against the law. After all, a man was killed to protect the secrets of HGVB, I understand that. Where I'm from, people will sometimes kill for a few hundred dollars, sometimes a few thousand. But oddly enough it doesn't seem possible that someone could kill for a billion. It doesn't seem possible that people could be rewarded with a billion dollars for breaking the law.

I look down at Lander, and even he seems amazed by the enormity of this. He turns in his seat and catches my eye. "There's still more."

I shake my head. How much more could there be?

"A few years ago, some of our special services customers, otherwise known as criminals, started pulling out of HGVB."

"Why?" I ask, still somewhat dazed.

"From what I can gather they were concerned with the potential crackdown of the American government. It was right after the banking crisis and there was a lot of talk about greater oversight and more regulations. And of course the criminals have options now, Bitcoin and the like."

I wave my hands in the air; this is getting too complicated.

"I think Sean has been feeling out some of our *special* clients. Once he's sure they're not informants or anything like that, he's been setting them up with Travis for meetings so he can calm their nerves. Keep the money flowing in."

"That's why he met with Javier?" I ask, my back still firmly against the wall. I need its firm pressure just to remind me that this isn't a dream. "And that . . . that Kliff guy? The arms dealer?"

"Yes . . . but now I'm speculating a bit. Nothing here spells that out. There's just a memo written by my father sent to a handful of people, including Travis and Sean, suggesting that we reassure nervous Cayman Islands account holders. And then I have an email from Sean saying he was going to investigate and identify the key point men who would be willing to discuss the security of their accounts with HGVB executives."

"What did Travis say to that?"

"That's the thing, I don't have a single email or memo *from* Travis here. I have things written to him, but that's it."

"Lander," I say softly, "there's something wrong here."

He nods, and when he looks up at me again I can tell he knows what I'm thinking. "You want to know why Travis would keep all this information," he says.

"Not just keep it, but store it in one place."

"Your brother is not a stupid man," I say emphatically. "And if all this is true, how could he possibly think that keeping *any* evidence of this around would be a good idea?" I shake my head. "Could we be being set up? Is this whole thing a trap?"

"No," Lander says definitively. "These files show me *exactly* where to look, and everything I've checked on so far has borne out. But you're right, Travis keeping all this is odd."

"I don't understand it," I say quietly.

"It's possible that he simply wanted to keep track of what could actually be found. After all, if Travis has a copy of this stuff, someone else must have a copy too."

"I guess that's possible," I say doubtfully. "But there's got to be more to it than that."

"There is more to it than that," Lander says, pushing his chair back from the desk. "There's the security that comes from blackmail."

"What?"

"Like I said, nothing here is written by Travis. If he were to release any one of these documents the person who did write it could end up in prison. He could easily be using this to keep people in line. Or, if he's caught, he could turn informant and cut a deal. If we didn't find this in Travis's home there'd be nothing here to fully implicate him as a willing participant."

"But . . . we did find it in his home." And now some of my shock fades away as a new sense of excitement kicks in. "He was hiding it and we found it and now we can prove that he knew about everything, *everything*, and at the very least he did nothing to stop it."

I start pacing the room, just like Lander did after the fund-raiser dinner, fueled by a sudden buzz of delight. "I bet he thought he was safe! I bet the reason he was meeting these guys in person is because he didn't want to leave *any* paper record! No emails, probably as few calls on his cell as possible. He thought he had covered his bases, but he *didn't*!" I whirl around to face Lander. I'm literally jumping up and down right now, clapping my hands. "We got him! We found the flash drive! And when we hand it over to the Feds . . ."

"Adoncia," Lander says, slowly rising to his feet. "You can't be involved in that."

I stop jumping, my hands hovering in the air mid-clap. "I . . . I don't think I understand."

"You can't be involved in handing over the USB. You can't be involved in reporting any of this to the authorities. You can't take any part in this at all."

"The hell I can't! I've dedicated years of my life to this! All those years building to this one day! You wouldn't even have these files if it wasn't for me! I'm the one who got you into Travis's place when he wasn't there. I'm the one who found the hiding spot. This is *my* baby."

"Your involvement isn't an option."

We stand there, facing off, his expression completely calm, confident, while I'm simply baffled.

"Not only is it an option," I say slowly, my voice icy cold, "it's the only option I'm giving you."

Lander studies me a moment and then puts his thumb through the belt loop of his jeans and stares at the edge of the area rug. "The only way we get Travis is if we let the Feds know that this was found in Travis's home. What do you think will happen if you tell the Feds that you found it? What happens when they find out that you've been working for Travis under a false name . . . and probably a false social security number, yes?"

"Oh, give me a break." I hold my hand up to stop him. "So I've been using some dead chick's social. That's bad, I'll admit it. But I haven't used it to ring up debt or open credit cards. I only used it to fool Travis. On the flip side Travis has been funding *fucking Al Qaeda*! That's worse, don't you think?"

"We don't know if it was officially Al Qaeda—"

"Billions of dollars, Lander! Billions of dollars in money laundering! Drug cartels, Russian gangsters, terrorists. The FBI isn't going to care that I used a false social in order to get them this information!"

"And where did you get that social?" Lander asks, still staring at the carpet. "Did Micah give it to you?"

I don't say anything. Micah hadn't known I was going to seek employment with Travis. He just knew that I wanted a new start, a new social security card, a new life. He didn't ask questions; he didn't care. In Micah's world the kind of favor I was asking was small.

"So," Lander continues, finally meeting my eyes. "A woman gets a social security number from a member of the Russian mafia, gets a job with Travis under false circumstances using a pseudonym, and she now claims that she just happened to find this USB flash drive in Travis's house. Oh, and did I mention that this mystery woman is the daughter of the woman who killed an executive at HGVB a little over ten years ago?"

"She didn't kill Nick Foley."

"I know that," Lander says, raising his voice for the first time. "But she was convicted, Adoncia. You have no *evidence* to clear her. You are not a credible witness and if you say that you found this in Travis's place, Travis will be able to make a convincing case

that you found a way to plant it there. God knows
you have motive and like you said, you've been working on finding ways to destroy him for *years*. You
try to be involved in this phase of the game and you
jeopardize *everything*. Sure, we'll still be able to give
HGVB a black eye, we might even get my father, and
we definitely get Sean, but if you insert yourself into
this process, Travis walks away completely unscathed.
Is that what you want?"

I stand there, staring at him, trying to find a flaw
in his logic.

"Is it?" Lander asks again.

"No," I whisper, shrinking into myself.

I feel like Jessica.

"Good, then you will go to Travis this afternoon
and you will quit. You will tell him that we broke up
and that you want to move on. And then you will
make yourself a ghost until this whole damn thing is
locked down."

"But . . . but why do I have to tell him we broke
up?" I hear the way that comes out. I sound weak,
like a child.

"We have to make him think that you're just gone,
out of the picture. If *I* go to the Feds right now with
this information and *I* tell them I found it at Travis's
place, he will try to say that I'm setting him up for the
benefit of my criminally minded girlfriend."

I nod, slowly, taking it in. "So . . . we have to lie to
Travis," I say. There's a tightness in my chest, but I try
to ignore it, try to see things in a way I can be okay
with. "Well, that's not new." I force a laugh. "And

quitting my job, that won't be suspicious either. Any sane person with half a brain would quit that job. If he didn't pay five times the going rate he wouldn't be able to get anyone to work for him at all."

Lander's posture relaxes and his mouth curves back into a small smile. "You'll still get to see their downfall. I promise you that. And it will be big and it will be public. You will still know that you caused it. Your mother will still be avenged."

"I . . . I want to prove that they killed her," I say, still struggling to keep my composure. "I want them to go to prison for *all* of it."

"One thing at a time," Lander assures me. "It might be easier to get the police to reopen that case once we can prove what kind of illegal activity the other members of my family have been up to."

He pauses a moment, his expression softening as he watches me. "I didn't mean to sound harsh," he adds. "But we've both worked too hard for this to snatch defeat from the jaws of victory."

"I know," I say quietly.

"I'm sorry."

"You don't have to apologize." I look around the room, at the desk, at the pictures on the wall, trying to collect myself. "I understand what you're saying and I agree. I won't interfere."

"No, that's not . . ." His voice fades off and he shakes his head as if trying to sort out his thoughts. "I'm sorry," he says again. "I'm sorry that your dreams were ripped away from you when you were young."

"My . . . my dreams?"

"And I'm sorry that my family made the world ugly for you at an age when it still should have been beautiful," he continues. "I'm sorry, so incredibly sorry that I had any part in that."

"Lander, you didn't know."

"But I should have. I believed my family when they told me your mother was guilty. I didn't ask questions, I just took their word for it. And as a result I helped them hurt you. I didn't mean to but I did. And now you *have* to let me apologize, for all of us. We crashed into your fairy tale when it was still alive and real for you. We had *no right*."

I wave my hand in the air as if waving away the apology. "It was my mother who was hurt, Lander."

"And it was you," he counters. "Maybe our tragedies make us stronger, but they're still tragedies. We can still grieve."

The comment startles me. *We can grieve.*

Have I ever grieved for my mother? I railed against her when I thought she was guilty and I railed against her accusers when I realized she wasn't. I've been angry for her, I've sought vengeance for her.

But when did I grieve?

"No," I say, stepping forward and putting my hand on his chest. "We just won. We *won*, Lander! Now is definitely not the time for grieving. We've come so far! To think that when I first met you, I thought I knew you." I let my hands slide over to his arms as he moves to hold me. I run them over the slopes of his muscles, feeling them tense and release under my touch. "When I first met you, I thought you were someone else. I guess I thought you were your brother."

"I'm definitely not that."

"No," I say with a little laugh. "You're not. You've been my partner, the perfect partner. You've helped me with so much . . . maybe even more than you know. And now, with your help, I'm going to finally have justice for my mother." I look up into his eyes, suddenly overcome with the enormity of what that means. "I'll let you handle this last part, but promise me we'll get them. Promise me, Lander. Promise me that my promise to myself will be kept." Tears are stinging my eyes now. God, I've become such a crybaby. And now I don't even know if I'm crying for joy, anxiety, or relief. Is it possible to feel all of that at once? Because that's almost what it's like . . . Like I'm experiencing every human emotion at the exact same time. Frustration and triumph, pain and comfort. Hate and love.

And as he holds me close to him I can hear him whispering into my hair. "I promise you. I promise you, my love."

My love. He said my love!

He pushes my hair from my face and now it's me who puts my hands on his face, staring at him with awe and need. *My love.* I heard him say the word. If he could only say more! If he could just tell me that this term of endearment means as much to him as it means to me! I lean forward and kiss him hard, holding on to him like he's a lifeline.

And in a way he is. He's taking away my revenge, taking ownership of it while I sit on the sidelines.

So he *must* give me this. He must give me love. He must give me what I need to fill this new void.

I feel his hands on the small of my back and I realize that I need him in every way. And I need him Right. Now.

I take his hand and lead him out of the office and into his bedroom.

"You want to consummate our victory?" he says with a teasing smile. But there's something else, something in his eyes. He looks wistful, maybe even a little sad.

But I must be wrong. There's nothing to be sad about now. I flip my hair, mimic his smile. "You think you know me so well."

"I do," he says, and now he's completely serious. "Perhaps better than I should."

I look at him, a bit puzzled, but again I dismiss it. Slowly I take off my shirt, then my bra, and peel off my pants so that I'm wearing nothing but my black panties. I stand before my lover, naked and bold, letting him drink me in, feeling like a warrior once more.

Keeping my eyes locked on him I step forward, reach out, and unbutton his shirt, carefully, meticulously, and once exposed I place my hand against his bare chest, feel the smoothness of his skin over the hardness of his muscles.

Slowly, my fingers begin to curl until my hand is not so much a hand as it is a claw. With precision I rake my nails over the tender skin, marking him, letting the world know that he is mine.

This is a different kind of need.

I back him up against the bed, and when I push he relents and falls back, but only after grabbing my arm, pulling me down with him so that I tumble over him. My kisses quickly find the marks of pain as I straddle his waist, then slide lower, unfastening his pants before pulling them lower and finally tossing them onto the floor with the rest of his discarded clothes.

His erection is straining against his Calvin Kleins.

I look him in the eye, letting my fingers outline the contours of what is waiting for me under that thin layer of cotton. "That's for me." It's not a question. I'm not playing that game anymore.

I pull off the boxer briefs and then kiss his thigh as I move back up his leg. I feel his hand reaching into my hair as I kiss the hard bone of his pelvis.

"Adoncia," he says, but I lift up my hand and place a silencing finger against his lips. I can see his erection becoming stronger, waiting for me. He is mine.

He has to be.

I let my tongue trace every ridge, every vein, and his groan only spurs me on as I finally trace a path around the tip with my tongue.

"Do you want me, Lander?"

"Yes," he breathes.

I wrap my lips around him, taste the salt of his skin as he shudders beneath me.

And I continue, slowly, steadily, until the shudder is practically a shake.

When I pull away he grabs me and whips me around so that I fall hard on my back. He tears off my panties, literally ripping them and throwing them to the floor. He kneels before me on the bed, savage, dangerous, perfect.

My eyes lock with his, almost defiantly. "You're *mine*," I say.

Lander responds by grabbing my legs and holding them firmly over one of his shoulders. He kneels before me on the bed, his chest pressed against my calves as he thrusts forward, entering me. By holding my legs together he makes me tighter; his angle hits new nerve endings that I didn't know I had. I'm writhing against the sheets as he watches me.

He doesn't tell me I'm his. He doesn't ask.

He just proves it.

I call out his name, my hands reaching for him, only to fall back onto the mattress, empty, knowing that he's in control. Slowly he begins to rise, pulling me with him. I press my hands into the mattress to support myself as my back lifts up into the air. He's now essentially standing on his knees; my legs are still over his shoulder, my lower body leaning into him as now only my shoulders and head are on the bed. He's holding my hips and I find myself grasping his thighs for support, the muscles of which are taught and trembling.

And he's still inside me.

The blood rushes from my thighs to where he moves inside me, intensifying everything, making me throb and whimper as he continues to move. This shouldn't even be possible, but it is . . . Lander has once again shown me how many rules we can break when we're together. How successful we can be.

When he pulls away and allows my body to fall gently back onto the bed, I moan in protest, but he's not done with me. In an instant he's inside me again, riding me hard, as I claw at his back. I want his blood, I want his soul . . .

I want his love.

"Lander," I cry as the orgasm comes, and with the utterance of his name he comes inside me, filling me, giving with his body what he won't give me with his words:

Confirmation, fulfillment, satisfaction.

This man, my prince, he can bring me to new heights of ecstasy. His body loves my body.

I wish I was as confident about his heart.

chapter twenty-two

Lander and I are standing on opposite sides of the bed, getting dressed. We've barely spoken since we made love. That was almost an hour ago. It's not like us. It's not like *him*.

"You've gone quiet," I say.

"Have I?" he asks, buttoning up his shirt. "I was just thinking."

But there's something heavy in his voice. I know it's not my imagination. "What are you thinking about?"

He pauses, his shirt still only half-buttoned. "I didn't tell you this, but last week I put in calls to the DA and to the Innocence Project."

"The Innocence Project?" I repeat.

"I . . . I want to prove that my family was behind Nick Foley's murder. I want to exonerate your mother. I want to do that for you."

My mouth forms the word *oh*, but no sound comes

out. No one has ever been willing to help me with that. Not the police, not my mother's public defender, no one. And here is this man, volunteering to do this, just for me. I start to walk around the bed, to throw my arms around him, to kiss him, to let him know how much this means to me, but he holds up a hand to stop me, freezing me in my place.

"I haven't gotten very far at all. I'm not even sure if I should be mentioning it at this point. I don't want to give you false hope. The Innocence Project is intent on getting wrongly convicted people out of prison, but your mother isn't in prison."

"No," I say. I've thought of this before. I know her suicide makes her look even more guilty and makes clearing her all the harder. "I like that you're trying," I finally say. "It means the world to me."

Lander holds my gaze for a moment before returning his attention to his shirt. "I owe you at least that." He fastens the button at his wrist. "So you'll go to HGVB now?" he asks, although it doesn't exactly sound like a question. "You'll hand in your resignation to Travis?"

"Yes." I grab my shirt off the floor and pull it over my head. "And I'll tell him we broke up. I guess we're going to have to be more sneaky from now on. Do you think it's still safe for me to come here? Or will Travis be watching? Maybe it would be better if you started coming to my place instead? I'll spruce it up for you. Maybe even put up a poster," I say with a light laugh.

"Adoncia, it can't be like that."

I look at him, not understanding. "Be like what? You want me to leave the place a mess?"

"We can't risk being seen together. Anywhere."

"But . . . I don't understand. Do you think we should meet in a hotel or something? Or maybe we . . ."

"*Anywhere*," Lander repeats, putting new emphasis on the word. He turns to me, looking so incredibly sad. "We can't see each other for a while."

I stare at him, one hand on the belt I've just now wrapped around my waist, my tongue pressed against the back of my teeth as I try to absorb this. "How long is a while?"

"Adoncia—"

"How long is a while, Lander?" I demand.

"These things can take time. The FDIC will have to do their own investigation, there will be hearings—"

He continues to talk but I can't hear him; his words have become part of a pervasive buzzing that is consuming the room. I know what he's telling me . . . but I can't know. He can't be saying these things.

"You don't get to take everything from me." It's my voice, but I barely recognize it. It's deeper and much more powerful than I'm feeling right now. "You don't get to tell me that I can't be there when Travis falls and I can't be here to hold your hand. Revenge has been my life. My *life*," I say, hissing that last word for emphasis. "And then you . . . you added on to that. You gave me something new. You gave me . . ."

. . . love. You placed love in my heart.

"You . . . you gave me more," I stammer. "And

now you want me to hand over my revenge to you and I can't see you either? No! Just *no*! You are not allowed to take everything from me!"

"Adoncia," he says, his expression so somber and so very, very sad. "I don't have the power to take everything from you. No one has ever been able to do that, and God knows they've tried."

"I don't understand you—"

"You are more than your revenge—"

"Why are you doing this? Do you really think—"

"*I can't be your everything!*"

The words slap me across the face. I can physically feel the sting. When I look at him the wild look in his eyes actually makes me take a step back.

His hands clench up into fists as he presses them against his temples. "I am not *worthy* of that! No one should ever be worthy of that!"

"Lander—"

"My father was my mother's *everything*!" he snaps. "She made her life all about her husband and his children. We weren't just her life, we were her *identity*. Look where it got her!"

"I'm not your mother, Lander."

"Of course you're not but . . ." His voice trails off and he takes a deep breath. Slowly, before my eyes, I see him regain his composure. He straightens his posture, his fists unclench, his expression becomes calm. "I'm just trying to explain to you that we can't be seen together for a while. This isn't forever, just . . . a while. Use this time to figure out what you want to do once this is all over. You have a whole life ahead of you. A life that won't just be about one thing. Take this time to expand. Figure out what you want."

I want you!

But I don't say it. I feel utterly and completely lost.

"Adoncia," he says gently. "Do you understand what I'm saying?"

"We can't be seen together," I say mechanically. And then look up at him, my eyes pleading. "But afterward; we'll come back to each other afterward, right?"

He meets my gaze, locking me in with his eyes. "Assuming you still want me. You may not."

"Why would you even say that?"

"You may decide to move on," he replies. "Once you have perspective you may begin to see me as who I am rather than what you want."

He's telling me something. Something that lies between and underneath his sentences. It's something important and something worrisome, part of me knows that.

And another part, a much *bigger* part of me, simply doesn't want to hear it.

"You're not breaking up with me," I say firmly. "When this is over we can be together."

"If you still want me," he qualifies.

It's enough. It simply has to be enough. I step forward again. Trembling, I place my lips against his. The kiss starts out so gentle, almost hesitant, but then, slowly, his hands move to my lower back, pressing me into him and I'm pulling him to me. It's the kind of kiss that you see in black-and-white posters, the kind that defines Hollywood's most passionate love stories.

And then I pull away again, stepping backward, toward the door. "I will never stop wanting you," I whisper.

And then I gather my things and I leave.

I leave before he can tell me that he might stop wanting me.

chapter twenty-three

Walking into HGVB this time feels so different than the first time I did it. I remember that day so clearly. Travis had just hired me and I had felt very clear about my purpose. I knew I had the upper hand because he didn't know who I was and I knew exactly who he was.

That's still true, but the clarity is completely gone. I don't know what's happening between Lander and me. I don't even have a full grasp on what's going to happen with my revenge. In the beginning I had total control over this process. Now I feel like I don't have any control at all.

Once I announce myself to security it only takes them a few seconds to get the order from Travis to send me right up. When I get to the floor where his office is his secretary escorts me to his office immediately.

Travis is notorious for making people wait. It's a power thing for him. So yesterday this kind of immediate access would have been incredibly encouraging. It implies that I've become important to Travis, maybe even that I've regained his trust.

But today? Today I'm not even sure if any of that matters.

"Sir, I have Ms. Dantès for you," the secretary says as she opens the door.

Travis is sitting at his desk on the phone, waving me in with one hand without bothering to look up. It's not until the secretary leaves that he wraps up his call. Leaning back in his chair, arms crossed over his chest, he takes me in, but this time his gaze isn't leering or even appraising. He's studying me the way a doctor might study an X-ray, looking for anything irregular, any sign of a problem.

"Do you have the flash drive?" he asks.

"What?" I had almost forgotten about that. "Yes, wait, I have it." I search in my purse and then walk over and slam it down onto his desk.

The hostility of the gesture causes him to raise his eyebrows. "Is there a problem?"

"A problem?" I parrot, and then tap my finger on my lip as I stare up at the ceiling, making an exaggerated display of thinking about the question. "Well, I guess that's a matter of perspective, Travis."

It's the first time I've ever called him by his first name and the shift causes his raised eyebrows to dive down into a furrow.

"You see," I continue, "that flash drive is as empty

as it was when you gave it to me. So that might be a problem for you. But for me?" I shrug. "I'm fine with it."

"What the hell is going on with you?"

"Your fucking brother broke up with me!" The words come out before I really have a chance to think them out, but I realize immediately that they work.

I also realize that talking like this to Travis feels *good*. And at this moment I desperately need that. Less than an hour ago Lander made me feel weak and vulnerable. But Travis? He makes me feel angry. And God bless him for it. God bless him for reminding me of what a healing balm rage can be.

"He . . ." Travis shakes his head as if to clear it and then gets to his feet. "That's not possible."

"Oh, I'm pretty sure it is," I snap. "He's had his fill and now he's moving on."

"But that doesn't make sense," Travis insists. "My brother is in . . . What I'm trying to say is . . . There's just no logical reason for him to do this."

"Please tell me you're kidding," I say dryly.

"Excuse me?"

"Life," I say between clenched teeth, "is not about logic. It's about people. And *people* aren't logical. Not where their emotions are concerned. Now, I realize that the ways of us humans are foreign to you, seeing that you're some kind of demented creature from hell, but just so you know, that's generally how we work."

All this time I've been playing a part. All this time I've been kowtowing and kissing Travis's ass for the cause, and now I'm not going to be there to see it through? Fuck it, at the very least I will have *this*.

"Are you angry with me?" he asks, somewhat baffled.

"No, Travis, I'm just tired of you."

I hold my breath, waiting for him to blow up in a rage, but I can tell he's too shocked for that.

And this silence is all the permission I need to let it all come roaring out.

"I'm tired of *all* of it!" I declare. "I'm tired of your brother's games. I'm tired of your wife, who is so fucked-up she would make Hemingway look like a model of sobriety. And I'm tired of you and your pathological need to demonstrate control over those you perceive to be weaker than you. I'm not familiar with what you're compensating for, but if it's *that* small, *buy a pump*!"

I stop, somewhat surprised with myself. I look at Travis, waiting for some kind of confirmation that I said what I think I just said.

And the confirmation is right there on his face. I have literally never seen Travis look this angry. For a second I think he's going to leap forward and strangle me, which would be great because I'd love nothing more than to get him on an assault charge. Plus then I could punch him back. Oh God, Travis, do it, do it, *do it*! I feel my fists clenching by my sides, anticipatory, hopeful.

But Travis, being Travis, manages to rein it in and hold on to his cool composure. Damn.

"Your pride has been hurt," he says testily. "I understand that. But I promise you, if you continue to work for me—"

"You still want me to work for you?" I ask, honestly taken aback.

"—if Lander *sees* you," Travis continues, ignoring my interruption, "and knows that you're still available to him, he will not be able to stay away from you."

"You think you know your brother that well?"

"I think I know men that well," Travis counters.

"*You* don't seem to have a problem staying away from me . . . At least you didn't last night," I point out. "Don't get me wrong, I am *infinitely* thankful for that."

"My feelings about you are different from my brother's," Travis says, his voice straining for control. The possibility of being strangled is definitely still there. "Lander is planning something and I need to figure out what it is. He's much more devious than our father gives him credit for. I realize that I may have . . . offended your sensibilities—"

I let out a derisive laugh.

"—but if you stick with me I will help you win Lander back. I guarantee you it won't be hard. All I ask in return is information."

I lean back on my heels and shake my head. "You're scared of Lander."

"That's ridiculous," he snaps.

"You're so afraid of him that you'll continue to employ me after everything I just said, all because you think I might be able to protect you from him."

"I don't need your protection."

"Mmm"—I cock my head to the side—"kinda

think you do. You wanted me to be your Paul Revere and let you know when the attack is coming, because you know it's coming, don't you, Travis?"

"As I said, what I know is that he's planning—"

"What you know is that he'll win. You play by your father's rules. You always have and you always will. But Lander?" I shrug. "One never knows what path he's going to take. He *might* follow Daddy's rules, or he might not. You can't predict him, and that's what makes him stronger than you." I smile and cluck my tongue. "Don't lose too much sleep over it, Trav. As far as I can tell, Lander isn't working on any major battle plan." I walk up to him and give his arm a little patronizing pat. "You really need to stop worrying about people in your own family coming after you. It makes you sound paranoid."

I take a deep breath and turn to leave. And as I do, I call over my shoulder, "After all, it's not like you're going to be able to stop them if they do."

As I walk through the lobby, I'm literally in *awe* of myself! That was *the* most satisfying exchange I've ever had in my *life*.

I just wish it was satisfying enough to distract me from how much pain I'm in.

chapter twenty-four

I'm almost out of the HGVB building when I spot her coming in through the rotating doors. Cathy Lind. She's wearing those big sunglasses movie stars wear when they don't want to be recognized. But not recognizing her would be hard because she is so very . . . Cathy, in her handkerchief-hem pale pink shirt, skintight white pencil skirt with a metallic silver belt, and heels to make it all pop.

"Cathy?" I call out as she blindly walks past me.

She stops at the sound of my voice and pivots toward me, taking her glasses off as she does, giving the whole move a bit of style. "Bell, right?" she asks, as if we didn't have a long tête-à-tête over vodka in her kitchen.

"Are you here to see Travis?"

"Oh? You two are on a first-name basis now?"

She's looking at me hard, but now I wonder, is she glaring at me, or is she just trying to see me?

"Mr. Gable," I correct myself. "I actually just quit."

Her mouth curls into an amused little smile as she toys with her glasses. "I assume he did something to provoke that."

"Well," I hedge, "he's not the easiest person in the world to work for."

"He's not the easiest person, period," she replies with a laugh. "But then, easy is boring. I'm attracted to challenges."

"And what about his wife?" I ask pointedly. As the doors open and close behind us we can hear the staccato swears of a homeless man sitting on the sidewalk.

Cathy's smile broadens. "What about her?"

"Is she . . . a challenge to overcome?" There is something so freeing about being able to ask the questions I want to ask without worrying about it getting back to Travis.

She looks slyly over her shoulder and then leans forward. "I shouldn't tell you this," she admits in something just above a stage whisper, "but he's going to leave her. Actually, you know what? The hell with it." She steps back and says in a full volume voice, "He's going to leave her, everyone!"

A few people passing give her curious looks, but I'm still the only one who seems interested in this news.

"He . . . he told you that?" I ask.

A slight shadow passes over her face, but she quickly brushes it away. "He says he's going to find a way. I know what you're thinking," she says, holding up her hand to stop me from interrupting, although I had no intention of doing so. "You're thinking that he shouldn't have said he was *going* to find a way. He should just do it. And you're right, but . . . but . . ." As she grabbles for the words she seems to get a little smaller. It's subtle, but I can see her shoulders curling in a bit as uncertainty and hope light up her eyes. "It's more than he's ever offered me before," she says, finally completing her thought.

It's hard for me to keep from shaking my head. What is it about love that makes the strongest among us weak?

"You're better than him," I tell her flatly. People are streaming past us, oblivious to the tragedy that this woman represents. "I don't know what your husband is like, but even if he is the wrong man for you, Travis has got to be worse."

She nods, although I can tell she's only indicating that she hears and understands my concern, not that she agrees with it. Her eyes now cast down as if examining her glasses. "Just over a year ago," she says, quietly, "I was diagnosed with something called gyrate atrophy. Some rare genetic condition. Apparently I've always had it, but other than a little nearsightedness it hadn't caused me any problems. But now . . . I'm losing my sight. And you know what?"

She looks up, and now for the first time I notice

that the light that reflects in her eyes isn't quite normal. Cataracts perhaps? Or something else . . . something even more damaging.

"My husband," she continues, "my husband—the *doctor*—didn't notice. I waited for four months after my diagnosis, my vision weakening a little more every few weeks, and he didn't notice a thing. When I finally told him he gave me a whole bunch of excuses about why he didn't *see* it. He talked about how I cover so well, refusing to make eye contact, moving around our home without ever bumping into a thing. But the truth is, he simply doesn't see me. But Travis?" She smiles. "He noticed after speaking to me for less than five minutes. Do you understand what I'm saying?"

Yes, you're saying that Travis is a man who sees who you are and what you're going through. You're saying that you can't let go of that.

I understand it, I really do. And it makes me wonder . . .

How am I ever going to be able to get through these months without Lander?

As I walk to my place from the subway I feel tired and there's a pounding in my head. In a thousand years I never would have predicted victory would feel like this.

"Whatcha doin'?"

I turn to see Mary sitting in an alley along my path. Mary, the closest thing I have to a friend.

She has another coloring book in her lap, one that depicts stained glass windows, the kind you might find in a church. Even as she addresses me she keeps her focus on the paper as she fills in the details with a stub of a green pencil and the quick, controlled movement of her hand.

"How are you, Mary?"

"I'm okay."

"Good, that's good . . . Well, I won't bother you . . ."

She glances up briefly and shakes her head. "You're sad," she declares as she drops the green and pulls a glittery gold crayon from her frizzy brown hair.

"How can you tell?"

"You didn't offer me a Clif Bar," she says sagely. "You always give me your Clif Bars. So I figure you're either sad or you're mad at me, and I didn't do nothin' to make you mad."

I laugh and look up at the sky. "I actually don't have any on me. My bad. But you're right, I'm sad."

"Someone die?"

"Yes," I whisper. "But that was a long time ago."

"Then is it a man? Men always making people sad around here."

"Men make people sad everywhere," I mutter.

"But this one who's making you sad . . . Is he in your family?" she asks, sharply this time. "You gotta talk to him if he's family."

"He's not family."

"A lover then?"

I nod, my voice now smothered by a renewed sense of loss.

"That's the worst kind of man," Mary says. In the dark shadows of the alley her colors lose their distinction, all blending together into something opaque and mysterious. "Strangers can hurt you. They'll hurt you bad sometimes. But a lover? They'll make you hurt yourself."

"I don't want to hurt myself anymore." I say it slowly, measuring the sentiment against my tongue, making sure that it's true.

"Oh I don't know," Mary says, shaking her head and making a few crayons she has stored in her hair go flying into the air. "If we feel pain we know we're alive. Gotta hang on to whatever it is that reminds us of that."

"Anger, hate, pain," I say hoarsely. "I'm ready to feel something else now. I'm really, really ready. But I just . . . I just need someone to help me with that."

"Girl," Mary laughs as she adds a touch of pink to a dove's wing. "Don't you know that if you want something in this world you gotta go out and grab it all on your own? Ain't nobody gonna help you if you don't help yourself. And even that doesn't work sometimes."

I look down at Mary, her head bowed, her fingers moving furiously over the paper. What brought her to this? Bad experiences with her family? With men? Was she self-destructive in her youth?

Was she like me?

For a moment I see Mary differently. I see how she must have looked twenty years ago. I imagine her standing defiant against the world, angry and distrustful.

And alone.

Just like me.

"I have to go," I mumble. I reach into my purse and hand her a twenty. "Get something better than a Clif Bar," I insist. "Try something new."

And as I leave her I realize that's exactly what we all need.

We all need to try something new.

chapter twenty-five

The next morning comes too soon. I pull the covers over my head, trying to hide from the sun. As far as I'm concerned, there's simply no reason for the sun to rise anymore. What is there for me to do? I try to think of angles I can work, ones that won't interfere with Lander's plan to bring in the FDIC on Travis, Sean, and Edmund's crimes. I could try to cause trouble for Cathy and Travis. Or I could call Micah. I'd have to call him eventually anyway to tell him I'm no longer in a position to spy on Travis for him. But I could call him and tell him more than that! I could tell him I saw Travis with Javier again. I could make sure that Micah really sees Travis as a threat. Maybe then Micah would just kill Travis. The thought should probably bother me but at the moment it doesn't.

Still, it doesn't delight me either. Neither does sabotaging whatever weak excuse of a relationship he has going on with Cathy. It all feels pointless. I'd actually rather see them all go to prison for funding terrorists and drug cartels. Travis won't do well in prison. And while I might not be able to be there when they take him away, I'll be damned if I'm not going to be there for the verdict. Of course there are other people involved in this. The list of people emailed about Edmund's plans isn't all that short. But the only three I care about are Edmund, Sean, and Travis. I wonder if they'll have separate trials. Three trials would mean triple the fun.

But how long will I have to twiddle my thumbs before that happens?

How long will I have to be without Lander?

What reason could I possibly have to get out of bed?

What do I do now that my anger has achieved its aim?

I turn restlessly against the mattress and squeeze my eyes closed tighter. I try to imagine that the covers are Lander's arms. I try to pull his voice out of the silence.

You're beautiful.

My warrior princess.

There's no one like you.

I love you.

But of course I can't quite conjure up that last one. I don't know what it would sound like for him to say that.

There's no reason to get out of bed at all.

The sound of my cell phone jars me out of my

musings, interrupting my depression with a shot of annoyance. I reach over and pick it up off the floor and pull it under the covers with me.

"Hello," I mutter.

"Hello, is this Adoncia Jiménez?"

I suck in a sharp breath as my heart leaps into my throat. No one calls me by my real name other than Lander. Aside from Micah, he's the only one who knows who I really am . . . or at least that's supposed to be the case.

"Hello? Are you still there?"

I clear my throat and find my voice. "Who is this please?"

"This is Mandy Simpson, the manager at Callow's Rare Books. Am I speaking to Miss Jiménez?"

"Yes!" I say, bolting up, the covers still over my head. I flail at them with my free arm until they fall to my waist and I can see the light. "This is Adoncia, can I help you?"

I have no idea why Callow's would be calling me, but those who work for Callow's are essentially the nuns of my house of worship. Anything they have to say, I want to hear.

"Adoncia, I'm so glad I caught you. I hope it's all right, but Mr. Gable gave me your number."

"Lander?"

"Yes." She laughs lightly. "That's the Gable I'm referring to. The associate he usually works with here—"

"Garda."

"Yes, Garda. Garda is retiring and we're looking

for someone who can fill her position. Mr. Gable is a very good client of ours, and he felt that you would be an excellent addition to our team. He said he would be very comfortable working with you . . . In fact he suggested that he might not be comfortable working with anyone else. And Garda, you met Garda, well, she had nothing but good things to say about you. Apparently you are extremely well versed in classic literature and . . . well, almost all literature according to both Mr. Gable and Garda."

Once again I've lost my voice. Is Lander devising a way that we can secretly see each other?

And . . . *am I going to be working at Callow's?*

"Of course, you'll have to come in for an interview, and if you could, bring your résumé. Do you have any experience in this field?"

"I . . . I've worked in a few bookstores." My cheeks turn red with shame as I add, "Used bookstores." As if selling a beat-up copy of *Harry Potter* is even in the same ballpark as selling an autographed first edition of . . . well, *Harry Potter*.

"Any experience with books is good," Mandy assures me. "Where did you go to college, Adoncia?"

My mind travels to Micah. He promised me he would help me fake any reference or résumé I needed to fake. He did that for me when I was applying for the job with Travis; he could do it again. I could make up more experience . . . maybe something with antiques! Maybe he could find a way to make it look like I have a college degree too!

But this is my church.

And I'm so very tired of pretending.

I bend my legs and rest my forehead on my knees as I admit the truth. "I went to Kingsborough," I say quietly.

"A good community college," Mandy says approvingly. "Where did you transfer to, dear?"

"I . . . I didn't."

"I'm sorry?"

Suddenly this dream is feeling like a nightmare. I can handle being humiliated in front of my enemies, but to shame myself in front of the manager of this place . . .

And it's all my fault. I haven't prepared myself for anything other than destroying other people's lives. How could I think for even a moment that I could do more than that? How could I think I deserved something like this?

"I only have a two-year degree," I manage to clarify as I curl up my toes and bring my knees tighter to my chest. "I'm sorry," I add, because at the moment not having more of an education feels like an offense.

"Oh . . . Most of our salespeople have their master's."

"I understand," I say hoarsely. There has to be an elegant way to get out of this conversation so I can climb under the covers again . . . this time to cry.

"But Mr. Gable is a *very* good client of ours. We really do need someone who he will feel comfortable with."

I lift my head. Did I hear her correctly?

"Tell you what. Why don't you come in tomorrow,

shall we say three? Bring your résumé listing whatever work experience and education you have. Let's see if we can find a way to make this work."

"Yes!" I say, leaping up. "I can make it at three tomorrow, absolutely."

"Wonderful, Adoncia. I look forward to meeting you."

As soon as she hangs up I start squealing and jumping up and down. I literally can't stop and I don't stop until the person living below me starts banging on their ceiling in protest.

It's only then that I fully register what's just happened . . .

. . . I found a reason to get out of bed.

chapter twenty-six

I got the job.

I know I didn't earn it. I certainly don't deserve it. It's a gift from Lander. I suppose some would feel guilty about that. They would think that taking a job that other people might be more qualified for is wrong. Maybe it is, maybe it isn't, but personally, I don't feel bad at all. So many people in this world are given breaks and advantages. They're born into money, they have a loving family to nurture them throughout their childhood and young adult years, they happen upon a mentor who takes a keen interest in them . . .

I didn't get any of that. I'm not complaining, I haven't lived the life of an angel. There's a reason why my foster families rejected me in all the various ways you can reject someone. But now that I've been given this break? This gift? Well, maybe it's not fair, but it's also about time.

Furthermore, I'm determined to earn what I've already been given. As the weeks progress, I settle into a new routine. When I'm not at Callow's, I'm at the library looking up and studying everything there is to know about rare and valuable books. I study the history of each piece we have—and we have a *lot* of pieces. Not just books, but collections of articles and letters by famous and distinguished figures in history dating all the way from the fifteenth century. Every single day leaves me breathless.

I've been told that because of the small number of people who make up our target market, getting sales can be difficult. I'm told it takes a while to build up a clientele.

Which is why everyone is so impressed when I make my first six-thousand-dollar sale in my first week of employment.

I make my first hundred-thousand-dollar sale after three weeks.

And I get commission. It's a good gig.

Plus, as it turns out, Jessica isn't as cautious about her security as Travis is (not that his precautions are going to do him a lot of good in the end). She doesn't change the passwords for her email after I leave her employ. So I check it regularly, looking for any hints that there might be trouble in the Gable household—new trouble, that is. But I also look at her invitations to events. And when she declines an invitation to an art opening at one of New York's premier galleries, I crash that party.

It's so easy. I just put on a cocktail dress—not too

flashy but just sexy enough to sweet-talk the guy at the door into believing that I belong there. And really, what does he care anyway? It's just a gallery showing.

Blending in is easy, I've been studying the ways of New York's elite for years. So I just stand back, position myself perfectly, exchange a few words with one guest, then another, kind of like a jaguar gently tapping the surface of the water, luring the fish to come to her. And they do come. Perhaps it's not a surprise, but it turns out I'm very good at engaging people, pulling them in, gaining their trust, making them want the things I want them to want.

And what I want is for them to enhance their lives by purchasing very rare books.

Within a week of that event three of the men I spoke to and one of the women come in to Callow's. The woman ends up spending more than a thousand dollars. Two of the men spend over ten thousand dollars each. The third man asks me to help him build a collection of literature and letters from the Napoleonic era.

It's sort of amazing. It honestly never occurred to me that I might be able to use the skills I've been cultivating toward a legitimate business endeavor!

Mandy is *ecstatic*.

By the second month of employment I decide that it's time to put down a first and last on a new apartment. Still in Harlem, but in the *nice* part of Harlem. And the place is cute. It's a small, sunny one-bedroom that I fill with decent used furniture along with a few Ikea bookcases. I frame the picture of my mother and me. I actually hang things on the walls. One poster is a picture made up of the words of Jane Eyre. Brontë's words are used to create the outline of the book's protagonists, locked in an embrace.

Another poster is of the Roman goddess Bellona, goddess of war.

I really like my new place.

All the good things in my life, they're *almost* enough to distract me from the fact that my enemies are unwittingly getting closer and closer to their downfall.

But it's nowhere near enough to distract me from thinking about Lander. Every day I wait for him to come into the bookstore. I wait for him to call, email, reach out to me in some way. But for the first month there's nothing. Then another week passes, then another month. Each day that passes without him adds an element of tension to my otherwise tranquil new life, a drop of longing to balance out whatever satisfactions my employment may bestow on me.

I miss him. I miss him in a way that I didn't think possible. I miss him almost as much as I miss my mother.

After fourteen weeks I can't stand it anymore. Sitting cross-legged on the floor of my apartment I call his cell, yearning to just hear him say my name.

I get his voice mail.

And my heart drops.

Still, I close my eyes tight and listen to his voice telling me he is unavailable, thinking about the times when that same voice was whispering in my ear, telling me something quite different. When the beep finally comes, I'm discombobulated and unprepared. "Hi . . ." I say awkwardly as I try to figure out what's safe to say and what's forbidden. "I . . . I just wanted to tell you . . . I wanted you to know . . ."

I want you.

". . . that Callow's has a new collection of letters by Winston Churchill . . ."

I love you.

". . . they're in beautiful condition, each signed by his own hand. If you would like to make an appointment to see them, I'll be at the store every day this week except Thursday . . ."

Please come back to me.

". . . Of course, if Thursday's the only day you're available, I can come in. We can make a private appointment for you to peruse the collection."

I just want you back.

When I hang up my hand is shaking.

It's pathetic really, almost inexplicable. After all, I should be used to being alone. Why is it so difficult now? *Why has he done this to me?* Living with anger had been motivating. But living with unrequited love? That's devastating.

And now, how can I *not* believe that it's unrequited? How else could he walk away so easily?

He had warned me: *There has never been a woman who has loved a Gable man who hasn't lived to regret it. Even when we don't mean to, we always end up crushing whatever heart has been handed to us.*

If only I had been able to hear him. If only I hadn't handed him my heart.

❧

It's not until the next day that I finally get a response to my call. I'm at Callow's; the store is empty as it often is. We're not a high-traffic place. I'm sitting at a table, letting my fingers dangle over the handwritten words of Napoléon, trying to understand his power to mesmerize and destroy by the slant of his cursive, when Mandy approaches me, a broad smile on her face.

"I have a call for you," she says, "from the office of Mr. Lander Gable."

In a second I'm on my feet, gladly abandoning a dictator for my captain of industry. I snatch up the phone and press it to my ear. "Lander?"

"Um, no, this is Darlene Simon, Mr. Gable's personal assistant. Is this Adoncia Jiménez?"

I can't move. It's like someone has poured ice-cold water down my throat. It's freezing my insides so that everything shivers and aches. "His personal assistant?" I repeat.

"Yes, Mr. Gable received your call that you have a few new original letters of Winston Churchill? Mr. Gable is quite interested. Will these be sold as a collection or individually?"

"It's . . . it's a collection. A correspondence between him and the postwar Lord Chancellor of Britain." She sounds old. Is she old? Maybe over sixty?

"I see. And which chancellor would that be exactly? Oh, and can you tell me how many letters there are in the collection?"

"Twelve, six from Churchill, and six replies by the chancellor." She sounds ugly too. Old and ugly.

"Wonderful, would you mind sending some more information about the pieces over to me? Do include the chancellor's name. He'll be needing that. And please include a photo and pricing information. Mr. Gable may not be able to make it into your establishment, but he feels confident that anything you would sell him will be of the highest quality and live up to its description. He thinks very highly of you, Ms. Jiménez."

I feel like the world is eroding under my feet, like I'm about to fall and be buried in bits of rubble and dust.

On my dinner break I wander the streets of the city, letting the sound of rush-hour traffic wash over me, hoping that the chaos of horns and curses of frustrated drivers will somehow distract me from the chaos inside. There are things I have to think about, and it's not just my heart.

I've heard nothing about an investigation into HGVB. Not one article. Not one word.

My mind travels back to the first night that Lander gained my trust. I was on the verge of killing him, literally. I had clawed at his skin, pounded his flesh. I was ready for violence.

And then Lander told me a story. A story about his saintly mother, about his evil father and brother, a story about his own desire for revenge and a story about his desire to seek it with me.

It was a good story. Every bit as good as the fairy tales my mother told me when I was little. I believed in those stories. A big part of me still does. I believe . . . or at least I want to believe, that there are people who really do live the fairy tale. It's just that those people aren't me. My path is different.

The story Lander told me had fit me better. It's a good story.

I stand in front of a movie theater, staring blankly at the poster for an upcoming horror flick. When I was a teen I saw *The Sixth Sense*. I spent the first 90 percent of the film thinking that Bruce Willis's character was an idiot. What kind of psychiatrist follows his patient around? He was practically stalking him! And then the movie ended with a twist, and I suddenly realized that I didn't know Bruce Willis's character at all. I hadn't even understood the true nature of the movie I had been watching. Nothing was as I thought it was at all.

Odd, that I should think of that now.

chapter twenty-seven

When I get back to Callow's, Mandy gets up from her desk, clearly excited. "Oh good, you're back! A gentleman is here to see you; he just went back to look at some of our framed letters and photos."

My stomach does a little flip, but then I realize, if the gentleman was Lander, Mandy would have said so. It must be one of the other clients I've been working with. Disappointed, I make my way to the back room . . .

. . . and then stop short as I see who it is.

Micah turns to me with a giant, welcoming grin and wide-open arms. "Sweet! It's been too long!"

"Micah," I say, stretching out the name. He pulls me into a bear hug, giving me a hard pat on the back.

"This place is brilliant!" he says excitedly. "You have documents of Thomas Cromwell, the Kangxi

Emperor, and King George here! You have an actual letter written by Vlad III, Prince of Wallachia! The real-life inspiration for Count Dracula! All kept in exquisite condition. Pristine! And look at this! A personal letter and signed photo of Albert Einstein! The creator of the theory of relativity! The father of modern physics! That," he says, pointing dramatically at Einstein, "is one smart motherfucker."

"What are you doing here, Micah?" I whisper, looking over my shoulder to make sure that Mandy isn't within hearing distance.

"I missed you, Sweet. I haven't talked to you since you abruptly left Travis's employ and started to use your real name. Bit of a switch for you, isn't it?" he notes as he continues to peruse the room with his eyes. "Although, I can see why after working for Travis you might long to be surrounded by the work of Vlad the Impaler."

"I just had enough," I say quietly. "Travis was awful to work for and Lander . . . Well, you were right about him."

"What, you mean in regards to his being like his brother?" he asks distractedly as he pulls out a book from the shelf.

"In a way, yes, that's basically what I mean."

"Well, they're both Edmund's sons, aren't they? The apple doesn't fall far from the tree and all that." He holds up the book he's currently looking at. "Maya Angelou. Now there's a woman who knew how to write! Beautiful, aching prose that will rip you to shreds. If those elitist pricks over at Columbia didn't have their heads shoved up their own arseholes she'd have been given at least three Pulitzers before she died."

"Are you in the market for a book?"

He shrugs, puts the book back, and pulls out another. "One never knows. I really wish you had spoken to me before you quit your last job."

I straighten my posture and clasp my hands behind my back. "Was that necessary?"

"Necessary? Maybe not. It would have been polite, though. You knew I was counting on you to keep an eye on your boss. For you to just up and quit without so much as giving me fair warning, well, it hurt my feelings, Sweet. I expect my friends to show me a little more consideration than that."

"I . . . I didn't mean to offend you."

"No, no, of course you didn't," he says with a big smile. "It's funny, though. Travis swears up and down that he didn't meet with Javier and Edmund without me. Edmund swears to it too."

"Oh?" I ask, trying to keep my voice steady, which is hard because I'm beginning to realize that I may be on very shaky ground.

"Javier says he's so offended by my lack of trust he now doesn't trust *me*, like I'm trying to hide something by distracting him with accusations . . . Of course, they could all be lying."

"I can't imagine any of them are known for their honesty," I say with a forced laugh.

"Good point." He pulls out yet another book. Every move is so casual and nonchalant it's terrifying.

"Faulkner," he notes. "This philandering piss-artist gets two Pulitzers and my girl Maya gets none. What kind of fucked-up world do we live in?"

"Are you still worried about what Javier's up to? I mean . . . his pharmacy?" Should I have responded to his comment about Faulkner? Am I playing this right?

"Hmm?" He flips through the Faulkner before putting it back in apparent disgust. "No, no. I haven't seen any evidence of that so far. No evidence of that and no evidence that he met with the Gables without me. Except of course your word on that, right, Sweet? You are swearing to that, aren't you?" He shoves his hands into his jacket pockets and cocks his head to the side. "You wouldn't lie to an old friend, would you?"

"No." The word comes out as a whisper.

"That's what I figured," he says, his smile returning as he again turns his attention back to the room. "I can see why you'd want to work here. You know, if you had called me I would have helped you make up some work experience."

"Thank you, but, um, it wasn't necessary."

"They didn't have a problem with your lack of an education?" he asks, now studying an engraved portrait of Ulysses S. Grant. "The fact that you don't have a four-year degree . . . You don't, right? Just junior college if I remember correctly."

"They decided to take a chance on me." I hate that he's handling these books. Hate that someone I fear is touching something I love.

"Did they? Well, that's generous of them. I like

that." He moves to the next framed photo. "The person who does the hiring, she's a woman, yes?"

"Yes, it's . . ." My voice trails off as I rethink the wisdom of telling him that the person who hired me is actually sitting in the front portion of the store, ready to be interrogated. "It was a woman," I finally finish.

"She a lesbian?"

"I'm capable of getting a job without sleeping with my employer," I say tersely. *Yes, Micah, make me angry. Give me some rage to get me through this.*

"Uh-huh. So, not a lesbian." He moves on to the next frame. "Bloody hell, is that really a letter from Thomas Jefferson?" He leans in closer. "Well, for forty-eight thousand dollars I believe it is." He looks at me. "Or at least the price tag makes the lie more believable."

I step forward, resting my weight on the back of a wooden chair near the center of the room, and look at the frame myself. "I didn't know you were so interested in American history and literature."

"No? It's interesting how there are so many things we don't know about each other, isn't it?"

He turns, locks me in his gaze. "I did tell you that I have some legitimate business with the Gables, didn't I?"

"Yes," I say softly. "You did."

"And I told you not to interfere with that."

I nod, no longer able to speak. Where is my anger? Where is my strength? How the fuck do I get out of this?

"Did you interfere with it, Sweet?"

"Micah, I'm here because I'm *done* with the Ga-bles. I don't want anything to do with them at all. I know they didn't hurt my mother now and—"

"You know what I find fascinating about people?" he asks, cutting me off.

I shake my head. I want to sit down in the chair but I know I can't afford to look any weaker than I already do.

"I find it fascinating that when people don't want to say something they almost always end up saying too much. They never embrace the right to stay si-lent, they just keep talking around the answer to the question they've been asked in a rather transparent attempt to distract the person asking the question."

"I didn't interfere with your business, or Travis's business," I say steadily. "The Gables are no longer on my radar."

"Uh-huh. How'd you get this job?"

"I . . ." But I falter. The lies aren't coming as eas-ily these days. I'm out of practice. Outside the room I hear approaching footsteps. Mandy? A customer? One of Micah's men? I'm too scared to even turn around and look.

"Am I interrupting?"

The sound of that voice is almost enough to make me lose my balance entirely.

It's the voice of Lander.

My first impulse is to literally throw myself into his arms, press my lips against his, and give him a wel-come suitable for a soldier returning from war. But I manage to hold myself back. And then, slowly, the full implications and complications of the timing of his appearance weigh on me. I don't *know* how to react. I just told Micah that I didn't want anything to do with Lander. On the other hand, I certainly don't want Mandy to see me being rude to the man she hired me to serve. I feel backed into a corner and there's literally no graceful way out of this.

And yet, it's *Lander.* To have him right here and not be able to tell him off for abandoning me for so long, or question him about the ugly suspicions that have been dancing in my mind of late . . .

. . . to not be able to hold him.

It's not fair. None of this is fair.

And it's also very dangerous.

My eyes slide to Micah, who is now in my peripheral vision. His hands are back in his pockets as if he's relaxed, casual.

But he's not. He jaw is tense and he's leaning forward just slightly, as if he is on the verge of an attack.

"Well, look who the cat dragged in," Micah says slowly.

In response, Lander looks at Micah. "Hello. I don't believe we've ever been introduced." Lander's wearing a gray suit with a lighter gray shirt; the tie he must have been wearing earlier has already been discarded. The look is expensive, and yet something about how he wears it, how he *carries* himself, is not quite civilized.

"Micah Romenov," Micah says, extending his hand. "And you're Lander Gable. The lady and I were just talking about you, in fact."

Lander looks at his hand but he doesn't shake it. Micah is clearly taken off guard by this, as am I. No one snubs Micah.

Slowly, Micah withdraws his hand. "It's funny," he says, crossing his arms over his chest. "She was telling me that the two of you weren't on speaking terms. But, well, here you are. No way to see that coming, right, Sweet?"

"I'm not here for her," Lander replies coolly. "I'm here to look at some letters written by Winston Churchill."

"Really! Now, don't that beat all? I spent twenty-one years in England and here I am looking at Americana, and you're a Yank here to look at letters written by the British Bulldog. Ironic, isn't it?"

"You work with my brother, don't you?" Lander asks, ignoring Micah's comment. "And my father?"

"At times, yes, yes I do."

Lander nods and then turns his attention to me. "Please don't take offense. I know it's been a while since we've seen one another, but since he's here, I'd like the opportunity to talk to Mr. Romenov alone."

I glance between Lander and Micah. This is ridiculous. We're in a rare bookstore. This is not the place for a showdown. I look at the Faulkner on the wall. "Do you think it might be better if—"

"We're just going to talk," Lander says softly, but solidly. "Whatever differences we may have, I think you know me well enough to know that I would never put a first-edition book in harm's way."

I suppress a smile and turn back to Micah.

"It's okay, Sweet," Micah says, his trademark smile completely gone now. "Let me talk to Mr. Gable."

Hesitantly, I step back and then turn and stride out into the front room, where Mandy is sitting at the desk, going over an invoice.

"I was wondering when he was going to come in," Mandy says as she makes a note on the paper. "Lander Gable was the main reason I hired you and we haven't seen hide nor hair of him since you started!" She finally looks up and offers me a reassuring smile. "Of course, I didn't realize then that you would become one of our top salespeople in less than three months. It's really quite impressive, Adoncia."

I nod and glance toward the back. "Lander knows the man I was speaking with," I hedge. "I hadn't realized they were acquainted."

She waves her hand dismissively and leans over to file the invoice away. "The population at that end of the income bracket is rather small. They're an insular bunch. We live in the world and they live in a village: Billionaire Village." She laughs, and then quickly checks herself. "That probably wasn't appropriate, and I don't even know the other gentleman's financial standing. I'm just making an assumption based on his acquaintance with Mr. Gable and the fact that he's shopping here. And he has that Russian British accent. I assumed *oligarch*." She rests her weight on her elbows, cups her chin in her hands. "He's actually rather attractive."

"Who?" I ask, finally dragging my eyes away from where I just came. "Micah?"

"We spoke while he was waiting for you. He's a very knowledgeable man. Quite well-read. And he has a . . . a down-to-earth quality."

She's got to be kidding. "He's really not your type."

"Oh, I saw the tattoo hiding under his sleeve. I glimpsed it when he was gesturing. But I actually find that rather charming. A well-educated man with a rebellious soul."

"He's married," I say quickly.

"Oh. Shame." She laughs and raises one of her hands to her cheek. "Look at me, I haven't made eyes at a client in decades. It's not appropriate at all. But he was so charming."

"Yes," I say, turning back again, "the forbidden ones always are."

She smiles and nods, thinking she knows what I'm referring to, but of course she doesn't. Not really.

And in that moment I realize that Mandy doesn't actually know me. She knows my real name. But she associates it with a nice, motivated, well-read young woman who has a way with customers and marketing. Micah knows Sweet (a nickname he came up with himself and the meaning of my name, Adoncia), the scrappy but seductive trickster, intent on cutting corners in order to survive. Travis . . . Well, Travis probably doesn't know what to think about me anymore. But he used to see me as the opportunist, a woman with no moral compass who will do anything he asks, including whoring herself out, if he pays her enough.

There are nuggets of truth in all of their assumptions, and their misjudgments can be forgiven, since

I'm the one who encouraged them. But even when you take out the parts that are wrong, none of them know the whole me. Not one of them.

Which means the only one who does is Lander.

Lander, the man I love. And the man I may have been a little too quick to trust.

Moments later Micah walks out. He looks . . . angry. No, scratch that, he looks *livid*. I have never seen Micah lose his cheery façade. I know he's a killer, but I always imagined him patting his victims on the back, telling them a joke, and offering them one last cigarette before blowing their brains out. But whatever transpired between him and Lander has him quaking with rage.

"Is everything all right, Mr. Romenov?" Mandy says, getting to her feet.

Micah simply stares at me. "This was a mistake," he says in a low voice. "People who betray my trust are making the biggest mistake of their lives."

"That's enough."

I turn to see Lander, leaning on a wall between the built-in bookshelves. He's completely composed, completely calm.

Micah doesn't say a word, but his lip curls up into a kind of snarl that actually makes me take a step back. And then, just like that, he walks out.

"What on earth . . ." Mandy's sentence fades out uncompleted as she watches her short-lived crush leave the premises.

"I believe you have some letters to show me, Adoncia," Lander says mildly.

Mandy glances at her watch. She's discreet about it but Lander catches it. "I know you're about to close."

"We'll stay open for you, Mr. Gable," Mandy says, as if that much is obvious.

"I'd appreciate that. But you should go home. You can trust Adoncia to lock up."

"Mr. Gable, I really can't do that. Adoncia is wonderful and you're one of our favorite clients, but there is millions of dollars of merchandise in here—"

"I know. I know because I've *spent* millions of dollars here over the years," Lander says evenly. "You can trust Adoncia to lock up."

Mandy stands there, virtually wringing her hands as she weighs the enormity of what he's asking against the enormity of what he spends. The play of conflict and distress across Mandy's face would almost be comical if it wasn't so disturbing.

Because really, who is Lander to put her in this kind of position? Who is *he* that people should change the rules for him at the drop of a hat?

He's rich. That's all. Just rich. And it's his money that allows him not to play fair.

And for the first time since I walked away from my own revenge, I feel a strong sense of real anger. *Everything* always has to be done by his ever-changing rules! He decides when I can't see him and *he* decides when I will and I get no notice about any of it. He decides how we're going to deal with *my* revenge. And worse yet, he just expects me to play along. He *knows* I'll let him set the rules because he's a Gable while I'm just me.

Mandy takes a deep breath and rolls her shoulders back. "I'm so sorry, Mr. Gable," she says, her voice as proper and quietly assertive as a school librarian's. "Everyone here values your patronage, but I'm afraid I do not have the authority to leave Adoncia or you in the store without a manager present. It's not an issue of trust, it's an issue of protocol."

My respect for this woman has just gone up by dozens of percentage points. Lander offers her a small, approving smile, clearly impressed in his own right. "Why don't you call the owner. Francis, right?"

Mandy wavers, but then turns back to her desk and makes the call.

"Mr. Callow? I'm sorry to disturb you, but one of our clients, Lander Gable . . . Yes, he—" But Lander gestures to her to give him the phone. Confused, Mandy complies as Lander takes over the conversation.

"Hello, Francis, I haven't seen you in a while . . . Yes, I think you're right, it was at Concours d'Elegance in Pebble Beach."

And in less than five minutes Mandy is showing me how to set the alarm, lock the doors, and close up. There's a new sadness etched into the creases around her mouth and eyes. A defeat.

And in this moment, mixed up in the love I feel for Lander, I feel something akin to . . . to *hatred*. I don't know if it's for him or for what he represents or just a product of my own frustration, but it's there.

We watch her leave and then I watch as Lander locks the door after her. After *her*, the manager of the store! This woman who has dedicated her life to Callow's.

I feel Lander move close behind me. The lapel of his jacket scrapes against my blouse. "I shouldn't be here," Lander says.

I scoff and step away. "Then tell me, Mr. Gable, why are you here?"

Lander blinks in surprise and then sighs in apparent exasperation. "I know you're angry."

I move to the wall and let my fingers run across the bindings, *the bindings of history* is what Mandy calls them. "What did you say to Micah?"

"We'll get to that in a moment."

I let out a rueful laugh. "Very well, we'll deal with the things you're concerned with first. So yes, you're right, I am angry," I finally say. "The problem is, you don't know why."

"No, I understand. I know you wanted me to reach out to you during this time. I didn't. It would have been too risky."

"Ah, but you're an investment banker," I point out as I trace the engraved gold font of an eighteenth-century treasure. "Minimal risk leads to minimal gain."

"And stupid risk will lead to ruin."

I pivot slowly, offering him a slow, menacing smile. "It's only stupid if the prize isn't worth it." I wait for that to sink in before adding, "I'm not angry that you didn't call. I'm hurt, Lander, but I'm not angry about that. I'm angry that you think you can decide when and how you come back. I'm angry that you think you can override the manager of this store in order to get what you want."

"I *can* override her." I can see his jaw tense as he's pushed into the defensive.

"And I can get away with stealing a shopping cart from a homeless person, but that doesn't mean I'm going to do it. I don't *need* the shopping cart and I don't need to humiliate people for no reason."

"You're on edge."

I close my eyes and silently count to ten. The worst thing any man can do is tell a woman how she's feeling when she's in the middle of telling him off. You'd think that would be obvious, but most men never get it, and Lander isn't an exception to that rule.

Which makes me wonder what other rules he's not an exception to. "I want a cutoff date."

"Excuse me?"

"When will the Justice Department be pressing charges? Give me a cutoff date, because after it's passed, if nothing's happened, I'm going to roll up my sleeves and do things my way."

"You don't trust me." For a second, and it really only does last a second, I think I see him deflate. But then immediately he's hardened again. The powerful Gable man who dishes it out but never, ever has to take it.

"Trust you?" I repeat. "You've made it hard."

"Have I?" he asks, a sharp edge creeping into his voice.

I look at the books in glass cases that are displayed behind him. Stories of battles and conquest. "You've always known," I say quietly. "You knew back when we were still gathering evidence. You *knew* you were going to ask me to step aside. You knew that even when you were first asking me to work with you. You never intended for this to be a full partnership—"

"That's not true."

"—and you never intended for the two of us to last."

"It's a relay race, Adoncia. You did most of the legwork for the first few laps. You gave us the head start we needed. Now this is my leg of the race. I'm just bringing it home."

"And the story you told me about *why* I had to step aside, it was so thought-out. So convenient. How could I argue with it?"

A new understanding crosses his face. "Care to tell me what you're suggesting?"

I raise my eyebrows, almost tauntingly. "Suggesting? You think I'm suggesting something?" I cluck my tongue. "What we have here is a failure to communicate. Let's start again, shall we?" I pull out a chair and sit down, crossing both my legs and my arms, leaning back so that I can glare up at him. "Tell me another story, Lander. Tell me a story about your mother."

He hesitates, clearly taken off guard. Ever so subtly he shifts his weight away from me. "My mother?"

"Yes, that's the reason you're so desperate for revenge, right? Your father led you to believe that your mother was being taken care of, that her cancer was in remission while you were at Oxford. And while you were there she died because it was all lies, right?"

Lander doesn't say anything. His posture has gone from straight to rigid.

"What I don't get is why your mother didn't just tell you herself. Why didn't she just pick up the phone and say, '*Lander, I'm sick and your father took away my insurance.*' "

"I told you, my father must have threatened her. Perhaps he told her he wouldn't pay for my education anymore if she was open with me."

"You already had a bachelor's at that point. What was there to freak out about? You could have taken out loans for Oxford if your father stopped paying. Oooh"—I push out my bottom lip in mock sympathy—"were you intimidated by the whole student loan process?"

"Why are you doing this?" His hands slip into his pockets. Is he restraining himself? Trying to keep from hitting me? Holding me? I don't know.

But I do know that he's in pain. I can hear it in his voice. I'm hurting him. I feel the pain in my own gut. It almost flattens me. But I don't know how to work with those feelings. Anger is something I've mastered. Falling back on that is easy, even instinctive. "The whole reason you want revenge, the reason you originally thought we were so suited as partners, is because of this one event, no? So I'd just like to get a better handle on that event."

"You're being ridiculous."

"Am I? See, here's the thing, Lander. I don't think your father had to threaten your mother. I think she kept her illness to herself because she *wanted* to keep it to herself. She wasn't forced to do anything; rather, she chose to make a sacrifice. And if *that's* the case, then you're not motivated by revenge. You're motivated by ambition."

He doesn't say a word. If someone were to walk by the store quickly they might mistake him for a mannequin. Even his expression has gone blank. The only movement I can see is the vein in his forehead quivering ever so slightly, silently letting me know I've hit my mark.

I wait, wait for his comeback, wait for him to argue. But then something in him shifts. His eyes drift toward the window. "I told Micah that over the last few months I've identified five separate HGVB bank accounts linked to his organization. I told him that I put a freeze on the accounts and that if anything happens to you, or if he gets within a mile of you again, I will alert the Feds and they'll simply seize the accounts and claim them as illegal funds. There's millions of dollars in those accounts, so I suspect he'll play ball. When I'm satisfied that he's behaving himself, I may let him withdraw some of the funds."

I don't know what this means, not exactly. Should I be flattered that he's trying to protect me? Or is this simply another magic trick, making me look this way when I should be looking that way?

"The US Justice Department will be announcing the charges against HGVB within the next forty-eight hours," he continues. "So there, there's your damned cutoff."

For a moment we just stare at each other. Was I really wrong? Is he the man he says he is? I want to ask him, I want to beg him to prove it to me. I want him to force me to trust him again.

But you can't force someone to trust you any more than I can force myself to be more trusting. So I hold my tongue, waiting for him to say something else, something that might fix this.

But he just turns his back and walks out into the darkness, leaving me here all alone with Einstein, Angelou, Faulkner, and Churchill.

chapter twenty-eight

The day it happens starts strangely. It's not that the weather is unseasonable, or that I woke up at an odd time or anything like that. But I did wake up with a feeling. Anticipation, fear, excitement, sorrow—it takes me a few minutes to place them all and figure out where they came from. Some came from the heartache of seeing Lander. Of turning our reunion into a confrontation. Some came from my exchange with Micah, because although Lander told me I'm protected from him I don't quite believe it. No one is ever safe from Micah once they make him an enemy.

But mostly? It's knowing that the charges are going to be brought against the Gables. Today, tomorrow, I don't know which, but if Lander is right it will be soon. Still in my nightshirt, I go searching for the remote control and then, with a shaking hand, I turn on the TV. The first news show I find is picking apart a Hollywood sex scandal. The next station is in the midst of covering racist remarks by the owner of a billion-dollar sports team.

But the next is talking about HGVB.

They're talking about HGVB!

They're saying that HGVB has allowed Iranian money to flow through its US branches. That it laundered money for banks associated with terrorists, drug cartels, and Russian gangsters. "This," the news anchor says ruefully, "could be a game changer."

Oh, but he has no idea.

Delighted, I hurry to get dressed. I don't have to be at work for another hour and a half, and I half run, half skip to a newsstand. I have to see this in black and white.

And when I do get to a newsstand, there it is! It's on the front page of the *New York Times* and the *Wall Street Journal*.

I literally squeal as I grab both papers off the shelf, making the cashier do an alarmed double take. I don't blame him. People shouldn't get this excited about bank corruption. But *oh my God!*

I take my papers to a Starbucks and, buying myself a twelve-ounce coffee, camp out at a small table and spread the *Times* out before me. It's all here. Everything I knew and a lot that I didn't. For instance, Russians who claimed to be used-car salesmen had been depositing up to five hundred thousand dollars a day into HGVB accounts via some crooked traveler's check operation based in Asia. More than seventeen thousand alerts were ignored by HGVB. There was some evidence suggesting that they had enabled clients in North Korea, Syria, and Cuba to evade sanctions and get their hands on US dollars.

It is beautiful.

I quickly turn from the front page to where the article is continued, savoring every detail. HGVB has yet to make a comment, but they'll have to say something soon, because according to the story, a Senate subcommittee is already being formed and they are expected to hold hearings within the month. No one wants to wait on this.

I read that last part again. A Senate subcommittee. They're going to bring executives of HGVB in front of a Senate subcommittee.

I look through the article again, searching for Edmund's name, Sean White's name, Travis's name.

But no one is named, and if anyone has been taken away in handcuffs today it's not in this paper.

I grab the *Wall Street Journal*. It's the same story, slightly different perspective. They talk more about what possible implications this is going to have on the financial sector overall. But they too say the revelations from the government's report are staggering. A Senate subcommittee is being formed.

I run my fingers over the words. Well, this is a big deal, isn't it? Travis, Edmund, White, they're all going to be brought in front of the Senate! Their guilt and humiliation will be televised! And I can hardly expect the names of those responsible to be printed in the paper on day one. After all, these articles were probably written right before the papers had to go to press. Iran, Cuba, *North Korea*? This is *bad*, which makes it good. The depth of their corruption is going to be exposed to the world.

And it's all thanks to Lander and me.

Lander and me . . . It's been so long since I've been able to link those words together, so long since I've thought of us connected like that. I probably have no right to. I lost faith in him, and he knows it. He did give me reason to. He could have handled things with me differently. Still, I hurt him . . .

But no, I'm not going to dwell on that. I can't. There's too much to be happy about. I go to the local liquor store and buy a bottle of champagne to celebrate with after work. My grin is so wide that when the clerk rings me up he says, with a quiet chuckle, "Whatever you're so giddy about, congratulations."

"Thank you!" I giggle.

It's not until I'm halfway to Callow's that I realize I have no one to drink with.

From work I call Lander. I have to apologize, I have to set things straight, and we have to celebrate! Surely an apology will be enough. We have to be strong enough to survive one fight. But once again I get his voice mail. I don't leave a message this time. He'll see the missed call. Either he'll call me back or he won't.

As the hours wear on it becomes clear that he won't.

Mandy is quiet today too. She doesn't ask me if I

have any appointments like she usually does. She just basically stays out of my way.

As closing time nears I try to break through the new layer of tension that has formed between us. "Are you doing anything after work?" I ask.

Mandy adjusts the clasp of her necklace, never meeting my eyes. "No, I'll just be going home."

"Come out with me!" I say in a way that I hope sounds more like an invitation than a plea.

"I'm really rather tired, Adoncia."

"That's because you've been sitting in here all day," I insist. "I love this place, but on days when it's slow like this? It isn't always energizing. Come on, we've never hung out outside of work. I know this great little BYOB place around here that serves the most amazing salmon rillettes."

"Well," Mandy says, wavering as she finally allows herself a small smile.

"And I already have the champagne chilling in back! Please, you have to come! Don't let me celebrate alone."

She finally makes eye contact and there's the gleam of friendship in her eyes. "What are we celebrating?"

"I'm celebrating—" I stop before I finish the sentence. I can't tell her. To her I'm Adoncia. She doesn't know about Bell. Only Lander knows how what's happening to HGVB affects me. If I want to celebrate with Mandy, I'll have to make up a different reason for my happiness.

I'll have to celebrate with lies.

Mandy sees the change in my face, sees that I'm

unwilling to share things with her. And immediately she closes up again, her eyes sliding back to the floor, her mouth pressing into a thin, disapproving line. "I'm really very tired, Adoncia," she says again. "I'm going to go home."

Home. It's funny, I have this new place, new furnishings, new neighborhood, but it's still not home.

The truth is, I've made my home inside of Lander.

And now that he's gone, I'm homeless.

But no, I can't be blue tonight . . . and I *can't* be alone. When work's over I go out and buy a few glass champagne flutes, a baguette, and some black caviar and take the subway back up to my old neighborhood.

I find Mary in her favorite spot, coloring a new coloring book with the same broken crayons and pencils, many of them worn down to stubs. As soon as I see her I'm overwhelmed by a sense of comfort. She's still here. She didn't leave me . . . even though I left her.

I walk right up and stand over her hunched figure. "Hi," I say softly.

She looks up, startled, as if she hadn't noticed me approaching. "Hi," she says uncertainly. "I'm Mary."

I swallow hard and look down at my painted toes, exposed and vulnerable in my new heeled sandals. "I . . . I remember your name. Do you remember mine?" I ask, trying to jog her memory. "Adoncia? I used to go by Bell?"

She looks at me without the faintest hint of recognition. "Bell's easier," she says.

"Yes," I agree sadly. "Bell was easier." I hold up my bottle of champagne. "I'm celebrating tonight."

"Oh? Well, you go and have a good time then."

"No, I mean, I was wondering if you would like to celebrate with me."

Mary looks up at me, a little bewildered at first, but then that fades into something else . . . something that looks like sympathy. "Well," she says, turning back to her coloring book, "sit down, then."

I sit on the ground by her side, not at all worried about what it'll do to my new skirt. I'm just grateful that someone will welcome my company. I open the champagne and the cork pops out, ricocheting off the alley wall, almost hitting me in the head.

"That thing's dangerous," Mary says, shaking her head. "They say alcohol will kill you every time."

"Yeah, but I'm not sure they're talking about flying champagne corks." I laugh as I pour her a glass and then one for myself. I hold up my flute and gesture for her to do the same. "Years ago some people hurt my family."

"That's no good," Mary interjects. "Family's important. Don't let nobody mess with your family, girl."

"Well, there wasn't much I could do about it at the time," I explain. "But I didn't let them get away with it. Today is the first day of my justice. The people who hurt me are now beginning to face the consequences of their actions. I've worked very hard for this, Mary, and today I'm finally beginning to see the rewards for my efforts. It's just gonna get better from here."

"Well, that's good, then," Mary says, clicking her glass against mine.

It's unclear if she understands what I'm saying, but she does seem to enjoy the champagne, and when I break out the baguette and caviar her whole face lights up. As we sit in the alley, eating and drinking like Manhattan elites, I can't help but think how easy it is to make some people happy.

And how easy it is to push some people away.

Anticipation, fear, excitement, sorrow—so many emotions. So much to celebrate.

And so much to grieve.

One day leads into another and still Lander doesn't call. I fluctuate between being horribly remorseful and unspeakably angry. What does he want from me? Can't he understand how his actions might have led to my being suspicious?

But whenever I get too angry or too sad I just turn on the news and then the day gets a whole lot better. By the end of the week, NPR is reporting that during one four-year period *trillions* of dollars in wire transfers had apparently gone through HGVB without anyone monitoring them. Billions of US dollars had been purchased from the bank and had been used in a peso exchange program that allowed drug cartels to convert their dirty money into US bucks. Drug dealers in Mexico had actually been building cash boxes that were custom made to fit the measurement of the

HGVB teller windows. Edmund Gable had finally gone on record and issued a terse statement acknowledging that "HGVB has sometimes failed to meet the standards that regulators and customers expect."

The statement actually made me burst out laughing.

I wish I could laugh with Lander.

I squeeze my eyes closed and shake the idea out of my head. *Focus on the news, Adoncia,* I tell myself. *Focus on the downfall of HGVB.*

And for a while that strategy works for me. The attacks on HGVB always make me laugh and smile . . .

But then, after a while, it stops being so funny.

Every day for three weeks I check every newspaper I can get my hands on. I watch CNN, FOX, MSNBC—*all of them* every chance I get. When away from the TV I listen to NPR through an app on my phone. I'm collecting bits of news the way some little girls collect stickers, always on the lookout for something new and cherishing all of them.

I love that Edmund's name is now out there and I've found a few articles mentioning Sean White. But those mentions are always in passing, like White's role is nothing but a minor detail. More often the articles refer to incriminating emails exchanged among executives . . . but they don't *name* the executives.

Why not? Usually if someone is arrested for a major robbery or is busted in a big crime ring people are publicly named. Even before it's clear if the people are guilty. How many times have I read that so-and-so was arrested for *allegedly* attacking her boyfriend while another so-and-so allegedly robbed a string of banks? But in these articles the individual names are almost never mentioned. "We are allowing organized criminals to launder their money," wrote one executive.

One executive. As if the executive wasn't actually a person, with a name, personal wealth, or, most importantly, personal responsibility. As if this *executive* was simply another anonymous mechanism of the bank.

You don't jail anonymous mechanisms, do you?

But of course they would. This isn't like the sub-prime mortgage crisis. These men are funding terrorists, and we live in a time where if you happen to have partied with a guy whose second cousin twice removed is married to a possible Al Qaeda operative you're going to have the FBI or a drone breathing down your neck. No, Travis and Edmund and Sean, they're all going down.

The following week, the *New Yorker* makes HGVB its cover story. And this time they name Edmund and Sean and a whole bunch of other people I don't really care about but who are clearly guilty as sin. They note Edmund's emails that prove he knew what was going on. That he had taken HGVB in a direction that pretty much ensured that the bank simply wouldn't differentiate between legal and illegal transactions. Scratch that, it actually seemed to *favor* illegal transactions. After all, I have a bank account and no one from HGVB has ever offered to hide my money from the IRS.

I keep waiting for them to mention Travis.

I keep waiting for someone to be arrested.

And then, two weeks after that, Edmund Gable is dragged before the Senate subcommittee. Of course I take the day off from work for that. No way am I going to miss a second of that testimony. So I pop some corn and dig in for an afternoon of C-SPAN.

Edmund's signature smile is nowhere to be seen as he and his band of lawyers approach the front of the hall. He sits staunchly in front of the committee, a prepared statement placed on the table in front of him.

"It would seem," he says in a strained voice, his eyes glued to the paper, "that despite the best efforts and intentions of many dedicated professionals, HGVB has fallen short of our own expectations, and for that everyone at HGVB is *profoundly* sorry."

Is he kidding?

He's sorry? Oops, seems that I've been knowingly laundering money for some of Mexico's most notorious drug cartels and a bunch of terrorists who may or may not be planning an attack on the United States. My bad! Profoundly sorry about that!

Except he's not saying he's sorry. He's saying *everyone* is sorry. Even in his apology he won't single himself out for scrutiny.

But the Senate isn't buying it. The first senator to question Edmund is a Democrat from Colorado who tears into Edmund for the complete lack of oversight regarding Mexico. "Five years ago the United States identified Rami Azar as a man with ties to certain terrorist organizations. He was placed on the list of individuals that banks operating in the United States are not supposed to do business with. The OFAC list, you're familiar with that list?"

"I am, Senator," Edmund says tersely. I don't remember his complexion being that rosy before. Maybe he's getting too much sun.

"At the time he had an account at HGVB. Azar then transferred his accounts to your Cayman Islands subsidiary. And then, you, sir, wrote an email to your compliance officer in which you said, and I'm quoting here, '*The accounts held in the Caymans are not in the jurisdiction of, and are not housed on any systems in, the United States. Therefore, there is no need to report this match to the OFAC.*' In other words, you *knew* this man was a terrorist, but because his accounts were in a place that we couldn't search you figured you'd just ignore your obligation to report."

"I informed my compliance officer of what the law was. That's all I intended to do."

"The *law* is that you report!" the senator snaps.

Then a Republican from Texas has his turn. He rips into Edmund about the Mexican drug cartel. "Billions of dollars!" he exclaims, his eyes flashing in indignation. "HGVB laundered billions for a drug cartel that has been responsible for kidnapping, torture, beheadings, and this is all in the backyard of the great state of Texas. This is a cartel that is a danger to our people, to *my* people!"

"As the CEO of HGVB, I am not in the position to personally oversee the specific business activities of our Cayman Islands account holders. However, I admit that our compliance with US regulations was not always as vigilant as it should have been."

"*Vigilant?* Forgive me, but it would seem that your compliance was the opposite of vigilant. It was non-existent!"

I smile and toss some more popcorn into my mouth. It's nice to see the Republicans and Democrats so united for once.

And then I get an extra treat. After Edmund vacates his seat he's replaced by my friend Sean White. White's movements are stiff and ungainly as he walks to his designated spot, like he has been thrown back into puberty and all the confidence he had built up as a man is suddenly gone.

And if the senators were harsh with Edmund, they are merciless with White. Was he in charge of staffing the compliance office in Delaware? *Yes.* Did he instruct the supervisor of that department to bypass any and all training that would educate the employees about how to identify money laundering? *Yes.* Did he see this as a problem, considering that the employees were hired to *find* money launderers? White agreed it was. Did he meet with a Raul Gonzales on April 26, 2006? White stammers that he can't be sure of the date. Did he recommend that Mr. Gonzales open an account in the Cayman Islands subsidiary? He admits that it's possible that he had. Was he aware that Mr. Gonzales is a leader in a drug cartel? *Mr. White? Mr. White, please answer the question.*

As I watch White sitting there at the table being grilled by senator after senator, I'm struck by how small he looks. More than small, he looks weak, help-less. It's disconcerting. The man who intimidated me, bullied my mother, destroyed my life—he's a . . . a *nothing*.

At one point in the hearing he starts crying. *Crying*. I've never seen anything like this on C-SPAN before. The senators seem utterly disgusted.

He's going to prison. The idea overwhelms me, knocking every other thought and emotion out of my mind and out of my heart. White is going to prison, not just because he's guilty, but because he's an easy target. Worse than that, he's not important.

But Edmund is.

And Travis is.

Travis . . . who hasn't even been called to testify.

I turn off the TV and stare at the black screen. Sean White, the man I came this close to feeding rat poison to, is going to prison. And he's an ex-cop.

I know what happens to ex-cops in prison.

I sit there awhile waiting for the glee to kick in. But it doesn't happen. Instead I feel hollow and cold.

White is a bad man. I have no sympathy for him at all, and God knows he deserves a long sentence. If he is brutalized by the other inmates I won't feel sorry for him.

But in the end, he's just a foot soldier.

And for some reason, I'm beginning to wonder if I'm as close to getting Travis and Edmund as I think I am.

But of course I'm just being paranoid. I don't care

how important Travis and Edmund are, what they did was blatantly criminal. They'll go to prison.

They have to go to prison.

Don't they?

Lander said they would. Did he mean it? He had to have meant it . . . Right?

You may not want me afterward.

Why had he said that? What had he thought I was going to find out?

For a few minutes I sit in silence, my hands folded in my lap. I want to push the thoughts I'm having out of my head.

And I can't.

But I *have* to! I should have trusted my mother, and when I didn't, I lost her. I lost myself. I have to learn to trust him.

I reach for my phone and call Lander. This time the recorded voice doesn't faze me.

"Lander, I need to talk to you. Tonight."

I hang up the phone.

It's not a choice anymore. I *have* to see him.

He has to *make* me trust him.

chapter twenty-nine

He doesn't call back, but somehow I know he's coming. I pace around the room throughout the day trying to see my new place through his eyes but I can't do it. I can't do it because I'm too distracted. My mind keeps replaying my brief history with Lander. My hatred, my passion, my love. Has there ever been a human being in this world about whom I have felt this consistently conflicted? The tenderness I feel toward him, the caring, the *weakness*—I can't shake any of that.

And yet I know he's not exactly the man I thought he was. Not in the beginning when I thought he was my enemy, and not later when I thought he was my partner.

Because to assume that Lander is my enemy would imply that he's working against me, that he wishes me harm. He isn't and he doesn't, I'm sure of that. But to say that he has ever been my partner would imply that the two of us have been on equal footing, that he's been working with me toward a common goal.

But I don't fully believe that anymore. I believe that Lander is working for himself and that would make him just like me . . . or at least just like the woman I used to be before he had the audacity to alter my worldview.

And I don't know what to do with that.

I imagine suspicion to be like the ghostly gray smoke you get once you blow out a bunch of birthday candles. Slow curling remnants of extinguished flames. You may be too distracted by the celebration to really notice it, unless you take a moment to stop, breathe in, and taste the air.

That's what I'm doing now. I'm tasting the air, and it's beginning to taste a little bitter.

He arrives at six. I spot him through the window, approaching my building as I sip my freshly brewed coffee. It doesn't surprise me that he knows where I live despite never being told. When have I ever *told* Lander anything? All this time he's expressed concern about Micah and the very real possibility that he's watching me. But no one has been watching me as close as Lander.

I buzz him in without bothering to address him through the intercom, put my coffee down on the island that divides the living room from the kitchen, and stand in front of the open door to my apartment, ready for anything.

When he appears he's not wearing a suit. Instead

he's in black denim wash jeans and a lightweight black long-sleeved sweater. There's something about him tonight that puts me in mind of a criminal.

"I assume you're still angry," he says.

I close the door slowly and turn to him, expecting him to be examining the changes that I've made in my life. The posters on the wall, the books organized on the shelves, the hanging fern. But his eyes stay with me, and for a moment I can't decide if his unwavering attention is a compliment or an insult.

"I don't think I'm angry. At least not at you . . . not yet." I go over and retrieve my coffee, sipping it slowly. "Who are you, Lander Gable?" I ask, careful to extract any venom or sarcasm that I might inadvertently express with that question. "What did I sign up for when I signed up with you?"

"People are going to jail, Adoncia. Sean White resigned tonight. And now there might be state charges brought against him as well since he met with this Gonzales person right here in the city."

"He met with Javier too."

"I'm having a hard time proving that. I don't have photos, and to be honest, although I'm pretty clear about what organization Javier works for, I can't really prove that either."

"So White is out of a job and he's *probably* going to jail. But what about Edmund?" I ask. "What about Travis? He hasn't even been called before the committee."

"He has," Lander corrects. "He was subpoenaed, but it didn't look like they were going to call him.

This afternoon they changed their minds. He'll be testifying tomorrow. I will be testifying as well."

"You." I put down my coffee. "And what do you plan to say? What is your goal?"

"You know my goal."

"I don't know that I do." I step forward, put both my hands on his cheeks as I guide his face toward mine. "Lander," I breathe, "I need you to tell me the truth, even if it's ugly. You can lie to every other person in the world, but not me. I need to be able to trust you. Right now I need that more than anything else in the world."

"I know you think I've been cold," he says quietly. "Please try to believe me when I tell you that I hate being away from you. I dream about you, I *fantasize* about you. But I'm just trying to make sure we win." His hands move to my waist. "If we play this right, we *can* win."

"What does winning look like, Lander?" I slide my hands under his shirt, feel the careful craftsmanship of his muscles. I had almost forgotten what he feels like. "What do you want? Do you want the destruction of your family?"

He pulls away, paces around the room. "I'm doing everything I can to ensure that you get your revenge. It's going to happen."

"Yes, but that's not what I asked. Tell me what you want, Lander. Tell me the truth this time. Please, I'm literally begging you, make me trust you."

He stops and turns to me. I can see the determination in his eyes, but I also see the worry. "There are things you may not want to hear . . . but if I can get you what you want—"

"What I want is the truth."

He inhales sharply and turns away, as if considering how to begin. "You may have been right about my mother. It's possible that she chose to make a sacrifice for me. It's possible that's why she didn't tell me about her illness or lack of care."

"Ah." I walk over to my poster of Bellona, as if seeking support from the one woman I've always channeled for strength.

"But," Lander adds vehemently, "without *them* there would have been no sacrifice to make. Travis could have helped her, my father might have been able to save her." He moves into my space, grips my wrist as if he's afraid that he's about to say something that might scare me, as if he needs to hold on to me to keep me from running away. "I want revenge, that wasn't a lie," he says quietly. "The only thing I didn't mention is that I also want more."

And now, with just those few words, I see it *all*.

"You want the company," I say as his grip tightens. "You want the Gable name all to yourself." I shake my head. "For me this has always been about one thing. But for you? It's been about everything. Because that's what you want, isn't it? You want everything."

He stares at me for a moment and now I see a new emotion. Relief.

In an instant his lips are against mine, he's grabbing me, pressing my back against the hard wall as my breasts are crushed against the only slightly more yielding pressure of his body. In that moment I know the source of his longing, I understand why, right now, his need for me is so great.

It comes from knowing that at long last I finally understand him. And I'm the only one who does. And for as long as that's true he will need me.

At times he may hate me for it too.

We have so much in common.

"When this is over, I want to come back to you. But things will be different." I use my free hands to feel the contours of his erection. "You don't make the rules, Lander Gable," I whisper. "You don't get to tell me when it's my turn to play."

"You still want me," he says in a low voice. It's a statement, not a question. "Do you want me now, Adoncia?"

I look into his eyes and whisper, "*Yes.*"

And with that one word the floodgates are released. Months of pent-up passion, frustration, desire, anger, longing . . . it all comes out *now.*

With one hand Lander rips my shirt open, destroying it. Letting go of my arm, he forces down the straps of my bra until it is down to my rib cage, my bra straps restraining my arms to my sides as he leans down to tease my hardening nipples with his tongue and fingers. I moan, arching my back, demanding more.

And he gives it to me. He rips the bra off, leaving it in no better condition than the shirt. I yank off his belt and reach into his pants. I take hold of him and, ever so gently, apply pressure. "My turn," I whisper. I ease my hold and with my free hand I push his pants and boxers to the floor.

He stays perfectly still for a moment, and then suddenly he moves, catching me off guard, pulling my hand away, and then with one leg he sweeps both of mine out from underneath me, like a wrestler. I fall backward, but he catches me before I hit the floor. For a moment I'm stunned, but then his kisses bring me back, making me insane as I claw at him. How dare he stay away for so long. How *dare* he! I claw at his back as he rips away the rest of my clothes and in an instant I feel him enter me as I cry out, pulling him closer, biting his skin. Our savagery is reckless and uncontrolled. As we tussle we roll over and I'm on top now, filled with passion and so much fury. I rock against him violently, and when he grabs my leg I press my hand against his chest, hard, as if holding him down. Fire lights up his eyes and he turns us over again. This time he holds my arms down against the floor as he thrusts inside me. I wrap my legs around him, embracing him, rocking with him even as I struggle to free my hands. And when I do I scratch my fingernails down his back, this time drawing blood.

He cries out in surprise and I immediately use the advantage to turn the tables again, pushing us over once more so that now I'm on top. I put my hand on his throat as I ride him forcefully, thrusting myself onto him. He grabs at my waist, but I grab him by the wrists and push his arms down onto the floor as I continue to set the rhythm. This is my territory, this is my game, this is my *life*. I move forward and back, rocking against him, pushing him so deep inside me that the explosion comes quickly, taking me over as he comes with me, pulsating, filling me, satisfying me with what can only be a victory.

I collapse by his side, staring up at the ceiling, still unable to catch my breath.

Yes, I need Lander. And he needs me.

God help us.

chapter thirty

When Lander left that night we agreed that we would be in contact every five weeks until the Justice Department finally reaches its verdict. Five weeks is too long . . . but so is ten years. Lander's right, I can't risk losing what I've worked for. But on the other hand, I need to know I can count on him. I need to know when I will see him, that I can trust him. That he's more than just a lost dream.

And the next day the loose grip I have on my trust for Lander becomes a little more secure as Travis is called in front of the committee. I make sure I'm in front of the television when it happens, but watching Travis be questioned by the Senate subcommittee isn't as riveting as I expected it to be. Partially because he's too good. Not one question trips him up. *Yes, yes, now that he's reminded, he did meet with this man. No, of course he didn't know he was a crimi-*

nal. He would never associate with criminals. All he knew was that man had been referred by Sean White. A man in Travis's position isn't in charge of verifying the employment of his investors. That's left to others. It would seem that their systems failed them though; anti-money-laundering compliance wasn't what it should be at HGVB.

"But Mr. Gable," one senator says plaintively. "We have been informed that some of the evidence of these criminal transactions was found in your home."

This is the only time that Travis seems genuinely irritated by a question. "I find that surprising since I have never once engaged in correspondence on this matter. Nor have I had any other type of communication that dealt with accounts that were not in compliance with US regulations. It's possible that I have saved some files and emails that I had yet to get around to reading or, in my haste, skimmed without ever fully grasping the meaning of what was being said."

"Are you suggesting that your work is rushed, Mr. Gable? That you aren't smart enough to understand emails from your own employees?"

There's a spattering of uncomfortable laughter from the congressional hall. Travis remains impassive, but I think I see his hand shake, just slightly, as he reaches for his water.

"I have many responsibilities at HGVB. I may, at times, not have been as diligent as I should have been."

I lean forward and wait for the senator to ask him why this information was found not only in Travis's home, but expertly hidden in his closet door. I wait for them to point out that some of the emails—emails *addressed* to him, some written by his own father—were extraordinarily straightforward in their purpose. He'd have to be more than hurried to misunderstand them; he'd have to be severely mentally challenged.

But they don't push *that* hard. They go on about how *people* at the bank knew but they don't specifically accuse Travis of knowing.

It's like some of the articles that cite "an executive" made this or that incriminating statement. The company got the responsibility, not the individuals involved.

But then, this is just a Senate hearing. The Justice Department is the one that will be bringing criminal charges against Travis and Edmund.

But the funny thing is, after all this time, the testimony I'm anxious to hear is not Travis's. And as Travis walks away I find myself sitting on the edge of my secondhand sofa, clutching the cushions beneath me, waiting for *him* to show up on my screen.

And then he does. Lander, walking toward the table, owning the room as if he's about to address eager shareholders, not angry senators. When he takes his seat I notice that he does not have a paper in front of him. The impression being that nothing has formally been prepared.

I know differently.

If he handles this the way I *think* he's going to handle this, I'll know exactly what I'm dealing with.

For once in my life, I feel like I'm one step ahead of Lander.

"HGVB is more than a bank to me," Lander begins. "It was founded in part by my great-great-grandfather, and while it is now a public company, I have always felt that I have a unique responsibility to ensure that it is fulfilling its obligations to its customers, to its shareholders, and to the community as a whole. And when you're talking about a multinational entity, the community is the world."

I shake my head, marveling at the skill with which he delivers his bullshit. "I am younger than my brother, Travis Gable. I have not been working for the bank for as long as he has. Nor am I as well versed on every HGVB policy and bank subsidiary as my father. However, in the short time that I have been building my career at HGVB I have found that there are things happening at this bank that are simply unacceptable. Our compliance officers have failed us. Many of our executives—"

There's that word again.

"—have failed us. Initially, I attempted to address our weaknesses internally, but as the scope of our failings became clear I realized that this had to be dealt with on a national level. As many of you here know, I have done my best to be helpful in this investigation. And while I may not have known about some of the mistakes that were made at HGVB, as a vice president, I feel that I too am responsible for this debacle. On behalf of HGVB Bank, *my* bank, I apologize, although I know that any apology at this point is horribly inadequate. I am here today to answer any questions and concerns you may have and that the American people may have, and to pledge to you that as one of the more recently appointed VPs I will do everything in my power to overhaul systems that are egregiously inefficient and put in place new policies and controls to ensure that nothing like this ever happens again."

"Wow." The word comes out of my mouth like a puff of air. His execution and delivery were perfect. He managed to associate Travis and Edmund with the old guard, the *corrupt* guard, and make himself look like the face of the future of international banking.

And from that moment on the senators are literally eating out of his hand. They throw him softball after softball. When they do slam HGVB, they seem to be almost apologetic about it. They don't want Lander to think they blame *him*.

And yet, while his skill has impressed me, he hasn't surprised me. I do know who I'm dealing with now. He values revenge.

But he values his own advancement more.

My heart is beating against my chest. I left my revenge in the hands of a man who will never care about it the way that I do.

And if something goes wrong, if the people who hurt my mother *don't* pay? I will hold Lander responsible. Before, he got the best of me by drawing me away from my anger. But if he betrays me, if he even fails me, summoning up the anger I'll need to make him suffer will not be a problem.

⚜

When the hearings are over the days begin to blend into one another again, until they become weeks, then a month. We've passed the five-week mark, but I don't know what to ask or what to say. I don't even know where we stand. I don't call Lander. Worse yet, he doesn't call me. But I'm so very aware of him. Sometimes, when I step out onto the streets of New York I think I can feel his presence wrapped up in the chaos and strength of the city. It's inescapable. One night I walk by his building, pausing only momentarily to look up at the towering skyscraper. The wind is unseasonably cold and I clutch at my jacket, pulling it tight, trying to protect myself from the chill.

This is where New Yorkers who rule the world live.

Perhaps the same could be said about where Travis lives and where Edmund lives.

But where does that leave the rest of us?

The question whirls around in my head until I'm dizzy, until I realize that I can't wait any longer for Lander, or the Justice Department, or even the US Senate. It's time to reclaim a little of what I've given away.

⚜

It begins the next day. I wait on the sidewalk on the Upper West Side. I've been reading her emails, I know their schedule.

And at 6:45, exactly when I expect them, Travis and Jessica exit their building. She's dressed for a cocktail party and he's dressed . . . well, like Travis. Crisp eight-thousand-dollar suit, thousand-dollar dress shirt, the only nod to the fact that this is officially a social occasion is his missing tie.

I step out of the shadows as they begin to walk to their waiting limo. "Hi!"

Both Jessica and Travis pivot at the sound of my voice.

It's the first time I've seen Jessica since I quit. She's aged years in the months we've been apart.

You're still young.

Only if you measure age in years.

"Take the limo to the party, I'll catch up with you soon," Travis says coolly to his wife.

"But they're expecting us—"

"Go."

Jessica chews on her cheek and then turns and goes to the limo, each one of her steps a little heavier than the one before.

He waits until the limo rolls away before he approaches.

"Where's Cathy?" I ask with faux innocence.

A flash of anger sparks in his eyes, but he doesn't take the bait. "So, this is what you were up to? You planted some files in my home to help my brother incriminate me?"

A low laugh escapes my lips and I look up at the clear, darkening sky. "I gotta hand it to you, Travis. You're good. You never let your guard down, always staying with the same story, always on the lookout for a wire tap and spies."

"I believe I can return that compliment," he says, not unpleasantly. "I may have found a worthy adversary in you. Speaking of which, I know why my brother is doing this, but what's in it for you?"

"Me?" I place my hands against my heart. "I'm just a concerned citizen, trying to protect my country from those who would exploit its laws for profit."

"I'm serious."

"Well, that's good, because I'm only partially joking. Laundering money for drug cartels, Travis? Do you know what those people do? People are dying, not just other drug dealers but farmers, journalists, innocents whose families can't afford to pay ransom. And you're also funding terrorists. You're a *New Yorker* funding terrorists. You work and live in highrises, for God's sake. Doesn't it ever bother you that the people you're helping might be planning on killing you? Your children? Your wi—actually scratch that one. We all know you're not worried about them killing your wife. But certainly you and your children."

"I have never solicited the money of terrorists."

"But you knew it was being solicited by people at your bank," I point out. "You knew that people at HGVB were scrubbing wire transfers for any mention of country of origin when that country was one that might be sponsoring terrorism."

"Who are you?" Travis asks, clearly unimpressed with my demonstration of moral outrage. "I assume Bell Dantès is your nom de guerre."

I smile, shrug.

"So what did Lander tell you?" he asks. "Did he tell you that this information was going to send me to prison?" The sinister smile that plays on his lips is so familiar it almost makes me nostalgic. "Let me explain the difference between you and me." He takes another step forward, moving more into my space. "If you launder money for a ring of small-time pot dealers and word gets out? The police are going to be on your doorstep within minutes. You'll be thrown in jail. If you've laundered ten thousand dollars or more you'll go to prison. No lawyer would be able to help you. But me? I could be caught laundering money for the most vile, violent crime organization on earth—"

"Which you were."

"—and I still wouldn't get so much as a slap on the wrist. Didn't they tell you? People like me are given get-out-of-jail-free cards at birth. When they look at you they see someone who might need to be straightened out. Someone who may need some discipline. When they look at me? They see someone important. Someone who is not suitable for incarceration."

"You know, Bernie Madoff probably told himself the same thing," I point out.

"Bernie Madoff pissed off some very powerful people."

"You've pissed off the US government."

Travis chuckles. "Yes, it seems I have. Maybe when

they send me another cease-and-desist letter I'll have it framed and give it to you as a gift."

"And you've also pissed *me* off."

Travis's smile shrinks on his lips. "I know that what's happening is part of Lander's plan," he says. "I won't get locked up for it, but he'll advance. And although I don't know exactly who you are, I suspect that your original plan for me was darker."

Again I shrug, refusing to acknowledge that he's right.

"Did he mislead you, Bell? That would be Lander's style." He puts his hand in his jacket pocket and surveys the stream of pedestrians as they hurry past each other, all focused on their destinations or their phones, never really seeing what's around them. "It's funny," he says. "You clearly think that I'm the bad brother. That I'm the one who deserves your wrath. But I've only misled you once, that time when I sent you to meet L.J., who sold you Tylenol crushed to look like cocaine. And even then I revealed the truth pretty quickly. On the whole I've been very straightforward with you, and to my memory I've never lied to you. Can you say the same about Lander?"

When I don't answer he releases an exaggerated sigh. "It would be a pity if it turns out you picked the wrong brother to ally yourself with. But if you're confident that Lander's going to come through for you and that I'll end up going to prison for this nonsense, perhaps you'd be interested in a little wager? If I go to prison I'll give you a hundred—no, let's say five hundred thousand dollars. If I get off without so much as a personal fine? Well, let's see . . . I assume you don't have half a million dollars at your disposal. But L.J. told me that you're in need of a spanking, and I'm beginning to think he's got a point. So if you lose I'll have both you and L.J. come into my office, you'll pull down whatever undergarments you have on, bend over his knee, and he'll give you a few good whacks for the entertainment of me and a few male HGVB shareholders who you've inconvenienced. Perhaps afterward we can all watch that tape of Lander fucking you in the conference room. What do you say, do we have a bet?" He pauses a moment. "No? Not that confident?" He smiles again and taps his finger lightly against the side of my head. "You see? You're not that stupid after all."

"Neither are you, Travis," I say, my voice so low he has to lean forward to hear me. "You know that I'm more dangerous than your brother ever was or ever will be, because unlike him, I have nothing to lose." I reach out and smooth his lapel. "You better pray that they do send you to prison for this. Because if the rules don't work for me, I'll change them. You won't see me coming. You won't know what to expect. This will get *dark*." I pause a beat, letting the weight of my words sink in. Then I smile the sweetest, most innocent smile in the world. I give his chest a light, friendly pat. "You should go. Your wife's waiting."

As I turn and walk away I feel satisfied that I've gotten my point across. But I pray that my small speech was simply showmanship for showmanship's sake. I pray that the Justice Department will do what it's meant to do: dole out justice. And of course it will. This is *bigger* than that whole Madoff thing. I try to imagine how I'll react when I receive the news that Travis is about to be locked up for money laundering. But I can't.

I can't quite imagine it happening at all.

chapter thirty-one

Exactly two weeks later I wake up to a newswoman's voice floating through my iHeartRadio alarm. "It's the biggest penalty every paid by a bank to the US government."

I jump out of bed, still half-dazed with sleep but aware that the world is shifting on its axis.

"HGVB will pay $1.9 billion dollars to settle allegations of money laundering."

I blink at my cell phone. Did she just say settle?

The voice switches to an audio clip of an announcement made by an official of the US Justice Department. "Today HGVB is paying a heavy price for its conduct."

What did she mean, *settle*?

"US officials also say that HGVB allowed countries such as Iran, Cuba, and Syria to do business in the United States," the newswoman continues, "allowing them to evade US sanctions."

And they switch to a Justice Department official: "In the end, HGVB's wholly inadequate anti-money-laundering practices and procedures left dangerous gaps that criminals readily exploited and abused."

I look around the room, looking for some kind of sign that I'm still asleep. Surely this can't be real; they're making it sound like HGVB was just careless, like they were inept and therefore taken advantage of. *But that's not what happened!* The Justice Department has emails proving that Edmund, Travis, Sean, and many others *knew* what was going on! Not only did they know, they did their best to accommodate the criminals, they *solicited* their business!

"As part of its settlement, HGVB has agreed to overhaul its compliance department," the woman's voice says. "In exchange the Justice Department agreed to defer prosecution indefinitely. They stopped short of leveling charges against individuals for criminal conduct."

Everything in the room falls out of focus. I can hear that the newswoman is still talking, but I have no idea what she's saying. I've lost the capacity to understand words.

I reach out my hand to steady myself against the wall.

There's a mistake. I heard them wrong, there's a mistake.

I blink my eyes a few more times, try to understand, try to focus on the woman's voice. "At a press conference, Justice officials were repeatedly questioned as to whether or not they thought the penalty went far enough."

"It's a fiction to suggest that this isn't a very robust result," I hear a man explain, his voice coming through scratchy and strained. "We've gone after the traffickers, we've gone after the cartels, and we've held a financial institution accountable."

But the cartels and traffickers were helped by individuals in the bank!

"However, if we had taken more extreme measures against HGVB, it would have had reverberations throughout the financial sector and cost thousands of jobs."

The financial sector? Thousands of jobs?

Only two jobs needed to be lost: Edmund's and Travis's.

They still had their jobs!

My breathing is coming too fast, I'm on the verge of hyperventilating.

And then everything just slows down; my breathing, my thoughts, my heart. I'm barely aware of having a pulse. The only thing that beats in my breast is a pounding, uncontrollable rage.

I place my hand against my poster of Bellona and with one hand I slowly rip it in half.

chapter thirty-two

I call in sick to work. It's the third day in a row I've done that and I can tell that Mandy is losing patience, but I don't care. For a short while my focus had been broadened. For a blink of an eye I had imagined a life that didn't center around revenge and justice. This is the consequence of a blink. But now my focus, my hatred, and my voracious appetite for vengeance—it's all back. And it's those things that are driving me to HGVB.

When I arrive I go straight to Lander's floor. As I ride up in the elevator the walls seem too close, the speed of my elevation too slow, like it's trying to contain me. When the doors open I burst out and stride to Lander's office as the receptionist at the front desk rushes after me, telling me I need permission to go to the executive offices.

The word *executive* crawls under my skin like a

hated parasite. I find myself clenching my fists and picking up my pace as the receptionist calls for help. I fling the door open to Lander's office. He's there, standing behind his desk as three other men in suits are in various positions around the room, all leaning in toward Lander.

Lander, impeccably dressed and perfectly in his element, is commanding the room like . . . like a *Gable*. Like he *belongs* here, running this evil empire! Everyone here is focused on him . . . until they hear that door open and slam against the wall, and then their focus turns to me.

Before I can even open my mouth security is there. Two guards grab me by the arms and try to pull me away as I struggle.

"It's all right," Lander says, raising his voice above the chaos. "Leave her be, I'll see her."

As the guards loosen their grip, Lander turns to the other men in the room. "We'll continue this later."

"But, Mr. Gable, this must be dealt with immediately. The press—"

"—will wait," Lander finishes for him. "Everyone can wait. Nothing in this settlement says that we have to work on a schedule set by CNN."

The men look at each other and then reluctantly file out of the room as the security guards back away.

When the last man is gone and the door is closed, Lander finally turns his full attention to me. "I know what you're thinking."

I walk up to his desk, let my fingers caress the phone, black with dozens of buttons all designed to immediately connect Lander to a different department in this evil institution. In one swift move I pick it up and hurl it across the room, so it crashes against the wall. I then use my arms to sweep almost everything else off his desk, watching it clatter to the floor. I reach for the computer monitor that is still resting there and shove it off too.

The door to Lander's office is flung open again. Once again it's the receptionist and a security guard by her side, but Lander holds up his hand to stop them. "Just had a little mishap," he explains to them sternly. "Please, no more interruptions."

Again, the intruders back out as I stand before him, my chest heaving, my teeth clenched.

He clasps his hands behind his back and surveys the damage on the floor. "I don't blame you for being angry."

"You promised me." The words come out as a growl. "You said we'd get them. You said they'd pay. This was the course that *you* put us on. This is *your* plan, a plan that you wanted me to leave in your hands for . . . what did you call it? The last lap of the relay? You lost the fucking race, Lander! You lost it for both of us!"

"It's not over," Lander says. His tone is soothing, gentle. It makes me want to scratch out his eyes. "I'm still looking for angles—"

"*We're not supposed to need another angle!*" I scream. "This *was* the angle! The truth! We get them on money laundering, on trading with the enemy, on working with *drug cartels*. You said we had enough.

That was you. My God, Travis and Edmund haven't even lost their jobs!"

"My father handed in his resignation less than twenty minutes ago," Lander says. "The board is insisting on it. It's a blow to him; he lives for his job."

"Oh, oh does he?" I put my hands over my heart in mock sympathy. "You know what my mother lived for? Me. She lived for me and she lived for the hope of a brighter future. They took *all* of that! She died alone and in disgrace! And wait, wait." I back up and hold my hand up as if anticipating an interruption. "Let me see if I can get this right. I'm guessing that Edmund is going to say that this resignation has nothing to do with the hearings. He's just getting a little too old for this shit and he wants to spend some chill time on his yacht."

"He's drafting a statement to give to the press now. It will undoubtedly be delicately worded."

"*He's* crafting the statement? So he gets to be the one to put the spin on this? Wow. That's just . . . Wow. What's his golden parachute?"

"Adoncia, try to hear me. I'm not done with these people."

"How much is the severance package, Lander?"

Lander hesitates a moment and then sighs heavily. "When you add it up, stock options and all, it comes to a little over sixty million dollars."

I stand there, stock-still.

"I know this looks bad."

"Oh my God." The words come out a little above a whisper.

"Like I said, this isn't over. And while Travis hasn't been pushed out yet, I am working on it."

"Why?" I ask, still too out of breath to raise my voice again. "So he can get a thirty-million-dollar severance package?"

"My father's reputation is destroyed," Lander continues. "He will no longer have any say in the company that his great-grandfather founded. He is no longer the almighty and powerful captain of industry. And when I find a way to reopen your mother's case—"

"HGVB had to pay $1.9 billion to the United States government. What percentage of profits is that for your company?"

"Don't do this, Adoncia. It was never about HGVB. It was about Travis, and Edmund and Sean."

"All of whom were brought together and motivated by HGVB. Everything they've done has been under the protective umbrella of this organization. What's the percentage?'

"I don't know the exact percentage."

"Lander."

He pauses, his eyes wandering to the window before coming back to me. "It's the equivalent of one month's profits."

Again I put my hand over my heart, but now it's not in mockery, it's in response to actual pain.

"The plan was never to bring down HGVB," Lander persists. "This is my company too, Adoncia. And now, with my father out of my way and Travis handicapped by scandal, I will be able to reshape this bank. I'm going to be a pivotal part of its leadership, and in the not-too-distant future I will be named the youngest CEO of a top-tier bank in the world. I'm going to run this place the way it *should* be run. I will reclaim and redefine the Gable name. Travis and Edmund, they will have nothing by the time I'm done and I . . . I . . ."

"You will have everything," I finish for him. "That's always what this has been about for you. Not revenge but ambition. I was right . . . I was right and I didn't stop you."

"You couldn't have stopped me."

I shake my head, almost in awe of his audacity. He's standing before me, the light of the city at his back, tapping his fingers against the bare surface of his desk. Part of my brain registers that he seems nervous, worried, maybe even hurt. But then, what does that matter? In a world where the rich and powerful can get away with crimes that if perpetrated by anyone else would result in life sentences, what is it exactly that matters?

"Micah's in a panic," Lander says, stepping to the side of the desk, bringing himself a little closer to me. "He knows that his accounts are this close to being confiscated by the Feds, which means he's in trouble with the other members of his organization. He also knows that the people of other crime organizations, like Javier, will feel that Micah misled them about the security of HGVB. He's left the country, and if he comes back I'll make sure he regrets it." Again, Lander moves closer. "I won't let him hurt you. I won't let any of them hurt you."

"They already have," I whisper.

"No, listen, I will do everything I can to get your mother's case reopened. I've hired an investigator. He'll be contacting you soon. And in light of White's current disgrace, I was finally able to convince the DA to look at the case again. It's still going to be tricky, because White was a cop, and sometimes cops look out for their own, so records may *disappear*." He uses his fingers to make quotation marks around that last word. "There are no guarantees, but there's a chance. And in the meantime I will bring my father and brother low at every opportunity. Do you hear me?" He steps forward once more and takes my face in his hands. "They will have *nothing*."

"Your definition of nothing is skewed," I say dully. "Sixty million dollars isn't nothing." I pull away from him, sink into a small leather sofa placed against the wall. "The only person who's leaving with nothing is me."

"No," Lander says sternly. He sits by my side, putting his hands over mine. "I won't allow that. And you don't need to leave. Not long ago you said that we could be together, and now it's true. Stay with me, Adoncia. I will protect you and I will work with you. We can claim the power that Edmund and Travis are being forced to relinquish, but we'll use it differently. We can have luxury and wealth and everything that comes with it without losing our souls. We won't let up on *them*, but we won't let them consume us either. We'll have rich, full lives. We'll be happy. And that, *that* can be part of our revenge."

I feel the tears stinging my eyes as I gently pull my hands away. "I'm sorry, Mr. Gable," I say, my voice hoarse with emotion. "But I would rather leave with my version of nothing than be part of your version of everything."

I think I hear him call after me as I rush out, but I can't be sure.

And besides, it doesn't really matter.

chapter thirty-three

Down in the subway station, waiting for the train, I study the backs of my hands. Holding them out before me, my fingers outstretched, looking at the veins, the bones, the skin, the things that make me *me*. I know what I've walked away from. I know most women would think I was crazy. Hell, there are probably people right here in the subway station who think I'm crazy, this quiet woman with decent clothes and wild hair who can't stop staring at her hands.

The thing is, I don't know how to live the life that Lander wants me to live. I don't know how to accept injustice. Part of me knows that my inability to do so is a flaw. There are so *many* injustices in this world. To paraphrase a line in Neil Gaiman's *American Gods*, if we let the pain and injustice of the world touch us too deeply we'll become cripples or saints . . . and I'm no saint.

And besides, Lander isn't asking me to simply find ways to live with *any* injustice. He's asking me to be by his side knowing that his brother and father have gotten away with heinous crimes. That among many other things, they're probably going to get away with locking up my mother. His suggestion that I satisfy myself with taking Edmund and Travis down a peg or two whenever the opportunity presents itself and hoping that *maybe* we'll find the evidence to prove that they set my mother up for murder, it's not enough for me.

It shouldn't be enough for anyone.

My train arrives and I step inside the nearest car, finding a seat on the sideways bench along the wall. I feel almost hollow, almost. Because there is *something* there. Deep down I feel it; it's the low, pulsing rhythm of my anger, just waiting for me to tap into it again, waiting for me to give it strength, direction, and purpose.

How very familiar.

I think back on how Lander told me that I had turned revenge into a reason to live. And now I really see it. Because every one of us needs a reason to live. We can't just exist. That doesn't work. Sometimes people survive simply because their particular battle for survival is so intense it becomes a war. If they live, they win. If they die, they don't. You see this phenomenon in refugees, in the homeless, in the oppressed.

People can live for war. *I* lived for war. It's such a tangible thing. A *vitalizing* thing. Anyone can tell you that if you want to really feel alive all you need to do is put your life on the line. But of course my war wasn't over my personal survival. I may have been torn from my mother, but I'm not a refugee. I made my war with the Gables.

But Lander isn't offering me a new war, only a watered-down version of the old one. I'm not even sure if he's offering me love. He's never said the words. I know who he is now, but I still don't really know how he feels.

Maybe, *maybe* I could live for love. But I can't live for ambiguity. More to the point, I can't live for an idea that can be so easily yanked away from me. Not again.

So I'll go back to my base camp and draw up a new battle plan, one just as fierce and challenging as the last one, but one more likely to end in a clear victory. Because when all is said and done, vengeance and war are the only things I can count on. They may challenge me, but they'll never leave me.

❧

After getting off the train, when I'm about a block away from home I notice someone sitting on the bottom step of my building. A woman. And as I draw closer I see who it is. Jessica. She has her legs stretched in front of her, crossed at the ankle, unmindful of the fact that she's sitting on the ground while wearing a twelve-hundred-dollar dress.

"Hi," she says when I finally reach her. "I was wondering if you might like to join me for a cup of coffee."

We take a cab all the way down to the Village. Her choice, not mine. But I'm literally bursting with curiosity now, so much so that if she had suggested we get coffee in New Jersey I might have agreed just for the opportunity to hear whatever it is she has to say.

We sit in a little independently owned café. Jessica is using both her hands to cradle a white porcelain cup, a perfectly crafted milky heart hovering on top of her specialty latte. I had opted for just plain old coffee. I'm done with putting on pretenses for Jessica.

She really does look worse for wear. There are dark circles under her eyes and new creases on her forehead. She's gained a little weight too, which isn't such a bad thing since she was ballerina-skinny before, but it's surprising. The one thing Jessica had always seemed to be in control of was her appearance, and designer clothing aside, it looks as if she's begun to let that go.

I wait for her to introduce a topic, but when she doesn't I sigh and tap the toe of my shoe against the dark wood floor impatiently. "You look like you haven't been getting a lot of sleep."

"I haven't had a drink or a pill in seventy-one days. Although Travis doesn't know that," she says tersely. "I swear, sobriety has very little to recommend it."

I look again at her dark circles and the way she's clutching her cup. She might be telling the truth. "If you hate being sober so much, why did you stop with all the . . ." I wave my hand in the air as if gesturing to all the substances Jessica likes to abuse.

"I had to. I had to be alert. I needed to be able to focus on what's going on."

"You mean the HGVB scandal?"

"Oh dear lord, why would I care about that?" She shakes her head impatiently. "No, no, my husband has been seeing Cathy Lind!"

"Ah." I sip my coffee. "Well, that can't surprise you. You were always accusing everyone of sleeping with your husband, why not her?"

"She's different."

"Yes, I agree," I say blandly, then glance over toward the register as one of the cashiers calls out a name for a ready order.

"Cathy Lind has a wealthy husband," Jessica goes on. "And I'm sure he had her sign an ironclad prenup before they married. If she's risking all that it's because she feels certain that Travis is about to get rid of me."

"I hear there are reviews for divorce attorneys on Yelp."

"I didn't say he was going to divorce me, I said he's going to get rid of me."

I pause, my coffee cup halfway to my lips.

"I know too much for him to let me just walk away, Adoncia."

Slowly, *very* slowly, I put my cup down, my eyes glued to hers. "You know my name," I say quietly.

"I've known it for some time," Jessica replies, falling back into her chair, looking suddenly bored. "I used to worry about you, you know. The little girl who had lost her mother to prison. I tracked you for a few years after the trial. I even donated money to a youth program one of your foster families tried to get you involved in. I *cared*. And then you show up with the clear intention of ruining my life. *That's* what I get for caring."

"You lied under oath." My voice is so low, so steady, so perfectly couched in anger.

Jessica shifts uncomfortably in her seat. "We all do what we have to do. That's the world we live in. That's how it *works*."

"My mother died in prison."

"Your mother was a home wrecker."

"She didn't deserve to die."

"Well, she didn't deserve a happy ending either." Jessica drums her fingers against the table. "Nick Foley had children, both still in their teens, when your mother started sleeping with him. Did you ever worry about what happened to *them*?"

"They both went to college. One's in advertising and the other's a podiatrist."

"Exactly! They could have been at the top of New York's social hierarchy, but they were so traumatized by their father's affair it affected their grades and they were forced to settle for second-rate universities. Now they have to spend their days listening to commercial jingles and touching other people's feet!"

"Jesus, you're a bitch."

Jessica raises her eyebrows in a passing indication of annoyance tempered with a degree of indifference.

I lean forward, resting my elbows on the table. "Forgive me for saying this, Jessica, but you don't come across as a woman who is legitimately in fear for her life."

Jessica's demeanor shifts to something steadier and more serious. Her gaze moves out to the street and for a moment she just watches the stream of pedestrians pass us by. "I'm not sure that I'm afraid," she says, her tone almost meditative. "I'm not sure that it won't be a relief . . . dying, that is. And yet, he's taken so much from me. I don't know if I have it in me to let him take anything more, not even a life I don't want. And if he does?" She turns her eyes back to me. "He's going to have to pay a very steep price for it. You can help me with that, but you can't be as clumsy or impetuous as you were last time."

I shake my head. "I'm not sure I know what you're referring to."

"The flash drive you found in the closet door. I could have told you that the information on there wasn't strong enough to get Travis indicted. The only reason I put it there is because those were all the files and evidence I had been able to gather to date, and if something happened to me I wanted to be sure that the police found *something*. And of course I wanted them to find the keys."

I can feel my mouth slowly dropping open. "You? You put it there?"

"Yes, that was me."

"And you've been gathering evidence against HGVB?"

"Oh dear God, are you slow? *Yes!* Obviously I did or I wouldn't have had anything to put on that flash drive!"

I stare at this woman who I have spent so much time with. This woman who I have given so little credit to. This woman who I imagined as a bitter but hapless victim of Travis's brutality.

And at the end of *The Sixth Sense* you realize that the movie you've been watching isn't the movie you thought it was at all.

"But you encrypted the files," I point out.

"If I didn't have them encrypted no one would have believed they belonged to Travis."

"You hid it so well. I only stumbled upon it by chance. It might *never* have been found."

"Yes, I worried about that, but if I didn't hide it well Travis would have found it. Anyway, I thought I had more time to work that detail out."

"Why the keys?"

Jessica lifts her chin. A few tables over someone's cell phone is ringing. In line a woman's rocking a crying child in her arms. But as far as I'm concerned the only two people here are Jessica and me.

"Have you seen it?" she hisses. "His little love nest?"

"It hasn't been used."

"It's being used now."

I mouth the word *oh* and pick up my coffee.

"There's a safe," Jessica continues. "It's behind the

books on the bottom row of the bookshelf. I'm a little worried about it. If Travis or Cathy decide to read any of those books they'll find it."

"Wait a minute, *you* had that safe installed?"

"Don't worry, I was very careful to make it look like Travis did that. I got his receptionist to convince him to consider buying a safe. He went to the store, talked to the merchant about it, but left without buying. Then his assistant"—Jessica points to herself to imply that she played the part of the assistant—"called the store to say Mr. Gable had changed his mind. I had it charged to his credit card and installed in his little . . . little . . ." She scrunches up her face as if she can't think of a term vile enough. "Den of iniquity!" she finally spits out, clearly unsatisfied with the phrase. "The combination is 5-7-01. That's the date they met. It's in some stupid little Valentine's Day card she gave him eons ago. Can you believe it? He's kept her *cards*!"

"Jessica, what's in the safe?" I ask urgently.

"Everything you need to put Travis and Edmund away for the conspiracy to commit murder. I do believe that's what they call it. Conspiracy? When someone helps to plan a murder but isn't necessarily the one to pull the trigger?"

"Wait . . . are you saying . . ."

"It's the evidence that will prove that Travis and Edmund were responsible, at least in part, for both Nick's death and your mother's incarceration. Unfortunately, it's probably enough to convict me too, for bearing false witness, that is." She pauses and sucks in a shaky breath as I sit across from her in stunned silence.

She has evidence. I try to make the words make sense in my mind. Try to find a hint of jest or deception in her face. But instead I just see her lower lip quiver. For a moment I think she's going to cry.

"I thought your mother was guilty," she whispers. "Travis, Edmund, they *assured* me she was guilty. And Travis . . . he framed it like it was some kind of test. That if I could just tell this one little lie in the name of justice, for his family, for *him*, then he would know I was the kind of woman he could spend the rest of his life with. I was so young, I thought I was in love. By the time I realized the truth . . . it was too late. I knew too much. I had *done* too much."

She looks at me, her eyes pleading for some kind of verbal response, some expression of understanding, but I can't even move.

"He took my youth," she continues. She's speaking so softly now I have to strain to hear her. "He took my innocence, my heart, my self-respect, and my future and he tore them all to shreds."

She reaches forward, puts her hand on top of mine. I jump, almost as shocked by the gesture as by what she's telling me. Jessica has never touched me before.

"Please," she says, "tell my children that. Tell my children that I made a mistake but that I wasn't evil. Please tell them that."

I'm still incapable of a response. It's all too much. I feel dizzy and sick and . . . and hopeful. This morning my world was in ruins and here, amid the rubble and dust, is hope.

"Make sure he is charged with both murders," she whispers. "It's time he pays for taking Nick's life." Then she stands up, hesitating only a moment before adding, "And it's time he pays for destroying mine."

chapter thirty-four

The coffee shop is exactly four city blocks away from the apartment Travis got for Cathy. I run the entire way. People look at me as if I might be running either to catch a purse snatcher or because I *am* a purse snatcher. But I don't care. I push past them, totally indifferent to their judgments. The hard soles of my flats pound against the pavement. I can already feel the blisters forming but *I just don't care*.

When I get to the front of the building, sweat is trickling from my hairline, my breathing is rapid, my pulse even faster. I fish in my bag for the key and let myself in. I take the stairs up to the fourth floor two at a time and I almost jam my key into the door to the apartment before my brain kicks in. I step back while I attempt to steady myself and then, as quietly as possible, I put my ear to the door. I wait, five seconds, ten, twenty. I don't hear anything. I have to take this chance. I press my key inside the lock and carefully, slowly, open the door. Once it's open a crack I wait again, listening.

Nothing.

"Thank God," I whisper. It's only then that I realize how close I am to tears.

When I step inside, the cobwebs are gone. The thick layers of dust have been wiped away and there are a few things that have clearly been handled and left out of place. Jessica's right, this apartment is getting used. How often is anyone's guess.

And again, *I don't care.*

I manage to move stealthily through the apartment until I get to the safe. In less than thirty seconds I have it open.

Inside is a digital voice recorder that looks like it's about seven or eight years old.

I retrieve a tissue from my purse, planning on using it as a barrier between the device and my skin. I don't know what's on this thing and until I do I can't risk having my fingerprints on it. But my hand is shaking so hard even unfolding a Kleenex proves difficult. I want to listen to it now. *Right* now.

But what if Travis shows up? Or Cathy? I can't risk it. I can't do anything that might screw this up.

Somehow I manage to get the recorder out of the safe without dropping it. I use another Kleenex to wipe my prints off the safe after I close it, and then, on unsteady feet, I make my retreat. I'm holding the recorder in my hand, and as I flag down a taxi on the street I'm struck by what that may mean.

My future, my past, my pain, and my justice . . . it all may now be in my hands.

I don't dare listen to the recording device while in the cab, but waiting is sheer torture. As soon as I get home I race to my apartment and find a spot on the living room floor, right beneath the torn Bellona poster. I put the recorder in front of me and stare at it, my finger hovering over the play button.

What truths will I discover? What lies? Was it all a trick? The very idea that I should trust Jessica about *anything* seems ludicrous. Am I being set up?

I put a hand to my hairline, pressing the base of my palm hard into my forehead. I'm so tired of constantly second-guessing everything. It's like I'm living inside the twilight zone, never knowing what reality is true and what is deception, always trying to find the implication of every gesture, always looking for the angle. Then again, maybe that's just normal, everyday life. All any of us can do is get as much information as we can and then we make decisions about who and what to trust based on that. Now all I need is the courage to get the information.

I close my eyes, silently count to ten, and then I press the play button.

"I lied for you, Travis! You asked me to lie under oath and I did it, for you!"

It's Jessica's voice. She sounds younger, but the

lilt and tone are an exact match. There's no mistaking it.

"*You did. And now you're guilty of perjury in a homicide case. What do you think will happen to you if you come forward with that information?*"

And that's definitely Travis. No one else has the ability to sound so sophisticated while simultaneously coming across as a complete asshole.

"*I felt like I had to! I was scared, and I was young . . . besides, you told me this Julieta woman was guilty!*"

"*I never said that,*" Travis says mildly. "*I told you what kind of woman she was, about her affair with Nick, and you jumped to your own conclusions.*"

"*No, no, no, you may not have said the words Julieta Jiménez is guilty, but you definitely led me to believe that! If I had known the truth I never would have lied under oath! Not even for . . . for . . .*"

"*For the promise of becoming a Gable?*" Travis's voice is icy. "*That's why you lied, not because you thought she was guilty or because you were afraid. You lied because you wanted to be Mrs. Travis Gable. And now you are. I don't see the problem.*"

"*You said you loved me!*" Jessica cries.

"*Yes, I did lie about that.*"

"*Who pulled the trigger, Travis? Was it you? Was it that sleazy Romenov person? Was it that disgusting little cop you paid off . . . What was his name, Whitman? Williams? No, White, was it White?*"

"*I doubt it, but you'd have to ask my father for*

confirmation on that. If it was up to me, Nick never would have died. There are neater and easier ways to keep people quiet. Ways that don't lead to spending a lifetime in hell with you."

"You said you loved me," she says again, softer this time.

"We've been over this."

"Do you still love her? *Are you in love with Cathy, Travis?"*

"This conversation has become dull."

"Julieta had a little girl . . . We took a mother away from her little girl!"

"I did no such thing. I did not testify in that trial. You did. If you want someone to blame, look in the mirror. Here." There's a pause, some rustling in the background. *"Take one of these."*

"What is it?" she asks weakly.

"Something to calm you. And by the way, Jessica? If you ever say a word about this to anyone you will live to regret it. I'll make sure that you're the one who goes to prison . . . that is, unless my father decides to deal with you first, his way."

Footsteps, someone leaving the room, Jessica's quiet sobs, and then . . . nothing.

Slowly, I reach for the recorder, pick it up, and press it against my heart. "Mamá." It's the only word I can manage to say.

How many years have I been looking for ways to get justice? How many devious plans have I come up with?

And now all of a sudden, I don't *need* a devious plan. I have the truth.

And this time the truth is going to fucking work for me. The Feds don't want to put the Gables away? Fine. Let New York's DA do it.

I get up and walk over to my phone and then stop. Lander told me about how the cops might try to cover for White. I don't know if I believe that or not, but perhaps this should go straight to the DA.

I pick up the phone and instead of dialing 911, I call Lander.

"Adoncia," he says, picking up on the first ring, not bothering with hello.

"I have it," I say quietly.

"Have it? Have what?"

"Everything."

He pauses, unsure of what I mean.

"I mean . . . I have my . . . my mother's justice. There's a . . . a recording and . . . Lander, it's all here. I can make them all pay: Travis, White, Edmund, Jessica . . ." My voice trails off.

"Adoncia, what are you talking about?"

But I barely hear him. Once again I'm staring at the recorder.

Why would Jessica give this to me? She knows what will happen to her. This was only supposed to come out in the event of her death and she hasn't died yet . . .

Make sure he is charged with both murders.

Oh no.

"Adoncia, are you still there?"

Tell my children that I made a mistake but that I wasn't evil. Please tell them that.

"Lander, we have to find Jessica."

"What?"

"I'm going to the penthouse. We have to get to Jessica right now."

chapter thirty-five

I give the cab driver an extra fifty dollars to get me to Travis and Jessica's building as quickly as possible. But it doesn't seem to help much. He stops at each stop sign and red light even as I scream at him to run them.

"You gonna pay me three hundred dollars on top of the fifty?" the driver asks. "Because that's the cost of running a red. How about my medallion? You gonna cover the cost of losing that? Or my medical bills if we get in an accident? This is my life we're talking about here!"

Yes, I want to scream. *That's exactly it! We're talking about the value of a life!* But I hold my tongue. The cabbie won't understand what I'm talking about and even if he does, he might not care. *I* shouldn't care!

But I do. Perhaps, as Lander once suggested, it's because I understand that all life has value. Or maybe it's something else, some deeply buried feeling or compulsion I don't understand. All I know is that I have to get to Jessica, now. So I keep egging on the driver until he's so sick of me he speeds up just so he can get rid of me faster. I clutch the door handle while he takes the fast turns and I try to will all the traffic lights away.

But when the cab finally comes screeching to a stop I can see that Lander has beaten me here. He's standing on the sidewalk across the street from the building.

In fact, there's a large crowd across the street from Travis's building, all staring at the police cars and ambulance that have assembled on the street.

The adrenaline that has been coursing through me slips away, just like that. Slowly opening the cab door, making my way to Lander's side through a crowd of whispering voyeurs, every move seems clumsy and futile.

"Lander," I whisper as I grab his arm. I don't know what else to say.

"She went through the window," Lander says dully. "Fell to her death."

I open my mouth but no sound comes out. I stare at the ambulance, stare at the yellow police tape blocking off a segment of the sidewalk.

Lander takes a deep breath. "Neighbors say they heard her screaming. Travis was there. From the little information I'm getting he's saying that she went crazy. That she lunged toward the window with that metal stepladder of theirs. He's claiming she broke the window with it, that she jumped before he had time to react to any of it."

"And the police?"

"I don't think they're buying it."

"Lander, where are the kids?"

"They've been out all day, school, then off with the nanny as usual. She has them at her place now. I don't think anyone's told them yet."

I sink down onto the pavement, pulling my knees to my chest. I'm surrounded by strangers, people who barely notice the woman who sits at their feet. My eyes follow the ambulance as it slowly pulls away. It's in no hurry at all. Not anymore.

Jessica lied about my mother under oath. She helped take my mother away from me. When I worked for her she never missed an opportunity to demean me.

She was not a good person.

But she gave me my justice.

Two police officers come out of the front entrance of the building. They're escorting a man in handcuffs. They're escorting the devil.

Slowly I rise again as Travis is brought toward a police car. He pauses a moment as they open the back door. His icy blue eyes look past the cops, past the car, all the way to the other side of the street.

And his eyes meet mine.

We just stand there, staring at each other, the hate, the anger, and the understanding that exist between us so strong they're almost tangible.

The moment lasts for five seconds. Five seconds that last forever.

And then the police help him in, pushing his head down so he doesn't accidentally bang it against the patrol car.

Lander puts his hand on my back, between my shoulder blades.

It's a horrible day.

But it's also the day that I am given my version of *everything*.

chapter thirty-six

Seventy-two hours passed before Lander called and requested to meet me. He didn't say why, and I didn't ask. He wants to see me and for the moment that feels like enough of a reason to oblige.

We agreed to meet at a café, but I'm fifteen minutes late. I was with a client at Callow's and I couldn't afford to pass him off to Mandy, not after missing so much work during the HGVB trials. But secretly I'm glad I'm late; it gives me a chance to observe him through the window as he sits at a table and meditatively stirs his coffee. It's an odd gesture because Lander takes his coffee black.

I step inside and as the door closes behind me he shifts his position. I think he senses me, but he doesn't look up until I'm at the table, until he's rising from his seat and pulling out my chair with the solicitude of a nineteenth-century gentleman.

"Thank you," he says as I sit. He doesn't say what he's thanking me for but I get the distinct feeling that he's simply thanking me for showing up. It's all very humble, and not like Lander at all.

I nod toward his cup as he takes his place across from me. "Is the coffee any good here?"

"I don't know," he says, his lips curving into a self-deprecating smile. "I haven't tasted it. I felt I should order something so . . ." He gestures to the cup before pushing it to me. "Take it if you like, It's not what I came for."

"And what did you come for, Lander?"

"I came for you, Adoncia."

Around us there is the sound of cups clicking against saucers, of the chatter and quiet laughter of other patrons, just the sounds of normal life.

Normality isn't something I've ever been comfortable with. I know Lander isn't either. It's why we fit . . . or at least, it's why I thought we fit.

"Braden and Mercedes?" I ask as I raise the coffee to my lips.

"They're in shock," he says quietly. He leans back in his chair, a subtle look of confusion crossing his features. "I'm a little shocked myself. The police told me they talked to you yesterday. That you told them that Travis had an apartment that no one knew about."

"Well, obviously I knew about it."

"And I didn't. Was that what the keys were for? The ones we found in his closet?"

I smile in acknowledgment of both the correct

assessment and my decision to keep him in the dark about Travis's hideaway. I reach for a packet of sugar placed in a small container in the middle of the table and dump the contents into my cup.

"I thought you took your coffee black, like me," Lander notes.

"I'm trying something new," I say smoothly. "I don't seem to have the same craving for bitterness that I did before."

Lander observes me for a moment, his expression completely unreadable. "Why didn't you tell me about the apartment?"

"Because I'm a secretive person," I answer simply before looking up, locking him in my gaze. "So are you. You've always said we are alike."

He gives me an almost imperceptible nod of acknowledgment. I can see from his face that he's accepted this simple truth, and his thoughts are now taking him in a different direction. "Jessica is dead," he finally states.

"She is."

"She was my sister-in-law, Doncia."

"You hated her. Anyway, I would have saved her if I could. I did try." The women at the table next to us break into giggles as they lean into the table, undoubtedly sharing some mundane secret that they think is scandalous.

"It's why you called me, right?" he asks. "You knew something was going to happen."

"She came by to see me earlier that day. She told me she was afraid of Travis. Afraid for her life. She indicated as much at the fund-raising dinner—you remember that, don't you?"

"But why would she come to see *you*?" Lander asks, ignoring my rhetorical question.

"Well, you know," I reply, "I worked for Jessica for a while. We bonded." There's not a hint of jest in my voice. If you didn't know the real history, you might believe me. The police certainly seemed to. Only Lander sees the obvious humor in it.

Only Lander. It's frightening to think of how many things those two words could be applied to. When things were at their darkest, *Only Lander* was able to make me think about something other than revenge when he took me in his arms. *Only Lander* made my heart race with something other than anger. *Only Lander* made me feel like I wasn't alone in the world.

There are so many ways in which this man is disastrously wrong for me . . . except in all the ways he's so incredibly right. Is love always like that? If so it's no wonder so many people are addicted to Xanax.

Lander leans forward, putting his forearms on the table. "The police say they found some kind of recording in that apartment. They didn't give me details. Do you know anything about that?"

I raise my eyebrows in mock surprise. "A recording? No. I don't know anything about it at all. At least not officially."

The truth is, the police didn't come to talk to me; I had gone to talk to them. But only after I had returned the recorder to the apartment. I put it back in the safe but I had also left the safe exposed to ensure that the police would find it.

I told the police that I knew about the apartment because Travis had taken me there before, when I worked for him. I said that once I understood that he had brought me there to seduce me, I had rejected him and quit shortly thereafter. If the police dust the place for prints they'll have an explanation for why mine are there. Travis, of course, will give them a different story, but he's not considered to be the most reliable source these days.

Lander is still holding my gaze; the intensity of his stare is a little unnerving but I don't offer up any more information as I once again raise the cup to my lips.

"Will you ever tell me all you know, Adoncia?" he asks softly. "Will you ever tell me the truth about what's going on?"

"In regards to Jessica and Travis?" I say. I put the cup back down and place my hands flat on the table. "No . . . no, I won't do that. I . . ." I falter for the first time before taking a deep breath to collect myself. "I will tell you this: Jessica did come to see me. And as you know, I did hate her. God, that woman gave me *every* reason to hate her," I add, shaking my head. My cool demeanor is slipping away as the memory of my last conversation with her comes back to me. "The thing is, she also gave me the most amazing gift anyone has ever given me. She gave me the truth and she gave me justice, or at least some version of it. So while she deserves my hate, she's also earned my loyalty. And Jessica wouldn't want me to talk to you about what we spoke of. She wouldn't want me to tell you more than I'm telling you and for that reason . . . and for *so* many others, I won't."

Across the room someone breaks a glass, and although I know the broken pieces are too far away to touch me, I feel as if the prickly shards are piercing my skin. I want to reach out to Lander but instead I just hold the cup he gave me a little tighter, trying to keep my hands from shaking. "Can you accept all that, Lander?" I finally add.

But I hold back the words that are reverberating through my skull. *Please, please don't reject me. Please accept me for who I am and for all the things I can and cannot do. Please find a way to be my* Only Lander *once more. And please, make me trust you again.*

Lander takes a deep breath and then slowly his hand moves forward, over mine. "That depends," he says softly. "Can *you* accept that I am never going to let go of HGVB? Can you accept my ambitions and my unwillingness to destroy everything my family has ever touched? Most of all . . ." His voice fades off and I watch as he swallows hard and looks away. Is he holding back tears? Lander? My Lander? I dig my teeth into my lower lip as I wait for him to continue.

"Most of all," he says again, "can you accept that I have . . . at times, misled you? Can you forgive me for not always being completely honest?"

I laugh. I can't help it. Who would have thought that after all we've been through he would be asking *me* to forgive *him* for dishonesty. "I wish to God you'd leave HGVB. But . . . I get it . . . or at least I want to get it. I'm *trying* to get it." *Because I can't sleep. Because I hate the idea of being without you.* But aloud I say, "You're a bad boy, Lander Gable. But the thing is . . . I think you might be good for *me*."

"There's a Solomon Burke song that goes something like that," he notes.

"Yeah, I know. I heard it on an oldies station this morning. I'm stealing the sentiment."

"You're a thief."

"You're just figuring that out?"

The corners of his lips twitch with amusement, and he lets go of my hand and reaches for his briefcase. "I'm sorry I didn't buy this *from* you, but I did buy it *for* you," he says inexplicably as he opens the case. "And please forgive Mandy for keeping this purchase a secret. I made her promise."

And then he pulls the book out of his briefcase, Hans Christian Andersen's *Fairy Tales Told for Children*.

For a moment I can't breathe. I had noticed that it had been sold. Of course I had. But I hadn't dared ask Mandy whom it was sold to. I was afraid that if I knew, I'd have to break into the poor man's house and steal it back.

"There's more." He takes out a page, ripped out from some other book. The page is now encased in plastic. On the page is a very old photo, a daguerreotype. It's of a bust of Hans Christian Andersen and there are some handwritten words scrawled across the page in what I presume is Danish, and there's a signature.

Hans Christian Andersen's autograph.

"We'll get it framed, of course," he adds as my mouth hangs open.

"Lander, it's too much. I can't . . ."

"You can't what?" he asks as the faint sound of honking horns leaks into the restaurant from the street. "Accept this?" He shakes his head dismissively. "I know how you live. You have a bed. You have clothes and food. What if life didn't have to always be about necessity? What if you could have things you don't need but that you desperately want?"

"Like a hundred-thousand-dollar book?" I laugh.

"Like me."

I look up from the book, startled.

He gestures to the gifts that now rest on the table. "It's excessive," he admits. "I can be excessive. I have my issues, just like you. We're both dangerous and damaged and the other bad 'D' words. Deceptive, damned, whatever. But you *want* me, Adoncia. And I *want* you."

"You want me?"

"I love you."

Is it possible for your heart to jump into your throat and drop into your stomach at the same time? It must be, because that's what it feels like. He loves me. It's what I've wanted. And it's what could destroy me.

But when have I ever run away from possible destruction?

"I do want you. I want you and I love you. But," I say as I gesture to the two of us, "I don't know if this will work."

"Neither do I. But I'd like to try. Will you try with me? Will you . . ." He pauses and then a small smile curls onto his lips. "Will you take this book and the man who gives it to you?"

I can feel the tears gathering in the corners of my eyes and I try unsuccessfully to blink them away. "I do," I whisper. "I really do."

I have my revenge. I have this amazing book. I have Lander . . . I even have a new understanding of myself.

I feel like a fairy-tale princess.

epilogue

Nothing is meant to be, there is only what *is*.

It's a philosophy that I developed many years ago, and it's one of the few that I continue to believe in.

If things were meant to be a certain way, surely Travis, Edmund, and Sean, along with many other people, would have gone to prison for the crimes they committed under the flag of HGVB. HGVB wouldn't even exist anymore.

Jessica would be alive.

But that's not the way things worked out. Edmund Gable and Sean White are going to prison, not for laundering money, but for their involvement in Nick Foley's death. Edmund ordered the hit; Sean covered it up.

It's not clear who it was who actually pulled the trigger. Edmund has pled the Fifth, and even if he was talking, it's doubtful that he had that information. He paid for a hit and let dark, invisible forces take care of the rest. What does seem clear is that it was one of Micah's men.

Micah, the man who claimed to be my friend. The man who offered his assistance and money because he owed a debt to my mom. I thought he was talking about what my mother did for his niece who shared a cell with her for a while.

But it would seem that his debt was much bigger than that.

If things were meant to be a certain way, I'd know where Micah is. He'd be in prison right now.

But that's not how things worked out.

If some things were meant to be, surely Nick Foley wouldn't have died to protect a secret that, as it turns out, didn't even need protecting.

C'est la guerre.

As for Travis—ah, Travis. Perhaps he really is the devil. Only the devil could be this difficult to destroy. He may still go to prison, but it hasn't happened yet. The tape that Jessica made isn't as incriminating as it should be. It proves her guilt, but his? Does he once fess up to asking her to lie under oath? Not really, not exactly. He doesn't admit to planning Nick's murder either. On the contrary, he says he wishes Nick had been allowed to stay alive. And I believe that Travis meant that. I believe him because, even now, I understand him. Travis likes to control people, and occasionally torture them, without ever lifting a finger. His favorite weapon is inside his head, and he's completely confident that it's the only weapon he'll ever need.

He's smarter than his father. He may even be smarter than Lander, although he's also much less complicated than Lander, which makes him much easier to predict. That said, Travis was involved in covering up Nick's murder. He was involved in setting up my mother for murder. I'd bet my life on that. But it might be hard to make those charges stick.

If there was a *meant to be*, that wouldn't be the case.

But of course there's another charge. The charge of killing his wife. Jessica had spoken to the police in the weeks leading up to her death. She told them that she was afraid of her husband. But since she was unwilling to say that he had ever laid a hand on her the police had blown her off. Now they wish they hadn't.

And of course, when they looked at Jessica's computer they found that she had been posting on a battered women's online forum. Perhaps I should tell the police that I'm the one who posted on that forum, using Jessica's computer. If I want to be good, I should tell them that I did so because I wanted to make Travis look bad. Yes, speaking up is definitely the right thing to do.

And I'm never going to do it. Jessica clearly wanted Travis to go to prison for murder, and who am I to interfere with the wishes of the deceased?

Plus, as I said before, he helped set up my mother. So fuck 'em.

That's not to say that he's definitely going to jail for Jessica's death. He's out on bail right now and he has the best lawyers in the United States working for him. He was pushed out of HGVB, but he still has plenty of money. And if anyone can beat the odds, it's Travis.

The last time I saw him it was in Central Park. We met early in the morning, in a clearing, surrounded by trees that had just begun to change color for fall. Lots of green with just the most subtle sprinkling of orange. Perhaps I should have been scared, meeting him at a time and place where there probably wouldn't be any witnesses. I didn't even tell Lander about it. He would have wanted to come and protect me, but I wanted to have this meeting alone. I wasn't afraid. I know Travis. If he's going to hurt me it won't be through traditional violence.

He arrived first, and I was impressed to see how collected he was, standing there in his four-thousand-dollar Loro Piana city trench, dark khaki pants, and hard, icy stare. He looked like a gangster who was about to be photographed for *GQ*.

"Are you wearing a wire?" he asked as I approached.

"No." And it was true, I wasn't.

"You know I can't risk believing you," he said.

I studied his face, noting that his crow's-feet were a little more pronounced, but other than that the stress of the last several months hadn't aged him much.

"Why am I here, Travis?"

"I wanted to congratulate you on a job well done. You weren't able to make the HGVB charges stick, at least not to me personally, so you conspired with my late wife and helped her make her suicide look like a homicide. And you made it all look very convincing. It's truly impressive, Bell. I was right when I said I had found a worthy adversary in you."

My lips curled into a bemused smile as I cocked my head to the side. "Are you wearing a wire, Travis?"

"No," he said sternly, but there was a glint of appreciation in his eyes.

"Yeah, well, you know I can't risk believing you."

"Touché," he said with a genuine smile.

"And my name's not Bell."

"You will always be Bell to me. Let Lander call you Adoncia. With him you can be sweet. But for me? You will always be the goddess of war."

I laughed and cast my eyes around the park. New high-rises filled with luxury condos and co-ops for the rich and famous have been built around here. They cast long shadows on the park in places where there used to be sun. "You know you deserve this, don't you?" I asked. "You set my mother up for murder, you worked with drug cartels and terrorists so you could boost your bank's profit margins. You're a very bad man, Travis Gable. You deserve to go to prison."

"But I'm not going to prison, Bell. People like me are given get-out-of-jail-free cards at birth, remember?"

"Yeah." I nibbled on my thumbnail thoughtfully. "But you only get so many of them, and you've been blowing through those things like Liz Taylor blew through husbands."

"If I run out I'll just buy more. Money can buy you almost anything."

"Did it buy you Cathy?"

Travis fell silent and I could almost see his energy shift.

"I hear she went back to her husband."

"She never left him, not officially."

"But she was going to," I pressed.

"Yes," he said quietly, "she was. But Cathy doesn't want just money. She wants respectability, she wants to be everyone's first priority, she wants to be the woman who everyone wants at their party."

"She wants everything," I said, summing it up for him.

"Yes, Cathy has always wanted . . . no, *expected* everything. And I can't make her my first priority while I'm battling murder charges. I'm not getting many party invitations these days, and it's hard to be seen as respectable when you're on the arm of a man who might be a murderer."

"In other words, she's less worried about the possibility that you might be a murderer and more worried about what people will think of *her* if she chooses to overlook that possibility."

"You have to know her like I know her to understand it. She's not being unreasonable.'

"Nonetheless, you lost her."

"Yes." His eyes were on the trees as they rustled with waking birds.

"That's the part you won't forgive me for. The lies I told to get into your home and gain your trust, the HGVB charges, even the murder charge—you see all of that as a game, right? Like some kind of weird form of chess. But that all this cost you Cathy . . . That's the thing you want revenge for."

Travis's eyes slowly slid down to me. "Yes," he said again, his voice almost a snakelike hiss as he studied me with those icy blue eyes.

For about a minute we just looked at each other as we worked out our own individual battle plans in our heads. "You're an evil man," I finally said, breaking the silence. "You feed off other people's humiliation and pain. You have no moral compass at all. But"—I lifted my finger in the air, adding one more observation—"you do know what love is. You are a nuanced devil."

Travis took that in without a word or a smile.

"I almost forgot." I reached into my oversized bag and pulled out a wrapped gift. "Lander and I bought you this. It's from that place where I work, Callow's Rare Books. We were going to have it delivered, but since I'm here . . ."

As he took the gift, Travis said, "I would have thought you would have found yourself a more powerful and well-paid position by now."

"No, I like it there. It suits me, the *real* me."

Travis gave me a weary look, but he tore back the wrapping paper anyway and studied the gift inside. "A little obvious, isn't it?"

"I don't think so. It's a first edition," I explained. "Signed by the author. Look." I opened the cover for him and showed him the inscription. "The minute we got it in I knew Lander and I had to give it to you."

I saw a spark of amusement in his eyes. Then he looked up at me, suddenly serious again. "How are they?"

"Good, they're good. Anytime you want to see them—"

He waved off the invitation, apparently disinterested. It pissed me off.

"I do hope they let you take that book to prison with you."

"I'm not going to prison, Bell."

"You are," I said simply. "If they don't get you for soliciting false testimony in a homicide case and paying off a cop, then maybe they'll get you for Jessica's murder, and if by some miracle they don't get you for that, there will be something else. You'll commit another felony and I'll find out about it." I stepped forward and tapped the book in his hand. "Count on me to always be there when you mess up, Travis. No matter what else I have going on, I promise to always make time for that. Bringing you down is one of the many things that makes my life worth living."

I got up on my tiptoes and sealed my promise with a light kiss on his cheek. And then I walked away, leaving him there, in Central Park, holding a first-edition copy of *The Count of Monte Cristo*.

⧓

That was two weeks ago. His trial is next week. I'm not sure how it's going to go, but I'm not too worried about it. Edmund and Sean are in prison, and as I told Travis, if I can't nail him on this I'll nail him on something else.

After I've finished my Saturday shift at Callow's, I

take a cab toward Lander's, but have it drop me off five blocks before I get there. I just want to walk for a while, feel the wind in my hair and all that. As I move down the sidewalk, my footsteps adding to the beat of the city, it's hard not to think about how much things have changed for me. My whole worldview is different. I still have moments of intense anger, but it's not all the time and I know how to control it.

And now, when I think about my mother, really think about her, I don't think about the day they took her from me. Instead I remember all those years that we did have together. The years of pixie dust and hope. They were good years. They're worth remembering.

I breeze through the lobby of Lander's new building, waving at security as I make my way up in the elevator. I like Lander's new place in SoHo. It's luxurious, but it's also comfortable. Elegant without pretension.

When I get to his penthouse, Lander throws open the door before I even have a chance to put my key in. Mercedes is riding him piggyback, her arms wrapped so tightly around her uncle's neck I'm worried she might strangle him.

"How you holding up?" I ask as I scoot by him.

"Uncle Lander's my horse and I'm a race jockey!" Mercedes cries, clearly thinking the question is meant for her.

I smile and lean in to give Lander a light kiss and also to adjust her hands, ensuring that she holds on to his shoulders rather than his throat. "Where's your brother?"

Mercedes points toward the living room, where I find Braden reading a graphic novel. I lean over his shoulder to see what it's about. "I can't believe you're able to read this; this should be way above your reading level."

"It's not," he says sullenly.

"Mmm, is it a scary one? It kind of has that look."

Braden turns the page without answering me.

He's angry. He doesn't really understand what's going on with his dad, but he knows it's bad or Travis wouldn't have consented to allow both him and Mercedes to live with their uncle.

Plus, even though he didn't get along with Jessica very often, she was still his mom. He misses her. And I know what it's like to lose your mom.

Which is why I make a point to spend a little time with Braden almost every day. I'm not going to let him push me away. I'm not going to let him come to think of himself as a problem child. That's simply not going to happen.

The doorbell rings and a moment later Lander enters the room with Lorella. "Ready to go to the movies?" the nanny asks Braden. He grunts his consent and I stand back as Lorella gets both him and Mercedes ready to go out. "So it's date night at home for you two?" Lorella asks quietly as Braden runs to his room to get his coat. "*Nice.*"

"Um, no, it won't be. Not even close," I correct her.

"Oh . . . so you're not—"

"Oh no, we are, I'm just saying it's going to be a lot better than nice."

Lorella laughs, and moments later she is walking out the door, a child holding each hand.

Lander's standing by the floor-to-ceiling windows, a sexy half smile gracing his lips. "You're good with them," he notes.

"So are you." I move over to him and rest my head against his chest.

I feel his hands move up to my hair. "You are so beautiful, Adoncia."

He pulls back a little, looks down into my eyes. "Will you dance with me?"

I smile my consent and he goes to put on some music, taking just long enough that I know he's lighting candles in the bedroom.

Sam Smith's song "Stay with Me" seeps through the speakers. When Lander comes back he wraps me up in his arms, and slowly we start to move. It's not a formal dance exactly. We're just moving together, my heart pressed against his heart, his lips by my ear as my lips find his neck. Just being here, swaying.

"Do you like this song?" he asks.

"It's sad," I say, breathing my sigh against his skin.

"Is it?"

"He wants her to stay with him, but he says he doesn't love her. He just *needs* her. He doesn't want to be alone."

Lander pulls back and looks down at me, brushing my hair away from my face. "You used to scare me, you know that?"

"Yes," I say with a light laugh, "I know that."

"You wanted to make me your world. I knew I

could never be that. I knew I had to let you go for a while, let you learn to stand on your own two feet, learn to live for something that isn't just revenge and . . . and isn't just me."

"You wanted me to live for myself."

"And other things . . . yes." He holds my face in his hands. "But I was never going to be able to stay away forever."

"I know that."

"Do you know why?"

I look at him long and hard, our bodies momentarily still. "Because," I finally say softly, "you love me."

"Because I love you."

And his lips find mine. I hold him so close I wonder if anyone who saw our silhouette from afar would be able to tell that we aren't one person. My hand slips under his shirt, moving up his back. He's so warm, so strong, so *real*.

And I know that as a real-life, flesh-and-blood man, he will be flawed. He will not be my world. But he will always be *part* of my world. He will always be part of my everything.

And as Lander lifts me up I'm reminded that you don't have to be a princess to live the fairy tale.

Slowly he lays me down on the couch and I cry out. Not because of the way he's touching me, but because there's a Barbie doll between the cushions and her plastic hands have jabbed my skin.

Lander and I both burst out laughing as we toss the doll to the other side of the room.

"Can you deal with this kind of chaos?"

"Lander, I *live* for chaos."

"Then will you move in with me, Adoncia Jiménez?"

"Yes, Lander Gable. I will."

And as his lips move to my ear, his tongue toying with that one spot that makes me shudder, I know that there are so many reasons to live. There's revenge, and children, and anger, and happiness and structure and chaos and work and passion . . .

. . . and there's war

. . . and there's love.

These days, most of all, I live for love.

acknowledgments

As usual, I need to thank *Cosmopolitan* magazine for giving me so many ideas for my sex scenes. Couldn't have done it without ya. And I continue to be both grateful and indebted to my amazing editor, Adam Wilson, whose guidance and support are truly invaluable to me.

I also want to thank Matt Taibbi for his incredibly well-researched *Rolling Stone* exposé on the misdeeds and transgressions of HSBC Bank. With the notable exception of the murder of Nick Foley, the vast majority of the crimes of the fictional HGVB Bank (from the scrubbing of Iranian wire transfers to the financial dealings with the cartels and other organized crime families) were heavily based on the actual actions of HSBC as revealed by Taibbi as well as such journalists and Ben Protess, Jessica Silver-Greenberg, and John Burnett. Their reporting was exemplary and succeeded not only in informing the public of what was going on in certain segments of our banking industry but also in giving me the foundation for what I hope is an entertaining novel. And yes, I realize that the former is more important than the latter. My ego isn't *that* big.

Last but absolutely not least I need to thank my husband, Rod Lurie, who is a tireless sounding board for my ideas and a constant source of inspiration. I'll never stop being grateful that the love of my life is also my partner in life. I'm a lucky gal.